TORCHY AS A PA

I0617635

SEWELL FORD

1st WORLD
LIBRARY
Literary Society

Torchy As A Pa

Sewell Ford

© 1st World Library, 2007
PO Box 2211
Fairfield, IA 52556
www.1stworldlibrary.com
First Edition

LCCN: 2007927872

Softcover ISBN: 978-1-4218-4573-9
Hardcover ISBN: 978-1-4218-4489-3
eBook ISBN: 978-1-4218-4657-6

Purchase *"Torchy As A Pa"*
as a traditional bound book at:
www.1stWorldLibrary.com/purchase.asp?ISBN=978-1-4218-4573-9

1st World Library is a literary, educational organization
dedicated to:

- Creating a free internet library of downloadable ebooks

- Hosting writing competitions and offering book
publishing scholarships.

Interested in more 1st World Library books?
contact: literacy@1stworldlibrary.com
Check us out at: www.1stworldlibrary.com

1st World Library Literary Society

Giving Back to the World

"If you want to work on the core problem, it's early school literacy."

- James Barksdale, former CEO of Netscape

"No skill is more crucial to the future of a child, or to a democratic and prosperous society, than literacy."

- Los Angeles Times

"Literacy... means far more than learning how to read and write... The aim is to transmit... knowledge and promote social participation."

- UNESCO

"Literacy is not a luxury, it is a right and a responsibility. If our world is to meet the challenges of the twenty-first century we must harness the energy and creativity of all our citizens."

- President Bill Clinton

"Parents should be encouraged to read to their children, and teachers should be equipped with all available techniques for teaching literacy, so the varying needs and capacities of individual kids can be taken into account."

- Hugh Mackay

CONTENTS

CHAPTER I

VEE TIES SOMETHING LOOSE

I forget just what it was Vee was rummagin' for in the drawer of her writin' desk. Might have been last month's milk bill, or a stray hair net, or the plans and specifications for buildin' a spiced layer cake with only two eggs. Anyway, right in the middle of the hunt she cuts loose with the staccato stuff, indicatin' surprise, remorse, sudden grief and other emotions.

"Eh?" says I. "Is it a woman-eatin' mouse, or did you grab a hatpin by the business end?"

"Silly!" says she. "Look what I ran across, Torchy." And she flips an engraved card at me.

I picks it on the fly, reads the neat script on it, and then hunches my shoulders. "Well, well!" says I. "At home after September 15, 309 West Hundred and Umpty Umpt street. How interestin'! But who is this Mr. and Mrs. Hamilton Porter Blake, anyway?"

"Why, don't you remember?" says Vee. "We sent them that darling urn-shaped candy jar. That is Lucy Lee and her dear Captain."

"Oh, then she got him, did she?" says I. "I knew he was a goner when she went after him so strong. And now I expect they're livin' happy ever after?"

Maybe you don't remember my tellin' you about Lucy Lee, the Virginia butterfly we took in over the week-end once and how I had to scratch around one Saturday to find some male dinner mate for her, and picked this hard-boiled egg from the bond room, one of these buddin' John D.'s who keeps an expense account and shudders every time he passes a millinery store or thinks what two orchestra seats and a double taxi fare would set him back. And, the female being the more expensive of the species, he has trained himself to be girl proof. That's what he lets on to me beforehand, but inside of forty-eight minutes by the watch, or between his first spoonful of tomato soup and his last sip of cafe noir, this Lucy Lee party had him so dizzy in the head he didn't know whether he was gazin' into her lovely eyes or being run down by a truck. Honest, some of these babidolls with high voltage lamps like that ought to be made to use dimmers. For look! Just as she's got him all wound up in the net, what does Lucy Lee do but flit sudden off to the Berkshires, where a noble young S. O. S. captain has just come back from the war and the next we know they're engaged, while in the bond room of the Corrugated Trust is one more broken heart, or what passes for the same among them young hicks.

And now here is Lucy Lee, flaggin' as young Mrs. Blake, livin' right in the same town with him.

"How stupid of me to forget!" says Vee. "We must run in and call on them right away, Torchy."

"We?" says I. "Ah, come!"

"We'll have dinner first at that cute little Cafe Bretone

you've been telling me about," says Vee, "and go up to see the Blakes afterwards."

Yes, that was the program we followed. And without the aid of a guide we located this Umpty Umpt street. The number is about half way down the block that runs from upper Broadway to Riverside Drive. It's one of the narrow streets, you know, and the scenery is just as cheerful as a section of the Hudson River tube on a foggy night. Nothing but seven-story apartment buildings on either side; human hives, where the only thing that can be raised is the rent, which the landlord attends to every quarter.

Having lived out in the near-country for a couple of years, I'd most forgotten what ugly, gloomy barracks these big apartment buildings were. Say, if they built state prisons like that, with no more sun or air in the cells, there'd be an awful howl. But the Rosenheimers and the Max Blums and the Gilottis can run up jerry built blocks with 8x10 bedrooms openin' on narrow airshafts, and livin' rooms where you need a couple of lights burnin' on sunny days, and nobody says a word except to beg the agent to let 'em pay $150 a month or so for four rooms and bath. I can feel Vee give a shudder as we dives into the tunnel.

"But really," says she, "I suppose it must be very nice, only half a block from the Drive, and with such an imposing entrance."

"Sure!" says I. "Just as cosy as being tucked away in a safety deposit vault every night. That's what makes some of these New Yorkers so patronizin' and haughty when they happen to stray out to way stations and crossroads joints where the poor Rubes live exposed continual to sunshine and fresh air and don't seem to know any better."

"Just think!" says Vee. "Lucy Lee's home down in

Virginia was one of those delightful old Colonial houses set on a hill, with more than a hundred acres of farm land around it. And Captain Blake must have been used to an outdoor life. He's a civil engineer, I believe. But then, with the honeymoon barely over, I suppose they don't mind."

"We might ask 'em," I suggests.

"Don't you dare, Torchy!" says she.

By that time, though, we're ready to interview the fuzzy-haired West Indian brunette in charge of the 'phone desk in one corner of the marble wainscoted lobby. And when he gets through givin' the hot comeback to some tenant who has dared to protest that he's had the wrong number, he takes his time findin' out for us whether or not the Blakes are in. Finally he grunts something through the gum and waves us toward the elevator. "Fourth," says he. And a slouchy young female in a dirty khaki uniform takes us up, jerky, to turn us loose in a hallway with a dozen doors openin' off.

There's such a dim light we could hardly read the cards in the door plates, and we was pawin' around, dazed, when a husky bleached blonde comes sailin' out of an apartment.

"Will you please tell me which is the Blakes' bell?" asks Vee.

"Blakes?" says the blonde. "Don't know 'em."

"Perhaps we're on the wrong floor," I suggests.

But about then a door opens and out peers Lucy Lee herself. "Why, there you are!" says she. "We were just picking up a little. You know how things get in an apartment. So good of you to hunt us up. Come right in."

So we squeezes in between a fancy hall seat and the kitchen door, edges down a three-foot hallway, and discovers Captain Blake just strugglin' into his coat, at the same time kickin' some evenin' papers, dexterous, under a davenport.

"Why, how comfy you are here, aren't you?" says Vee, gazin' around.

"Ye-e-es, aren't we?" says Lucy Lee, a bit draggy.

If you've ever made one of these flathouse first calls you can fill in the rest for yourself. We are shown how, by leanin' out one of the front windows, you can almost see the North River; what a cute little dinin' room there is, with a built-in china closet and all; and how convenient the bathroom is wedged between the two sleeping rooms.

"But really," says Lucy Lee, "the kitchen is the nicest. Do you know, the sun actually comes in for nearly an hour every afternoon. And isn't everything so handy?"

Yes, it was. You could stand in the middle and reach the gas stove with one hand and the sink with the other, and if you didn't want to use the washtub you could rest a loaf of bread on it. Then there was the dumbwaiter door just beside the ice-box, and overhead a shelf where you could store a whole dollar's worth of groceries, if you happened to have that much on hand at once. It was all as handy as an upper berth.

"You see," explains Lucy Lee, "we have no room for a maid, and couldn't possibly get one if we did have room, so I am doing my own work; that is, we are. Hamilton is really quite a wonderful cook; aren't you, Hammy, dear?

Of course, I knew how to make fudge, and I am learning to scramble eggs. We go out for dinner a lot, too."

"Isn't that nice?" says Vee, encouragin'.

Gradually we got the whole story. It seems Blake wasn't a captain any more, but had an engineerin' job on one of the new tubes, so they had to stick in New York. They had thought at first it would be thrilling, but I gathered that most of the thrills had worn off. And along towards the end Lucy Lee admits that she's awfully lonesome. You see, she'd been used to spendin' about six months of the year with Daddy in Washington, three more in flittin' around from one house party to the other, and what was left of the year restin' up down on the big plantation, where they knew all the neighbors for miles around.

"But here," says she, "we seem to know hardly anyone. Oh, yes, there are a few people in town we've met, but somehow we never see them. They live either in grand houses on Fifth Avenue, or in big hotels, or in Brooklyn."

"Then you haven't gotten acquainted with anyone in the building here?" asks Vee.

"Why," says Lucy Lee, "the janitor's wife is a Mrs. Biggs, I believe. I've spoken to her several times—about the milk."

"You poor dear!" says Vee.

"It's so tiresome," goes on Lucy Lee, "wandering out at night to some strange restaurant and eating dinner among total strangers. We go often to one perfectly dreadful little place because there's a funny old waiter that we call by his first name. He tells us about his married daughter, whose husband is a steamfitter and has been out on strike for nearly two months. But Hamilton always tips him more than he should, so it makes our dinners quite expensive. We have to make up, next night, by having fried eggs and bacon at home."

*   *   *   *   *

Well, it's a tale of woe, all right. Lucy Lee don't mean to complain, but when she gets started on the subject she lets the whole thing out. Life in the great city, if you have to spend twenty hours out of the twenty-four in a four-and-bath apartment, ain't so allurin', the way she sketches it out. Course, she ain't used to it, for one thing. She thinks if she had some friends nearby it might not be so bad. As for Hamilton, he listens to her with a puzzled, hopeless expression, like he didn't understand.

Vee seems to be studyin' over something, but she don't appear to be gettin' anywhere. So we sits around and talks for an hour or so. There ain't room to do much else in a flat. And about 9:30 Mr. Blake has a brilliant thought.

"I say, Lucy," says he, "suppose we make a rinktum-diddy for the folks, eh?"

"Sounds excitin'," says I. "Do you start by joinin' hands around the table?"

No, you don't. You get out the electric chafing dish and begin by fryin' some onions. Then you melt up some cheese, add some canned tomatoes, and the result is kind of a Spanish Welsh rabbit that's almost as tasty as it is smelly.

It was while we was messin' around the vest pocket kitchen, everybody tryin' to help, that we spots this face at the window opposite. It's sort of a calm, good natured face. You wouldn't call the young lady a heart-breaker exactly, for her mouth is cut kind of generous and her big eyes are wide set and serious; but you might guess that she was a decent sort and more or less sociable. In fact she's starin' across the ten feet or so of air space watchin' our maneuvers kind of interested and wistful.

"Who's your neighbor?" asks Vee.

"I'm sure I haven't an idea," says Lucy Lee. "I see her a lot, of course. She spends as much time in her kitchen as I do, even more. Usually she seems to be alone."

"Why don't you speak to her some time?" suggests Vee.

"Oh, I wouldn't dare," says Lucy Lee. "It—it isn't done, you know. I tried that twice when I first came, with women I met in the elevator, and I was promptly snubbed. New Yorkers don't do that sort of thing, I understand."

"But she's rather a nice looking girl," insists Vee. "And see, she's half smiling. I'm going to speak to her." Which she does, right off the bat. "I hope you don't mind the onion perfume?" says Vee.

The strange young lady doesn't slam down the window and go off tossin' her head, indignant, so she can't be a real New Yorker. Instead she smiles and shows a couple of cheek dimples. "It smells mighty good," says she. "I was just wondering what it could be."

"Won't you come over and find out?" says Vee, smilin' back.

"Yes, do come and join us," puts in Lucy Lee. "I'll open the hall door for you."

"Why, I—I'd love to if—if I may," says the young lady.

And that's how, half an hour or so later, when all that was left of this rinktum-diddy trick was some brown smears on five empty plates, we begun hearin' the story of the face at the window. She's young Mrs. William Fairfield, and she's been that exactly three months. Before that she had been Miss Esther Hartley, of Turkey Run, Md., and Kaio Chow, China. Papa Hartley had been a medical missionary and Esther, after she got through at Wellesley, had joined him as a nurse and kindergarten teacher. She'd been living in Kaio Chow for three years and the mission outfit was getting along fine when some kind of a Boxer mess broke out and they all had to leave. Coming back on an Italian steamer from Genoa she met Bill, who'd been in aviation, and there'd been some lovely moonlight nights and—well, Bill had persuaded her that teaching young Chinks to learn c-a-t, cat, wouldn't be half as nice as being Mrs. William Hartley. Besides, he had a good position waiting for him in a big wholesale leather house right in New York, and it would be such fun living among regular people.

"I suppose it is fun, too," says Esther, "but somehow I can't seem to get used to it. Everyone here gives you such, cold, suspicious looks; even the folks you meet in the hallways and elevator, as though they meant to say, 'Don't you dare speak to me. I don't know who or what you are, so don't come near.' They're like that, you know. Why, the street gamins of Kaio Chow were not much worse when I first went there. Yes, they did throw stones at me a few times, but in less than a month they were calling me the Doctor Lady and letting me tell them how wrong it was to spend so much time gambling around the food carts. Of course, they kept right on gambling for fried fish and rice cakes, but they would grin friendly when they saw me. Up to tonight no one in New York has even smiled at me.

"It's such a wonderful place, too; and so big, you would almost think there was enough to share with, strangers. But they seem to resent my being here at all, so I go out very little now when I am alone. And as Bill is away all day, and sometimes has to work evenings as well, I am alone a great deal. About the only place I can see the sky from and other people is this little kitchen window. So I stay there a lot, and I am sorry to say that often I'm foolish enough to wish myself back at the mission among all those familiar yellow faces, where I could stand on the bamboo shaded galleries and hear the hubbub in the compound, and watch the coolies wading about in the distant rice fields. Isn't that silly? There must be something queer about me."

"Not so awfully queer," says Vee. "You're lonesome, that's all."

"No more than I am, I'm sure," says Lucy Lee. "I wonder if there are many others?"

"Only two or three million more," says I. "That's why the cabarets and movie shows are so popular."

That starts us talking over what there was for folks to do in New York evenings, and while we can dope out quite a lot of different ways of passin' the time between 8 p. m. and midnight, nearly every one is so expensive that the average young couple can't afford to tackle 'em more'n once a week or so. The other evenings they sit at home in the flat.

"And yet," says young Mrs. Fairfield, "hardly any of them but could find a congenial group of people if—if they only knew where to look and how to get acquainted with each other. Why, right in this block I've noticed ever so many who I'm sure are rather nice. But there seems to be

16   Sewell Ford

no way of getting together."

"That's it, precisely!" says Vee. "So why should you wish yourself back in China?"

"I beg pardon?" says Mrs. Bill.

"I mean," says Vee, "that here is a missionary field, right at your door. If you can go off among foreigners and get them to give up some of their silly ways and organize them into groups and classes, why can't you do something of the kind for these silly New York flat dwellers? Can't they be organized, too?"

"Why," says Mrs. Bill, her eyes openin' wider, "I never thought of that. But—but there are so many of them."

"What about starting with your own block?" suggests Vee. "Perhaps with only one side of the street at first. Couldn't you find out how many were interested in one particular thing—music, or dancing, or bridge—and get them together?"

"Oh, I see!" says Mrs. Bill, clappin' her hands, enthusiastic. "Make a social survey. Why, of course. One could get up a sort of questionnaire card and drop it in the letter boxes for each family to fill out, if they cared to do so, and then you could call meetings of the various groups."

"If I could find a few home folks from Virginia, that's all I would ask," says Lucy Lee.

"Then we would start the card with 'Where born?'" says Mrs. Bill. "That would show us how many were Southerners, how many from the West, from New England, and so on. Next we would want to know something about their ages."

"Not too much," suggests Hamilton Blake. "Better ask 'em if they're over or under thirty."

"Of course," says Mrs. Bill. "Let's see how such a card would look. Next we would ask them what amusements they liked best: music, dancing, theatre going, bowling, bridge, private theatricals, chess and so on. Please check with a cross. And are you a high-brow; if so, why? Is it art, books, languages, or the snare drum?"

"Don't forget the poker fiends and the movie fans," I puts in.

Mrs. Bill writes that down. "We will have to begin by electing ourselves an organizing committee," says she, "and we will need a small printing fund."

"I'll chip in ten," says Mr. Blake.

"So will we," says Vee.

"And I am sure Bill will, too," says Mrs. Fairfield, "which will be quite enough to print all the cards we need. And tomorrow evening we will get together in our apartment and make out the questionnaire complete. Shall we?"

So when we left to catch a late train for Long Island it looked like West Hundred and Umpty Umpt street was going to have something new sprung on it. Course, we didn't know how far these two young couples would get towards reformin' New York, but they sure was in earnest, 'specially young Mrs. Bill, who seems to have more or less common sense tucked away between her ears.

That must have been a week or ten days ago, and as we hadn't heard from any of them, or seen anything in the papers, we was kind of curious. So here yesterday I has to call up Lucy Lee on the 'phone.

"Say," says I, "how's that block sociable progressin'?"

"Oh, perfectly wonderful!" says Lucy Lee. "Why, at our first meeting, in a big dance hall, we had nearly 300 persons and were almost swamped. But Esther is a perfect wizard at organizing. She got them into groups in less than half an hour, and before we adjourned they had formed all kinds of clubs and associations, from subscription dance clubs to a Lord Dunsany private theatrical club. Everyone in the block who didn't turn out at first has been clamoring to get in since and it has been keeping us busy sorting them out. You've no idea what a difference it makes up here. Why, I know almost everybody in the building now, and some of them are really charming people. They're beginning to seem like real neighbors and I don't think we shall ever pass another dull evening while we live here. Even folks across the street have heard about it and want Esther to come over and organize them."

So I had quite a bulletin to take home to Vee.

"Isn't that splendid!" says she.

"Anyway," says I, "I guess you started something. If it spreads enough, maybe New York'll be almost fit to live in. But I have my doubts."

CHAPTER II

WHEN HALLAM WAS RUNG UP

It ain't often Mr. Robert starts something he can't finish. When he does, though, he's shifty at passin' it on. Yes, I'll say he is. For in such cases I'm apt to be the one that's handiest, and you know what that means. It's a matter of Torchy being joshed into tacklin' any old proposition that may be batted up, with Mr. Robert standin' by ready to spring the grin.

Take this little go of his with the Hallam Beans—excuse me, the F. Hallam Beans. Doesn't that sound arty? Well, that's what they were, this pair. Nothing but. I forget where it was they drifted in from, but of course they couldn't have found each other anywhere but in Greenwich Village. And in course of time they mated up there. It was the logical, almost the brilliant thing to do. Instead of owing rent for two skylight studios they pyramided on one; besides, after that each one could borrow the makin's off the other when the cigarettes ran out, and if there came pea-green moments when they doubted whether they were real geniuses or not one could always buck up the other.

If they had stuck to the Village I expect we'd never heard anything about them, but it seems along early last spring

Sewell Ford

F. Hallam had a stroke of luck. He ran across an old maid art student from Mobile who was up for the summer and was dyin' to get right into the arty atmosphere. Also she had $300 that her grip wasn't any too tight on, and before she knew it F. Hallam had sub-let the loft to her until Sept. 15, payable in advance. Two days later the Beans, with more'n half of the loot left, were out on Long Island prospectin' around in our locality and talking vague about taking a furnished bungalow. They were shown some neat ones, too, runnin' from eight to fifteen hundred for three months, but none of 'em seemed to be just right. But when they discovered this partly tumbled down shack out on a back lane beyond Mr. Robert Ellinses' big place they went wild over it. Years ago some guy who thought he was goin' to get rich runnin' a squab farm had put it up, but he'd quit the game and the property had been bought up by Muller, our profiteerin' provision dealer. And Muller didn't do a thing but soak 'em $30 a month rent for the shack, that has all the conveniences of a cow shed in it.

But the Beans rented some second-hand furniture, bought some oil lamps and a two-burner kerosene stove, and settled down as happy and contented as if they'd leased a marble villa at Newport. From then on you'd be liable to run across 'em most anywhere, squattin' in a field or along the back roads with their easels and paint brushes, daubin' away industrious.

You might know it would be either Mrs. Robert or Vee who would pick 'em up and find out the whole story. As a matter of fact it was both, for they were drivin' out after ferns or something when they saw the Beans perched on a stone wall tryin' to unbutton a can of sardines with a palette knife and not having much success. You know the kind of people who either lose the key to a sardine can or break off the tab and then gaze at it helpless! That was them to the life.

And when Mrs. Robert finds how they're livin' chiefly on dry groceries and condensed milk, so's to have more to blow in on dinky little tubes of Chinese white and Prussian blue and canvas, of course she has to get busy slippin' 'em little trifles like a dozen fresh eggs, a mess of green peas and a pint of cream now and them. She follows that up by havin' 'em come over for dinner frequent. Vee has to do her share too, chippin' in a roast chicken or a cherry pie or a pan of doughnuts, so between the two the Hallam Beans were doin' fairly well. Hallam, he comes back generous by wishin' on each of 'em one of his masterpieces. The thing he gives us Vee hangs up over the livin' room mantelpiece, right while he's there.

"Isn't that perfectly stunning, Torchy?" she demands.

"I expect it is," says I, squintin' at it professional, "but—but just what is it supposed lo be?" And I turns inquirin' to F. Hallam.

"Why," says he, "it is a study of afternoon light on a group of willows. We are not Futurists, you see; Revertists, rather. Our methods—at least mine—are frankly after the Barbizon school."

"Yeauh!" says I, noddin' wise. "I knew one once who could do swell designs on mirrors with a piece of soap."

"I beg pardon," says Hallam. "One what?"

"A barber's son," says I. "I got him a job as window decorator, too."

But somehow after that Hallam sort of shies talkin' art with me. A touchy party, F. Hallam. The least little thing would give him the sulks. And even when he was feelin' chipper his face was long enough. As a floorwalker in a mournin' goods shop he'd be a perfect fit. But you couldn't suggest anything that sounded like real work to Hallam. He claims that he was livin' for his art. Maybe so, but I'll be hanged if he was livin' on it. I got to admit, though, that he dressed the part fairly well; for in that gray flannel shirt and the old velvet coat and the flowin' black tie, and with all that stringy, mud-colored hair fallin' around his ears, he couldn't be mistaken for anything else. Even a movie audience would have spotted him as an artist without a leader to that effect.

Mrs. Hallam Bean was a good runnin' mate for him, for she has her hair boxed and wears paint-smeared smocks. Only she's a shy actin', quiet little thing, and real modest. There's no doubt whatever but that she has decided that F. Hallam is going to be a great painter some day. When she ain't sayin' as much she's lookin' it; and Hallam, I suspect, is always ready to make the vote unanimous.

I judged from a few remarks of Mr. Robert's that he wasn't quite as strong for the Hallams as Mrs. Robert was, but seein' 'em around so much he couldn't help gettin' more or less interested in the business end of their career.

"Yes," says he, "they seem to be doing fairly well this summer; but how about next winter, when they go back to town? You know they can't possibly sell any of those things. How are they going to keep from starving?"

Mrs. Robert didn't know. She said she'd mention the matter to F. Hallam. And she found he wasn't worrying a bit. His plans were vague enough. He was doing a head of Myrtle—that being Mrs. Bean—which he thought he might let some magazine have as a cover picture. And then, other things were bound to turn up. They always had, you know.

But toward the end of the season the Beans got shabbier than ever. Myrtle's smocks were torn and stained, with a few cigarette burns here and there, and her one pair of walking boots were run over at the heel and leaky in the sole. As for Hallam, that velvet coat had so many grease spots on it that it was hardly fit to wear outside of a stable, and his rubber-soled shoes gave his toes plenty of air. The Beans admitted that their finances were down to the zero point and they had to be asked in for dinner at least three times a week to keep 'em from bein' blue in the gills.

"Hang it all!" says Mr. Robert, "the fellow ought to have a regular job of some kind. I suppose he can draw after a fashion. I'll see what I can do."

And by rustlin' around among his friends he finds one who runs a big advertisin' agency and can place another man in the art department. You'd 'most thought F. Hallam would have been tickled four ways at the prospect of draggin' down a pay envelope reg'lar and being able to look the rent agent in the face. But say, what does he do but scrape his foot and wriggle around like he'd been asked to swallow a non-skid headache tablet. At last he gets out this bleat about how he'd always held his art to be too sacred a thing for him to commercialize and he really didn't know whether he could bring himself to drawin' ad. pictures or not. He'd have to have time to think it over.

"Very well," says Mr. Robert, restrainin' himself from blowin' a fuse as well as he could. "Let me know tomorrow night. If you decide to take the place, come over about 6:30; if you find that your views as to the sacredness of your art are too strong, you needn't bother to arrive until 8:30—after dinner."

I expect it was some struggle, but Art must have gone down for the full count. Anyway the Beans were on hand

Sewell Ford

when the tomato bisque was served next evenin', and in less'n a week F. Hallam was turnin' out a perfectly good freehand study of a lovely lady standin' graceful beside a Never-smoke oil stove—no-wicks, automatic feed, send for our catalogue—and other lively compositions along that line. More'n that, he made good and the boss promised him that maybe in a month or so he'd turn him loose with his oil paints on something big, a full page in color, maybe, for a leadin' breakfast food concern. Then the Beans moved back to town and we heard hardly anything more about 'em.

I understand, though, that they sort of lost caste with their old crowd in Greenwich Village. Hallam tried to keep up the bluff for a while that he wasn't workin' reg'lar, but his friends began to suspect. They noticed little things, like the half pint of cream that was left every morning for the Beans, the fact that Hallam was puttin' on weight and gettin' reckless with clean collars. And finally, after being caught coming from the butcher's with two whole pounds of lamb chops, Myrtle broke down and confessed. They say after that F. Hallam was a changed man. He had his hair trimmed, took to wearin' short bow ties, and when he dined at the Purple Pup, sneaked in and sat at a side table like any tourist from the upper West Side.

Course, on Sundays and holidays he put on the old velvet coat, and set up his easel and splashed away with his paints. But mostly he did heads of Myrtle, and figure stuff. It was even hinted that he hired models.

It must have been on one of his days home that this Countess Zecchi person discovered him in his old rig. She'd been towed down there on a slummin' party by a club friend of Mr. Robert's who'd heard of Hallam and had the address. You remember hearin' about the Countess, maybe? She was Miss Mae Collins, of Kansas

City, originally, and Zecchi was either the second or third of her hubbies, or hobbies, whichever you'd care to call 'em. A lively, flighty female, Countess Zecchi, who lives in a specially decorated suite at the Plutoria, sports a tiger cub as a pet, and indulges in other whims that get her more or less into the spotlight.

Her particular hunch on this occasion was that she must have her portrait done by a real Bohemian artist, and offhand she gives F. Hallam the job.

"You must paint me as Psyche," says she. "I've always wanted to be done as Psyche. Can't we have a sitting tomorrow?"

Hallam was almost too thrilled for words, but he managed to gasp out that she could. So he reports sick to his boss, blows in all his spare cash buyin' a big mirror and draperies to fix up a Psyche pool in the studio, and decides that at last luck has turned. For three days the Countess Zecchi shows up reg'lar, drapes herself in pink tulle, and Hallam paints away enthusiastic.

Then she don't come any more. For a week she stalls him off and finally tells him flat that posing as Psyche bores her. Besides, she's just starting south on a yachting party. The portrait? Oh, she doesn't care about that. She hadn't really given him a commission, just told him he might paint her. And he mustn't bother her by calling up again. Positively.

So Hallam hits the earth with a dull thud. He reports back on the advertisin' job and groans every time he thinks how much he spent on the mirror and big canvas. He'd been let in, that's all. But he finishes up the Psyche picture durin' odd times. He even succeeded in unloadin' it on some dealer who supplies the department stores, so he quits about square.

Then an odd thing happens. At the advertisin' agency there's a call from a big customer for a picture to go with a Morning Glory soap ad. It's a rush order, to be done in six colors. Hallam has a bright little thought. Why wouldn't his Psyche picture fit in? The boss thinks it's worth lookin' up, and an hour later he comes back from the dealer's with the trade all made. And inside of three weeks no less than two dozen magazines was bindin' in a full page in colors showin' the fair form of the Countess Zecchi bendin' over a limpid pool tryin' to fish out a cake of Morning Glory soap. It was a big winner, that ad. The soap firm ordered a hundred thousand copies struck off on heavy plate paper, and if you sent in five wrappers with a two-cent stamp you'd be mailed a copy to tack up in the parlor.

Whether or not the general public would have recognized the Countess Zecchi as the girl in the soap ad. if she'd kept still about it is a question. Most likely it wouldn't. But the Countess didn't keep still. That wasn't her way. She proceeds to put up a holler. The very day she discovers the picture, through kind friends who almost swamped her with cut-out copies and telegrams, she rushes back to New York and calls up the reporters. All one afternoon she throws cat fits for their benefit up at her Plutoria apartment. She tells 'em what a wicked outrage has been sprung on her by a wretched shrimp of humanity who flags under the name of Bean and pretends to be a portrait painter. She goes into details about the mental anguish that has almost prostrated her since she discovered the fiendish assault on her privacy, and she announces how she has begun action for criminal libel and started suit for damages to the tune of half a million dollars.

Well, you've seen what the papers did to that bit of news. They sure did play it up, eh? The Psyche picture, with all its sketchy draperies, was printed side by side with half tones of the Countess Zecchi. And of course they didn't neglect F. Hallam Bean. He has to be photographed and interviewed, too. Also, Hallam wasn't dodgin' either a note-book or a camera. As a result he is mentioned as "the well-known portrait painter of Greenwich Village," and so on. One headline I remember was like this: "Founder of American Revertist School Sued for Half Million."

I expect I kidded Mr. Robert more or less about his artist friend. He don't know quite how to take it, Mr. Robert. In one way he feels kind of responsible for Hallam, but of course he ain't worried much about the damage suit. The Countess might get a judgment, but she'd have a swell time collectin' anything over a dollar forty-nine, all of which she must have known as well as anybody. But she was gettin' front page space. So was F. Hallam. And the soap firm was runnin' double shifts fillin' new orders.

Then here one afternoon, as Mr. Robert and me are puttin' the finishin' touches to a quarterly report, who should drift into the Corrugated general offices but F. Hallam Bean, all dolled up in an outfit that he must have collected at some costumers. Anyway, I ain't seen one of them black cape coats for years, and the wide-brimmed black felt hat is a curio. Also he's gone back to the flowin' necktie and is lettin' his hair grow wild again.

"Well, well!" says I. "Right off the boulevard, eh?"

"Why the masquerade?" demands Mr. Robert.

He don't seem a bit disturbed at our josh, but just smiles sort of satisfied and superior. "I suppose it is different," says he, "but then, so am I. I've just been having some new photos taken. They're to be used with an article I'm contributing to a Sunday paper. It is to be entitled, 'What is a Revertist?' They are paying me $100 for it. Not bad, eh!"

"Pretty soft, I'll say," says I. "Soak 'em while the soakin's good."

"Still getting on well with your job?" asked Mr. Robert.

"Oh, I've chucked that," says Hallam airy. "No more of that degrading grind for me. I've arrived, you know."

"Eh?" gasps Mr. Robert. "Where?"

"Why," says F. Hallam, "don't you understand what has happened during these last two weeks? Fame has found me out. I am known as the founder of a new school of art—the original Revertist. My name has become a household word. And before this absurd libel suit is finished I shall be painting the portraits of all the leading society people. They are already asking about me, and as soon as I find a suitable studio—I'm considering one on West 59th Street, facing Central Park—I shall be over-whelmed with orders. It's bound to come."

"You're quite sure this is fame, are you?" asks Mr. Robert.

F. Hallam smiles and shrugs his shoulders. "Quite," says he.

And Mr. Robert can't tell him it's anything else. Hasn't he got his pockets full of newspaper clippings to prove it? Don't people turn and stare after him in the street and nudge each other in the subway cars? Aren't his artist friends giving him a banquet at the Purple Pup? So why should he work for wages any more, or save up any of the easy money that's coming his way? And he sails out indignant, with his cape overcoat swayin' grand from his narrow shoulders.

"I give him up, Torchy," says Mr. Robert. "That is, unless you can suggest some way of making him see what an ass he is. Come, now!"

"All right," says I, gettin a sudden hunch. "I don't know as it will work in his case, for he's got it bad, but suppose we tow him out for a look at Private Ben Riggs?"

"By George!" says Mr. Robert, slappin' his knee. "The very thing. Sunday, eh?"

It was easy enough stagin' the affair. All he had to do was to ask the Beans out for the week-end, and then after Sunday dinner load 'em into the tourin' car, collect me, and drive off about 20 miles or so to the south shore of Long Island.

Maybe, though, you don't remember about Private Ben Riggs? Oh, of course the name still sticks. It's that kind of a name. But just what was it he did? Uh-huh! Scratchin' your head, ain't you? And yet it was less than two years ago that he was figurin' more prominent in the headlines than anybody else you could name, not barrin' Wilson or Von Hindenburg.

One of our first war heroes, Ben Riggs was, and for nearly two weeks there he had the great American people shoutin' themselves hoarse in his honor, as you might say. There was editorials, comparin' his stunt to what Dewey did at Manila Bay, or Hobson at Santiago, and showin' how Private Ben had a shade the best of it, after all. The Sunday illustrated sections had enlarged snapshots of him, of his boyhood home in Whositville; of his dear old mother who made that classic remark, "Now, wasn't that just like Ben"; and of his girlish sweetheart, who was cashier at the Acme Lunch and who admitted that "she always had known Ben was going to be a great man some day."

Then when the governor of Ben's state worked his pull and got Ben sent home right in the midst of it all there was another grand hooray—parades, banquets and so on. And they raised that testimonial fund for him to buy a home with, and presented him with a gold medal. Next, some rapid firin' publishin' firm rushed out a book: "Private Ben Rigg's Own Story," which he was supposed to have written. And then, too, he went on in a vaudeville sketch and found time to sign a movie contract with a firm that was preparin' to screen his big act, "True To Life."

It was along about that stage that Private Ben, with more money in the bank than he'd ever dreamed came from all the mints, got this great scheme in his nut that a noble plute like him ought to have a big estate somewhere and build a castle on it. So he comes out here on the south shore, lets a real estate shark get hold of him, and the next thing he knows he owns about a hundred acres of maybe the most worthless land on the whole island. His next move is to call in an architect, and inside of a month a young army of laborers was layin' the foundations for what looked like a city hall, but was really meant to be Riggsmere Manor, with 78 rooms, 23 baths, four towers, and a dinin' room 65 feet long and a ceiling 16 feet in the clear.

Then the slump came. I forget whether it was a new hero, or another submarine raid. Anyway, the doings of Private Ben Riggs ceased to be reported in the daily press. He dropped out of sight, like a nickel that rolls down a sewer openin'. They didn't want him any more in vaudeville. The movie producer welched on his proposition. The book sales fell off sudden. The people that wanted to name cigars or safety razors after him, or write songs about him, seemed to forget.

For a few days Private Ben couldn't seem to understand what had happened. He went around in a kind of a daze. But he had sense enough left to stop work on the Manor, countermand orders for materials, and pull out with what he could. It wasn't such a great pile. There was a construction shed on the property, fairly well built, and by running up a chimney and having a well sunk, he had what passed for a home. There in the builder's shack Private Ben has been living ever since. He has stuck up a real estate sign and spends most of his time layin' out his acres of sand and marsh into impossible buildin' lots. As he's way off on a back road, few people ever come by, but he never misses a chance of tacklin' those that do and tryin' to wish a buildin' plot on 'em. That's how we happen to know him so well, and to have kept up with his career.

On the way out we sort of revived F. Hallam Bean's memories of Private Ben Riggs. First off he thought Ben had something to do with the Barbara Freitchie stunt, or was he the one who jumped off Brooklyn Bridge? But at last he got it straight. Yes, he remembered having had a picture of Private Ben tacked up in his studio, only last year. Then we tried him on Jack Binns, and Sergeant York and Lieutenant Blue and Dr. Cook. He knew they'd all done something or other to make the first page, but his guesses were kind of wide.

"I would like to see Private Ben, though," says F. Hallam. "Must be an interesting chap."

"He is," says Mr. Robert. "His scrap books are interesting,

too. He has ten of them."

"By Jove!" says Hallam. "Good idea. I must tell Myrtle about that."

But after we'd been hailed by this lonesome lookin' party in baggy pants and the faded blue yachtin' cap, and we'd let him lead us past the stone foundations where a fine crop of weeds was coming up, and he'd herded us into his shack and was tryin' to spring a blueprint prospectus on us, F. Hallam sort of put his foot in his mouth by remarkin':

"So you are Private Ben Riggs, are you?"

"I was—once," says he. "Now I'm just Sand-Lot Riggs. Who are you?"

"Oh, pardon me," puts in Mr. Robert. "I thought you would know. This is Mr. Hallam Bean, the celebrated founder of the Revertist school of art."

"Oh, yes!" said Riggs. "The one who painted the corset picture ad."

"Soap picture," I corrects hasty, "featurin' the Countess Zecchi."

"That's so, it was soap," admits Riggs. "And I was noticin' in the mornin' paper how the Countess had decided to drop them suits."

"What?" says Hallam, starin' at him. "Where was that? On the front page?"

"No," says Riggs. "It was a little item on the inside mixed up with the obituary notes. That's always the way. They start you on the front page, and then—" Private Ben shrugs his shoulders. But he proceeds to add hasty, with a shrewd squint at Hallam: "Course, it's different with you. Say, how about buyin' the estate here? I'd be willin' to let it go cheap."

"No, thank you," says F. Hallam, crisp.

"Part of it then," insists Riggs. "I'd been meanin' to write you about it. I generally do write 'em while—while they're on the front."

"No," says Hallam, and edges toward the door.

He seemed to get the idea. Before he starts back for town that night he asks Mr. Robert if he could say a word for him at the advertisin' agency, as he thought it might be just as well if he hung onto the job. It wasn't such a poor thought, for Hallam fades out of public view a good deal quicker than he came in.

"Maybe it wasn't Fame that rung him up, after all," I suggests to Mr. Robert.

He nods. "It might have been her step-sister, Notoriety," says he.

"Just what's the difference?" says I.

Mr. Robert rubs his chin. "Some old boy whose name I've forgotten, put it very well once," says he. "Let's see, he said that Fame was the perfume distilled from the perfect flowering of a wise and good life; while Notoriety was—er—"

"Check!" says I. "It's what you get when you fry onions, eh?"

Mr. Robert grins. "Some day, Torchy," says he, "I think I shall ask you to translate Emerson's Essays for me."

It's all josh, all right. But that's what you get when you're a private sec. de luxe.

CHAPTER III

THE GUMMIDGES GET A BREAK

This news about how the Gummidges had come back is 'phoned in by Vee here the other afternoon. She's some excited over it, as she always is when she sees another chance of extendin' the helpin' hand. I'll admit I wasn't quite so thrilled. You see, I'd been through all that with the Gummidges two or three times before and the novelty had sort of worn off. Besides, that last rescue act we'd pulled had been no common charity hand-out. It had been big stuff, nothing less than passing the hat among our friends and raising enough to send the whole lot of 'em so far West that the prospects of their ever gettin' back to New York was mighty slim. Maybe that was one reason I'd been so enthusiastic over puttin' the job through. Not more'n eighteen months ago that had been, and here they all were back in our midst once more.

"At the same old address," adds Vee, "so you can guess what that means, Torchy."

"Uh-huh!" says I. "The Patricia apartments has a perfectly punk janitor again and we're due to listen to another long tale of woe."

"Oh, well," says Vee, "it will be interesting to see if Mrs.

Gummidge is still bearing up cheerful and singing that 'When the Clouds Are Darkest' song of hers. Of course, I am coming right in as soon as I can pack a basket. They're sure to be hungry, so I'm going to put in a whole roasted chicken, and some jars of that strawberry jam Rowena likes so much, and heaps of bread and butter sandwiches. Probably they'll need a few warm clothes, too, so I hope you don't mind, Torchy, if I tuck in a couple of those khaki shirts of yours, and a few pairs of socks, and—"

"Say," I breaks in, "don't get too reckless with my wardrobe. I ain't got enough to fit out the whole Gummidge family, you know. Save me a dress tie and a change of pajamas if you can."

"Silly!" says she. "And listen: I will call for you about 5 o'clock and we'll go up to see them together."

"Very well," says I. "I'll try to hold myself back until then."

At that, I expect I was some curious to find out just how the Gummidges had managed it. Must have been Ma Gummidge who found a way. Hen. Gummidge never would, all by himself. About as helpless an old Stick-in-the-Mud, he was, as I'd, ever helped pry out of the muck. And a chronic crape hanger. If things were bad, he was sure they were going to be worse.

"I never have no luck," was his constant whine. It was his motto, as you might say, his Fourteen Points of Fate.

I never could make out whether he got that way on account of his face, or if his face had lengthened out as his disposition grew gloomy. It was a long face, almost as long and sad as a cow's. Much too long for his body and legs as he was only medium height up as far as the chin.

Kind of a stoop shouldered, hollow chested, thin shanked party, too. Somewhere in the fifties, I should judge, but he might have been sixty by his looks and the weary way he dragged around.

When I first knew him he was assistant engineer in the Corrugated buildin' and I used to see him risin' solemn out of the sidewalk on the ash elevator, comin' up from the basement like some sad, flour-sprinkled ghost. And then before he'd roll off the ash cans he'd lean his elbows on the safety bar and stare mournful up and down Broadway for a spell, just stallin' around. Course, I got to kiddin' him, askin' what he found so comic in the boiler-room and why he didn't let me in on the joke.

"Huh!" he'd grunt. "If there's any joke down there, young feller, I'm it. I wonder how much grinnin' you'd do if you had to slave ten hours a day in a hole like that. I ought to be up sittin' on the right side of an engine cab, fast freight, and drawin' my three hundred a month with time and a half overtime. That's what I set out to be when I started as wiper. Got to be fireman once, but on the second run we hit a weak rail and went into the ditch. Three busted ribs and my hospital expenses was all I pulled out of that with; and when I tried to get damages they put my name on the blacklist, which finished my railroadin' career for good. Maybe it was just as well. Likely I'd got mashed fair in the next wreck. That's me. Why say, if it was rainin' soup I'd be caught out with a fork."

Yes, he was some consistent gloom hound, Henry Gummidge. Let him tell it and what Job went through was a mere head-cold compared to his trials and tribulations. And the worst was yet to come. He knew it because he often dreamed of seeing a bright yellow dog walkin' on his hind legs proud and wearin' a shiny collar. And then the dog would change into a bow-legged policeman

Sewell Ford

swingin' a night-stick threatenin'. All of which a barber friend of Henry's told him meant trouble in the pot and that he must beware of a false friend who came across the water. The barber got it straight from a dream book, and there must be something in it, for hadn't Henry been done out of $3 by a smooth talkin' guy from Staten Island?

Well, sure enough, things did happen to Gummidge. He had a case of shingles. Then he dropped the silver watch he'd carried for fifteen years and before he knew it had stepped square on it with the iron plated heel of his work boots, squashin' the crystal into the works. And six weeks later he'd carelessly rested a red hot clinker rake on his right foot and had seared off a couple of toes. But the climax came when he managed to bug the safety catch on the foolproof ash elevator and took a 20-foot drop with about a ton of loaded ash cans. He only had a leg broken, at that, but it was three or four months before he came limpin' out of the hospital to find that the buildin' agent didn't care to have him on the payroll any more.

Somehow Henry got his case before Mr. Robert, and that's how I was sent scoutin' out to see if all this about a sufferin' fam'ly was a fairy tale or not. Well, it was and it wasn't. There was a Mrs. Gummidge, and Rowena, and Horatio, just as he'd described. And they was livin' in a back flat on a punk block over near the North river. Their four dark rooms was about as bare of furniture as they could be. I expect you might have loaded the lot on a push cart. And the rations must have been more or less skimpy for some time.

But you couldn't exactly say that Ma Gummidge was sufferin'. No. She'd collected a couple of fam'ly washes from over Seventh avenue way and was wadin' into 'em cheerful. Also she was singin' "When the Clouds Are Darkest," rubbin' out an accompaniment on the wash board and splashin' the suds around reckless, her big red face shinin' through the steam like the sun breakin' through a mornin' fog.

Some sizable old girl, Ma Gummidge; one of these bulgy, billowy females with two chins and a lot of brownish hair. And when she wipes her hands and arms and camps down in a chair she seems to fill all one side of the room. Even her eyes are big and bulgy. But they're good-natured eyes. Oh my, yes. Just beamin' with friendliness and fun.

"Yes, Henry's had kind of a hard time," she admits, "but I tell him he got off lucky. Might have been hurt a lot worse. And he does feel downhearted about losin' his job. But likely he'll get another one better'n that. And we're gettin' along, after a fashion. Course, we're behind on the rent, and we miss a meal now and then; but most folks eat too much anyway, and things are bound to come out all right in the end. There's Rowena, she's been promised a chance to be taken on as extra cash girl in a store. And Horatio's gettin' big enough to be of some help. We're all strong and healthy, too, so what's the use worryin', as I say to Henry."

Say, she had Mrs. Wiggs lookin' like a consistent grouch, Ma Grummidge did. Rowena, too, is more or less of an optimist. She's about 16, built a good deal on her mother's lines, and big enough to tackle almost any kind of work, but I take it that thus far she ain't done much except help around the flat. Horatio, he's more like his father. He's only 15 and ought to be in school, but it seems he spends most of his time loafin' at home. They're a folksy fam'ly, I judge; the kind that can sit around and chat about nothing at all for hours at a time. Why, even the short while I was there, discoverin' how near they was to bein' put out on the street, they seemed to be havin' a whale of a time. Rowena, dressed in a saggy skirt and a shirt waist with one sleeve partly split out, sits in the corner gigglin' at some of her Ma's funny cracks. And then Ma Gummidge springs that rollin' chuckly laugh of hers when Rowena adds some humorous details about a stew they tried to make out of a piece of salt pork and a couple of carrots.

But the report I makes to Mr. Robert is mostly about facts and finances, so he slips a ten spot or so into an envelope for 'em, and next day he finds a club friend who owns a row of apartment houses, among them the Patricia, where there's a janitor needed. And within a week we had the Gummidges all settled cozy in basement quarters, with enough to live on and more or less chance to graft off the tenants.

Then Vee has to get interested in the Gummidges, too, from hearin' me tell of 'em, and the next I knew she'd added 'em to her reg'lar list. No, I don't mean she pensions Pa Gummidge, or anything like that. She just keeps track of the fam'ly, remembers all their birthdays, keeps 'em chirked up in various ways, shows Rowena how to do her hair so it won't look so sloppy, fits Horatio out so he can go back to school, and smooths over a row Pa Gummidge has managed to get into with the tenant on the second floor west. It ain't so much that she likes to boss other peoples' affairs as it is that she gets to have a real likin' for 'em and can't help tryin' to give 'em a boost. And she's 'specially strong for Ma Gummidge.

"Do you know, Torchy," she tells me, "her disposition is really quite remarkable. She can be cheerful and good natured under the most trying circumstances."

"Lucky for her she can," says I. "I expect she was born that way."

"But she wasn't born to live in a basement and do janitor's

work," says Vee. "For you know Gummidge puts most of it on her. No, her people were fairly well-to-do. Her father ran a shoe store up in Troy. They lived over the store, of course, but very comfortably. She had finished high school and was starting in at the state normal, intending to be a teacher, when she met Henry Gummidge and ran off and married him. He was nearly ten years older and was engineer in a large factory. But he lost that position soon after, and they began drifting around. Her father died and in the two years that her mother tried to manage the shoe store she lost all that they had saved. Then her mother died. And the Gummidges kept getting poorer and poorer. But she doesn't complain. She keeps saying that everything will turn out all right some time. I hope it does."

"But I wouldn't bank heavy on it," says I. "I never studied Hen. Gummidge's palm, or felt his bumps, but my guess is that he'll never shake the jinx. He ain't the kind that does. He's headed down the chute, Henry is, and Ma Gummidge is goin' to need all her reserve stock of cheerfulness before she gets through. You watch."

Well, it begun to look like I was some grand little prophet. Even as a janitor Hen. Gummidge was in about the fourth class, and the Patricia apartments were kind of high grade. The tenants did a lot of grouchin' over Henry. He wouldn't get steam up in the morning until about 8:30. He didn't keep the marble vestibule scrubbed the way he should, and so on. He had a lot of alibis, but mostly he complained that he was gettin' rheumatism from livin' in such damp quarters. If it hadn't been for Vee talkin' smooth to the agent Gummidge would have been fired. As it is he hangs on, limpin' around gloomy with his hand on his hip. I expect his joints did pain him more or less. And at last he gives up altogether and camps down in an easy chair next to the kitchen stove.

It was about then he heard from this brother of his out in Nebo, Texas. Seems brother was an old bach who was runnin' a sheep ranch out there. Him and Henry hadn't kept close track of each other for a good many years, but now brother Jim has a sudden rush of fraternal affection. He wants Henry and his family to come out and join him. He's lonesome, and he's tired of doin' his own cookin'. He admits the ranch ain't much account, but there's a livin' on it, and if Henry will come along he'll make him an equal partner.

"Ain't that just my luck?" says Henry. "Where could I scrape up enough money to move to Texas, I'd like to know?"

"Think you'd like to go, do you?" I asks.

"Course I would," says Gummidge. "It would do my rheumatism good. And, then, I'd like to see old Jim again. But Gosh! It would take more 'n a hundred dollars to get us all out there, and I ain't had that much at once since I don't know when."

"Still," says I, "the thing might be financed. I'll see what can be done." Meaning that I'd put it up to Mr. Robert and Vee.

"Why, surely!" says Vee. "And wouldn't that be splendid for them all?"

"You may put me down for fifty," says Mr. Robert. "If he'll move to China I'll double it."

But Nebo seemed to be far enough off to be safe. And it was surprisin' how easy we stood it when the tickets was all bought and the time came to say good-bye to the Gummidges. As I remember, we was almost merry over it. Even Mr. Robert has to shoot off something he thinks is humorous.

"When you all get to Nebo," says he, "perhaps the old mountain will be a little less lonely."

"And if anybody offers to give you a steer down there," says I, "don't refuse. It might be just tin-horn advice, but then again he might mean a long-horn beef."

As usual Henry is the only gloom in the party. He shakes his head. "Brother Jim only keeps sheep," says he, "and I never did like mutton much, nohow. Maybe I won't live to git there, though. Seems like an awful long ways to go."

But they did land there safe enough, for about a week or ten days later Vee gets a postcard from Ma Gummidge sayin' that it was lucky they got there just as they did for they found Brother Jim pretty sick. She was sure she'd have him prancin' around again soon, and she couldn't say how much she thanked us all for what we'd done.

And with that the Gummidges sort of fades out. Not another word comes from 'em. Must have been a year and a half ago they went. More, I expect. We had one or two other things to think of meanwhile. You know how easy it is to forget people like that, specially when you make up your mind that they're sort of crossed off for good. And after a spell if somebody mentioned Texas maybe I'd recall vague that I knew someone who was down there, and wonder who it was.

Then here the other afternoon comes Vee with this announcement that the Gummidges were back. Do you wonder I didn't give way to any wild, uncontrolled joy? I could see us goin' through the same old program with 'em; listenin' to Pa Gummidge whine about how bad he felt, tryin' to keep his job for him, plannin' out a career for Horatio, and watchin' Rowena split out more shirtwaists.

Vee shows up prompt a little before closin' time. She's in a taxi and has a big suit case and a basket full of contributions. "What puzzles me," says she, "is how he could get back his old place so readily."

"Needn't worry you long," says I. "Let's go on up and have it over with and then go somewhere for dinner."

So, of course, when we rolls up to the Patricia apartment we dives down into janitor's quarters as usual. But we're halted by a putty-faced Swede person in blue denims, who can converse and smoke a pipe at the same time.

"Yah, I bane yanitor here long time," says he.

"Eh?" says I. "What about Gummidge then?"

"Oh, Meester Gummidge," says he. "He bane new tenant on second floor, yes? Sublet, furnished, two days ago yet. Nice peoples."

Well, at that I stares at Vee and she stares back.

"Whaddye mean, nice?" I demands.

"Swell peoples," says the Swede, soundin' the "v" in swell. "Second floor."

"There must be some mistake," says Vee, "but I suppose we might as well go up and see."

So up we trails to the elevator, me with the suitcase in one hand and the basket in the other, like a Santa Claus who has lost his way.

"Mr. Henry Grummidge?" says the neat elevator girl. "Yes'm. Second."

And in another minute Vee was being greeted in the dark hallway and folded in impetuous by Ma Grummidge herself. But as we are towed into the white and gold living room, where half a dozen pink-shaded electric bulbs are blazin', we could see that it wasn't exactly the same Mrs. Gummidge we'd known. She's about the same build, and she has the same number of chins. Also there's the old familiar chuckly laugh. But that's as far as it goes. This Mrs. Gummidge is attired—that's the proper word, I expect—in a black satin' evenin' dress that fits her like she'd been cast into it. Also her mop of brownish hair has been done up neat and artistic, and with the turquoise necklace danglin' down to her waist, and the marquise dinner ring flashin' on her right hand, she's more or less impressive to behold.

"Why, Mrs. Gummidge!" gasps Vee.

"I just thought that's what you'd say," says she. "But wait 'till you've seen Rowena. Come, dearie; here's comp'ny."

She was dead right. It was a case of waitin' to see Rowena, and we held our breaths while she rustled in. Say, who'd have thought that a few clothes could make such a difference? For instead of the big sloppy young female who used to slouch, gigglin' around the basement who should breeze in but a zippy young lady, a bit heavy about the shoulders maybe for that flimsy style of costume, but more or less stunning, for all that. Rowena had bloomed out. In fact, she had the lilies of the field lookin' like crepe paper imitations.

And we'd no sooner caught our breath after inspectin' her than Horatio makes an entrance, and we behold the youngster whose usual costume was an old gray sweater and a pair of baggy pants now sportin' a suit of young hick raiment that any shimmy hound on Times Square would have been glad to own. Slit pockets? Oh my, yes; and a soft collar that matched his lilac striped shirt, and cuff links and socks that toned in with both, and a Chow dog on a leather leash.

Then Pa Gummidge, shaved and slicked up as to face and hair, his bowlegs in a pair of striped weddin' trousers and the rest of him draped in a frock coat and a fancy vest, with gold eyeglasses hung on him by a black ribbon. He's puffin' away at a Cassadora cigar that must have measured seven inches over-all when it left the box. In fact, the Gummidges are displayin' all the usual marks of wealth and refinement.

"But tell me," gasps Vee, "what on earth has happened? How did—did you get it?"

"Oil," says Pa Gummidge.

Vee looks blank. "I—I don't understand," says she.

"Lemme guess," says I. "You mean you struck a gusher on the sheep ranch?"

"I didn't," says Gummidge. "Them experts I leased the land to did, though. Six hundred barrels per, and still spoutin' strong. They pay me a royalty on every barrel, too."

"Oh!" says I. "Then you and Brother Jim—"

"Poor Jim!" says Henry. "Too bad he couldn't have hung on long enough to enjoy some of it. Enough for both. Lord, yes! Just my luck to lose him. Only brother I ever had. But he's missin' a lot of trouble, at that. Having to eat with your coat on, for one thing. And this grapefruit for breakfast nonsense. I'm always squirtin' myself in the eye."

"Isn't that just like Henry?" chuckles Ma Gummidge. "Why, he grumbles because the oil people send him checks so often and he has to mail 'em to his bank. But his rheumatism's lots better and we're all havin' the best time. My, it—it's 'most like being in Heaven."

She meant it, too, every word. There wasn't an ounce of joy that Ma Gummidge was missin'.

"And it's so nice for you to be here in a comfortable apartment, instead of in some big hotel," says Vee.

"Henry's notion," says Mrs. Gummidge. "You remember the Whitleys that complained about him? He had an idea Whitley's business was petering out. Well, it was, and he was glad enough to sub-let to Henry. Never knew, either, until after the lease was signed, who we were. Furnished kind of nice, don't you think?"

"Why, Ma!" protests Rowena. Then she turns to Vee. "Of course, it'll do for a while, until we find something decent up on Riverside Drive; one with a motor entrance, you know. You're staying for dinner, aren't you?"

"Why," begins Vee, glancin' doubtful at me, "I think we—"

"Oh, do stay!" chimes in Ma Gummidge. "I did the marketing myself today; and say, there's a rib roast of beef big enough for a hotel, mushrooms raised under glass, an alligator pear salad, and hothouse strawberries for dessert. Besides, you're about the only folks we know that we could ask to dinner. Please, now!"

So we stayed and was waited on by two haughty near-French maids who tried to keep the Gummidges in their places, but didn't more than half succeed.

As we left, Rowena discovers for the first time all the hand luggage. "Oh!" says she, eyeing the suitcase. "You are in town for the week-end, are you?"

"Not exactly," says' I. "Just a few things for a fam'ly that Vee thought might need 'em."

And Vee gets out just in time to take the lid off a suppressed snicker. "Only think!" says she. "The Gummidges living like this!"

"I'm willing," says I. "I get back my shirts."

CHAPTER IV

FINDING OUT ABOUT BUDDY

The best alibi I can think up is that I did it offhand and casual. Somehow, at the time it didn't seem like what people would call an important step in my career. No. Didn't strike me that way at all. Looked like a side issue, a trifle. There was no long debate over whether I would or wouldn't, no fam'ly council, no advice from friends. Maybe I took a second look, might have rubbed my chin thoughtful once, and then I said I would.

But most of the big stuff, come to think of it, gets put over like that; from gettin' engaged to havin' the news handed you that you're a grand-daddy. Course, you might be workin' up to it for a long time, but you're so busy on other lines that you hardly notice. Then all of a sudden— Bing! Lots of young hicks' start in on a foxtrot all free and clear, and before the orchestra has swung into the next one-step they've said the fatal words that gets 'em pushing a baby carriage within a year. Same with a lot of other moves that count big.

Gettin' Buddy wished on us, for instance. I remember, I wasn't payin' much attention to what the barber was sayin'. You don't have to, you know; 'specially when they're like Joe Sarello, who generally has a lot to say.

He'd been discoursin' on several subjects—how his cousin Carmel was gettin' on with his coal and wood business up in New Rochelle, what the League of Nations really ought to do to the Zecho-Slovacks, how much the landlord has jumped his rent, and so on.

Then he begun talkin' about pups. I was wonderin' if Joe wasn't taking too much hair off the sides, just above the ears. He's apt to when he gets runnin' on. Still, I'd rather take a chance with him than get my trimmin' done in the big shop at the arcade of the Corrugated Buildin', where they shift their shear and razor artists so often you hardly get to know one by sight before he's missin'. But Joe Sarello, out here at Harbor Hills, with his little two-chair joint opposite the station, he's a fixture, a citizen. If he gets careless and nicks you on the ear you can drop in every mornin' and roast him about it. Besides, when he opens a chat he don't have to fish around and guess whether you're a reg'lar person with business in town, or if you're a week-end tourist just blown in from Oconomowoc or Houston. He knows all about you, and the family, and your kitchen help, and about Dominick, who does your outside work and tends the furnace.

He was tellin' me that his litter of pups was comin' on fine. I expect I says "Uh-huh," or something like that. The news didn't mean much to me. I was about as thrilled as if he'd been quotin' the f. o. b. price of new crop Brazil nuts. In fact, he'd mentioned this side line of his before. Barberin' for commuters left him more or less time for such enterprises. But it might have been Angora goats he was raisin', or water buffalo, or white mice.

"You no lika da dogs, hey?" asks Joe, kind of hurt.

"Eh?" says I, starin' critical into the mirror to see if he hadn't amputated more from the left side than the right.

"Oh sure! I like dogs well enough. That is, real doggy dogs; not these little imitation parlor insects, like Poms and Pekes and such. Ain't raisin' that kind, are you, Joe?"

Joe chuckles, unbuttons me from the apron, brushes a lot of short hair down my neck, and holds a hand mirror so I can get a rear elevation view of my noble dome. "Hah!" says he. "You must see. I show you dogs what is dogs. Come."

And after I've retrieved my collar and tie I follows him out back where in a lean-to shed he has a chicken wire pen with a half dozen or so of as cute, roly-poly little puppies as you'd want to see. They're sort of rusty brown and black, with comical long heads and awkward big paws, and stubby tails. And the way they was tumbling over each other, tryin' to chew with their tiny teeth, and scrimmagin' around like so many boys playin' football in a back lot—well, I couldn't help snickerin' just watchin' 'em for a minute.

"All spoke for but dees wan," says Joe, fishing out one of the lot. "Meester Parks he pick heem first wan, but now he hafta go by Chicago and no can take. Fine chance for you. With beeg place like you got you need good watch dog. Hey? What you say?"

"What's the breed, Joe?" I asks.

Joe gawps at me disgusted. I expect such ignorance was painful. "Wot kind?" says he. "Wot you t'ink? Airedale."

"Oh, yes! Of course, Airedales," says I, like it was something I'd forgotten.

And then I scratches my head. Hadn't I heard Vee sayin' how she liked some particular kind of a dog? And wasn't it this kind? Why, sure, it was. Well, why not? Joe says they're all ready to be delivered, just weaned and everything.

"I'll go you," says I. "How much?"

Say, I had to gasp when Joe names his bargain price. You see, I'd never been shoppin' for dogs before, and I hadn't kept track of the puppy market quotations. Course, I knew that some of these fancy, full-grown specimens of classy breeds brought big money at times. But little pups like this, that you could hold in your hand, or tuck into your overcoat pocket—why, my idea was the people who had 'em sort of distributed 'em around where they would have good homes; or else in the case of a party like Joe you might slip him a five or a ten.

No, I ain't tellin' what I paid. Not to anybody. But after sayin' what I had I couldn't back out without feelin' like a piker. And when Joe says confidential how he's knockin' off ten at that I writes out the check more or less cheerful.

"Ought to be good blood in him, at that figure," I suggests.

"Heem!" says Joe. "He got pedigree long lak your arm. Hees mothair ees from Lady Glen Ellen III., hees father ees blue ribbon winner two tam, Laird Ben Nevis, what was sell for—"

"Yes, I expect the fam'ly hist'ry's all right," I breaks in. "I'll take your word for it. But what do we feed him—dog biscuit?"

"No, no!" says Joe. "Not yet. Some bread wit' milk warm up in pan. T'ree, four tam a day. Bymeby put in leetle scrap cook meat an' let him have soup bone for chew.

Mus' talk to heem all tam. He get wise quick. You see."

"You flatter me, Joe," says I. "Nobody ever got wise from my talkin' to 'em. Might be interestin' to try it on a pup, though. So long."

And as I strolls along home with this warm, wriggly bunch of fur in the crook of my arm I get more and more pleased with myself. As I dopes it out I ought to make quite a hit, presenting Vee with something she's been wantin' a long time. Almost as though I'd had it raised special for her, and had been keepin' it secret for months. Looked like I was due to acquire merit in the domestic circle, great gobs of it.

"Hey, Vee!" I sings out, as soon as I've opened the livin' room door. "Come see what I've brought you."

She wasn't long coming, and I got to admit that when I displays Mr. Pup the expected ovation don't come off. I don't get mixed up in any fond and impetuous embrace. No. If I must tell the truth she stands there with her mouth open starin' at me and it.

"Why—why, Torchy!" she gasps. "A puppy?"

"Right, first guess," says I. "By the way you're gawpin' at it, though, it might be a young zebra or a baby hippopotamus. But it's just a mere puppy. Airedale."

"Oh!" says Vee, gaspier than ever. "An—an Airedale?"

"Well?" says I. "Wasn't that the kind I've heard you boostin' all along?"

"Ye-e-es," says she, draggy, "I—I suppose it was. And I do admire them very much, but—well, I hadn't really thought of owning one. They—they are such strenuous dogs, you know; and with the baby and all—"

"Say, take a look!" I breaks in. "Does this one size up like he was a child eater? Here, heft him once." And I hands him over.

Course, it ain't five minutes before she's cuddlin' him up and cooin' to him, and he's gnawing away at her thumb with his little puppy teeth.

"Such a dear!" says Vee. "And we could keep him out in the garage, and have Dominick look after him, couldn't we? For they get to be such big dogs, you know."

"Do they?" says I.

I didn't see quite how they could. Why, this one was about big enough to go in a hat, that's all, and he was nearly two months old. But say, what I didn't know about Airedale pups was a heap. Grow! Honest, you could almost watch him lengthen out and fill in. Yet for a couple of weeks there he was no more'n a kitten, and just as cute and playful. Every night after dinner I'd spend about an hour rollin' him over on his back and lettin' him bite away at my bare hand. He liked to get hold of my trouser leg, or Vee's dress, or the couch cover, or anything else that was handy, and tug away and growl. Reg'lar circus to see him.

And then I begun to find scratches on my hands. The little rascal was gettin' a full set of puppy teeth. Sharp as needles, too. I noticed a few threads pulled out of my sleeve. And once when he got a good grip on Vee's skirt he made a rip three inches long. But he was so cunnin' about it we only laughed.

"You young rough houser!" I'd say, and push him over.

He'd come right back for more, though, until he was tuckered and then he'd stretch out on something soft and sleep with one paw over his nose while we watched admirin'.

We had quite a time findin' a name for him. I got Joe to give his pedigree all written out and we was tryin' to dope out from that something that would sound real Scotch. Vee got some kennel catalogues, too, and read over some of those old Ian MacLaren stories for names, but we couldn't hit on one that just suited. Meanwhile I begins callin' him Buddy, as the boys did everybody in the army, and finally Vee insists that it's exactly the name for him.

"He's so rough and ready," says she.

"He's rough, all right," says I, examinin' a new tooth mark on the back of my hand.

And he kept on gettin' rougher. What he really needed, I expect, was a couple of cub bears to exercise his teeth and paws on; good, husky, tough-skinned ones, at that. Not havin' 'em he took it out on us. Oh, yes. Not that he was to blame, exactly. We'd started him that way, and he seemed to like the taste of me 'specially.

"They're one-man dogs, you know," says Vee.

"Meanin'," says I, "that they like to chew one man at a time. See my right wrist. Looks like I'd shoved it through a pane of glass. Hey, you tarrier! Lay off me for a minute, will you? For the love of soup eat something else. Here's a slipper. Now go to it."

And you should see him shake and worry that around the room. Almost as good as a vaudeville act—until I discovers that he's gnawed a hole clear through the toe.

"Gosh!" says I. "My favorite slipper, too."

At four months he was no longer a handful. He was a lapful, and then some. Somewhere near twenty-five pounds, as near as we could judge by holding him on the bathroom scales for the fraction of a second. And much too lively for any lap. Being cuddled wasn't his strong point. Hardly. He'd be all over you in a minute, clawin' you in the face with his big paws and nippin' your ear or grabbin' a mouthful of hair; all playful enough, but just as gentle as being tackled by a quarterback on an end run.

And he was gettin' wise, all right. He knew to the minute when mealtime came around, and if he wasn't let out on the kitchen porch where his chow was served he thought nothing of scratchin' the paint off a door or tryin' to chew the knob. Took only two tries to teach him to stand up on his hind legs and walk for his meals, as straight as a drum major. Also he'd shake hands for a bit of candy, and retrieve a rubber ball. But chiefly he delighted to get a stick of soft wood and go prancin' through the house with it, rappin' the furniture or your shins as he went, and end up by chewin' it to bits on the fireplace hearth rug. Or it might be a smelly old bone that he'd smuggled in from outside. You could guess that would get Vee registerin' a protest and I'd have to talk to Buddy.

"Hey!" I'd remark, grabbin' him by the collar. "Whaddye think this is, a soap fact'ry? Leggo that shin-bone."

"Gr-r-r-r!" he'd remark back, real hostile, and roll his eyes menacin'.

At which Vee would snicker and observe: "Now isn't he the dearest thing to do that, Torchy? Do let him have his booful bone there. I'll spread a newspaper under it."

Her theory was good, only Buddy didn't care to gnaw his bone on an evening edition. He liked eatin' it on the Turkish rug better. And that's where he did eat it. That was about the way his trainin' worked out in other things. We had some perfectly good ideas about what he should do; he'd have others, quite different; and we'd compromise. That is, we'd agree that Buddy was right. Seemed to me about the only thing to do, unless you had all day or all night to argue with him and show him where he was wrong. I could keep it up for an hour or two. Then I either got hoarse or lost my disposition.

You remember there was some talk of keepin' him in the garage at first. Anyway, it was mentioned. And he was kept there the first night, until somewhere around 2 A. M. Then I trailed out in a bathrobe and slippers and lugged him in. He'd howled for three hours on a stretch and seemed to be out for the long-distance championship. Not havin' looked up the past performances in non-stop howlin' I couldn't say whether he'd hung up a new record or not. I was willin' to concede the point. Besides, I wanted a little sleep, even if he didn't. I expect we was lucky that he picks out a berth behind the kitchen stove as the proper place for him to snooze. He might have fancied the middle of our bed. If he had, we'd camped on the floor, I suppose.

Another good break for us was the fact that he was willin' to be tethered out daytimes on a wire traveler that Dominick fixed up for him. Course, he did dig up a lot of Vee's favorite dahlia bulbs, and he almost undermined a corner of the kitchen wing when he set out to put a choice bone in cold storage, but he was so comical when he tamped the bone down with his nose that Vee didn't complain.

"We can have the hole filled in and sodded over next

spring," says Vee.

"Huh!" I says. "By next spring he'll be big enough to tunnel clear under the house."

Looked like he would. At five months Buddy weighed 34 pounds and to judge by his actions most of him was watchspring steel geared in high speed. He was as hard as nails all over and as quick-motioned as a cat. I'd got into the habit of turnin' him loose when I came home and indulgin' in a half hour's rough house play with him. Buddy liked that. He seemed to need it in his business of growin' up. If I happened to forget, he wasn't backward in remindin' me of the oversight. He'd developed a bark that was sort of a cross between an automobile shrieker and throwin' a brick through a plate glass window, and when he put his whole soul into expressin' his feelin's that way everybody within a mile needed cotton in their ears. So I'd drape myself in an old raincoat, put on a pair of heavy drivin' gauntlets, and frisk around with him.

No doubt about Buddy's being glad to see me on them occasions. His affection was deep and violent. He'd let out a few joy yelps, take a turn around the yard, and then come leapin' at me with his mouth open and his eyes rollin' wild. My part of the game was to grab him by the back of the neck and throw him before he could sink his teeth into any part of me. Sometimes I missed. That was a point for Buddy. Then I'd pry his jaws loose and he'd dash off for another circle. I couldn't say how the score averaged. I was too busy to keep count. About fifty-fifty would be my guess. Anyway, it did Buddy a lot of good and must have been fine practice. If he ever has to stop an offensive on the part of an invadin' bull-dog he'll be in good trim. He'd tackle one, all right. The book we bought says that an Airedale will go up a tree after a mountain lion. I can believe it. I've never seen Buddy tuck his tail down for anything on four legs. Yet he ain't the messy kind. He don't seem anxious to start anything. But I'll bet he'd be a hard finisher.

And he sure is a folksy dog with the people he knows around the house. Most of 'em he treats gentler than he does me, which shows that he's got some sense. And when it comes to the baby; why, say, he'll gaze as admirin' at young Master Richard toddlin' around as if he was some blood relation; followin' him everywhere, with that black nose nuzzled under one of the youngster's arms, or with a sleeve held tender in his teeth. Any kid at all Buddy is strong for. He'll leave a bone or his play any time he catches sight of one, and go prancin' around 'em, waggin' his stubby tail friendly and inviting 'em to come have a romp.

Maybe you wouldn't accuse Buddy of being handsome. I used to think Airedales was about the homeliest dogs on the list. Mostly, you know, they're long on nose. It starts between their ears and extends straight out for about a foot. Gives 'em kind of a simple expression. But you get a good look into them brown eyes of Buddy's, 'specially when he's listenin' to you with his head cocked on one side and an ear turned wrong side out, and you'll decide he must have some gray matter concealed somewhere. Then there's that black astrakan coat-effect on his back, and the clean-cut lines of his deep chest and slim brown legs, which are more or less decorative. Anyway he got so he looked kind of good to me.

Like people, though, Buddy had his bad days. Every once in a while his fondness for chewin' things would get him in wrong. Then he'd have to be scolded. And you can't tell me he don't know the meanin' of the words when you call him a "bad, bad dog." No, sir. Why, he'd drop his head and tail and sneak into a corner as if he'd been struck with a whip. And half an hour later he'd be up to the same sort of mischief. I asked Joe Sarello about it.

"Ah!" says Joe, shruggin' his shoulders. "Hees puppy yet. Wanna do w'at he lak, all tam. He know better, but he strong in the head. You gotta beat him up good. No can hurt. Tough lak iron. Beat him up."

But Vee won't have it. I didn't insist. I didn't care much for the job. So Buddy gets off by being informed stern that he'd a bad, bad dog.

And then here the other day I comes home to find Buddy locked in the garage and howlin' indignant. Vee says he mustn't be let out, either.

"What's the idea?" I asks.

Then I gets the whole bill of complaint. It seems Buddy has started the day by breakin' loose from his wire and chasin' the chickens all over the place. He'd cornered our pet Rhode Island Red rooster and nipped out a mouthful of tail feathers. It took the whole household and some of the neighbors to get him to quit that little game.

This affair had almost been forgiven and he was havin' his lunch on the back porch when Vee's Auntie blows in unexpected for a little visit. Before anybody has time to stop him Buddy is greetin' her in his usual impetuous manner. He does it by plantin' his muddy forepaws in three places on the front of her dress and then grabbin' her gold lorgnette playful, breakin' the chain, and runnin' off with the loot.

I expect that was only Buddy's idea of letting her know that he welcomed her as a member of the fam'ly in good standin'. But Auntie takes it different. She asks Vee why we allow a "horrible beast like that to run at large." She's a vivid describer, Auntie. She don't mind droppin' a word of good advice now and then either. While she's being sponged off and brushed down she recommends that we get rid of such a dangerous animal as that at once.

So Buddy is tied up again outside. But it appears to be his day for doing the wrong thing. Someone has hung Vee's best evenin' wrap out on a line to air after having a spot cleaned. It's the one with the silver fox fur on the collar. And it's hung where Buddy can just reach it. Well, you can guess the rest. Any kind of a fox, deceased or otherwise, is fair game for Buddy. It's right in his line. And when they discovered what he was up to there wasn't a piece of that fur collar big enough to make an ear muff. Parts of the wrap might still be used for polishin' the silver. Buddy seemed kind of proud of the thorough job he'd made.

Well, Vee had been 'specially fond of that wrap. She'd sort of blown herself when she got it, and you know how high furs have gone to these days. I expect she didn't actually weep, but she must have been near it. And there was Auntie with more stern advice. She points out how a brute dog with such destructive instincts would go on and on, chewin' up first one valuable thing and then another, until we'd have nothing left but what we had on.

Buddy had been tried and found guilty in the first degree. Sentence had been passed. He must go.

"Perhaps your barber friend will take him back," says Vee. "Or the Ellinses might want him. Anyway, he's impossible. You must get rid of him tonight. Only I don't wish to know how, or what becomes of him."

"Very well," says I, "if that's the verdict."

I loads Buddy ostentatious into the little roadster and starts off, with him wantin' to sit all over me as usual, or else drapin' himself on the door half-way out of the car. Maybe I stopped at Joe Sarello's, maybe I only called at the butcher's and collected a big, juicy shin-bone. Anyway, it was' after dark when I got back and when I came in to dinner I was alone.

The table chat that evenin' wasn't quite as lively as it generally is. And after we'd been sitting around in the livin' room an hour or so with everything quiet, Vee suddenly lets loose with a sigh, which is a new stunt for her. She ain't the sighin' kind. But there's no mistake about this one.

"Eh?" says I, lookin' up.

"I—I hope you found him a good home," says she.

"Oh!" says I. "The impossible beast? Probably as good as he deserves."

Then we sat a while longer.

"Little Richard was getting very fond of him," Vee breaks out again.

"Uh-huh," says I.

We went upstairs earlier than usual. There wasn't so much to do about gettin' ready—no givin' Buddy a last run outside, or makin' him shake a good night with his paw, or seein' that he had water in his dish. Nothing but turnin' out the lights. Once, long after Vee should have been asleep. I thought I heard her snifflin', but I dozed off again without makin' any remark.

I must have been sawin' wood good and hard, too, when I wakes up to find her shakin' me by the shoulder.

"Listen, Torchy," she's sayin'. "Isn't that Buddy's bark?"

"Eh? Buddy?" says I. "How could it be?"

"But it is!" she insists. "It's coming from the garage, too."

"Well, that's odd," says I. "Maybe I'd better go out and see."

I was puzzled all right, in spite of the fact that I'd left him there with his bone and had made Dominick promise to stick around and quiet him if he began yelpin'. But this wasn't the way Buddy generally barked when he was indignant. He was lettin' 'em out short and crisp. They sounded different somehow, more like business. And the light was turned on in the garage!

First off I thought Dominick must be there. Maybe I wouldn't have dashed out so bold if I'd doped it out any other way. I hadn't thought of car thieves. Course, there had been some cases around, mostly young hicks from the village stealin' joy-rides. But I hadn't worried about their wantin' to take my little bus. So I arrives on the jump.

And there in a corner of the garage are two young toughs, jumpin' and dodgin' at a lively rate, with Buddy sailin' into 'em for all he's worth and givin' out them quick short battle cries. One of the two has just managed to get hold of a three-foot length of galvanized water pipe and is swingin' vicious at Buddy when I crashes in.

Well, we had it hectic for a minute or so there, but it turns out a draw with no blood shed, although I think Buddy and I could have made 'em sorry they came if they hadn't made a break and got past us. And when we gets back to where Vee is waitin' with the fire-poker in her hand Buddy still waves in his teeth a five-inch strip of brown mixture trousering.

"You blessed, blessed Buddy!!" says Vee, after she's heard the tale.

Oh, yes, Buddy finished the night behind the stove in the kitchen. I guess he's kind of earned his right to that bunk. Course, he ain't sprouted any wings yet, but he's gettin' so the sight of a switch waved at him works wonders. Some day, perhaps, he'll learn to be less careless what he exercises them sharp teeth of his on. Last night it was the leather covering on the library couch—chewed a hole half as big as your hand.

"Never mind," says Vee. "We can keep a cushion over it."

CHAPTER V

IN DEEP FOR WADDY

And all the time I had Wadley Fiske slated as a dead one! Course, he was one of Mr. Robert's clubby friends. But that don't always count. He may be choosey enough picking live wires for his office staff, Mr. Robert, as you might guess by my bein' his private sec; but when it came to gettin' a job lot of friends wished on him early in his career, I must say he couldn't have been very finicky.

Not that Waddy's a reg'lar washout, or carries a perfect vacuum between the ears, or practices any of the seven deadly sins. He's a cheerful, good-natured party, even if he is built like a 2x4 and about as broad in the shoulders as a cough drop is thick. I understand he qualifies in the scheme of things by playin' a fair game of billiards, is always willing to sit in at bridge, and can make himself useful at any function where the ladies are present. Besides, he always wears the right kind of clothes, can say bright little things at a dinner party, and can generally be located by calling up any one of his three clubs.

Chiefly, though, Waddy is a ladies' man. With him being in and out of the Corrugated General Offices so much I couldn't help gettin' more or less of a line on him that way, for he's always consultin' Mr. Robert about sendin' flowers to this one, or maneuverin' to get introduced to the other, or gushin' away about some sweet young thing that he's met the night before.

"How does he get away with all that Romeo stuff," I asks Mr. Robert once, "without being tagged permanent? Is it just his good luck?"

"Waddy calls it his hard luck," says Mr. Robert. "It seems as if they just use him to practice on. He will find a new queen of his heart, appear to be getting on swimmingly up to a certain point—and then she will marry someone else. Invariably. I've known of at least a half dozen of his affairs to turn out like that."

"Kind of a matrimonial runner-up, eh?" says I.

Oh, yes, I expect we got off a lot of comic lines about Waddy. Anyway we passed 'em as such. But of course there come days when we have other things to do here at the Corrugated besides shoot the gay and frivolous chatter back and forth. Now and then. Such as here last Wednesday when Mr. Robert had two committee meetin's on for the afternoon and was goin' over with me some tabulated stuff I'd doped out for the annual report. Right in the midst of that Wadley Fiske blows in and proceeds to hammer Mr. Robert on the back.

"I say, Bob," says he, "you remember my telling you about the lovely Marcelle Jedain? I'm sure I told you."

"If you didn't it must have been an oversight," says Mr. Robert. "Suppose we admit that you did."

"Well, what do you think?" goes on Waddy, "She is here!"

"Eh?" says Mr. Robert, glancin' around nervous. "Why the deuce do you bring her here?"

"No, no, my dear chap!" protests Waddy. "In this country, I mean."

"Oh!" and Mr. Robert sighs relieved. "Well, give the young lady my best regards and—er—I wish you luck. Thanks for dropping in to tell me."

"Not at all," says Waddy, drapin' himself easy on a chair. "But that's just the beginning."

"Sorry, Waddy," says Mr. Robert, "but I fear I am too busy just now to—"

"Bah!" snorts Waddy. "You can attend to business any time—tomorrow, next week, next month. But the lovely Marcelle may be sailing within forty-eight hours."

"Well, what do you expect me to do?" demands Mr. Robert. "Want me to scuttle the steamer?"

"I want you to help me find Joe Bruzinski," says Waddy.

Mr. Robert throws up both hands and groans. "Here, Torchy," says, he, "take him away. Listen to his ravings, and if you can discover any sense—"

"But I tell you," insists Waddy, "that I must find Bruzinski at once."

"Very well," says Mr. Robert, pushin' him towards the door. "Torchy will help you find him. Understand, Torchy? Bruzinski. Stay with him until he does."

"Yes, sir," says I, grinnin' as I locks an arm through one

of Waddy's and tows him into the outer office. "Bruzinski or bust."

And by degrees I got the tale. First off, this lovely Marcelle person was somebody he'd met while he was helpin' wind up the great war. No, not on the Potomac sector. Waddy actually got across. You might not think it to look at him, but he did. Second lieutenant, too. Infantry, at that. But they handed out eommissions to odder specimens than him at Plattsburg, you know. And while Waddy got over kind of late he had the luck to be in a replacement unit that made the whoop-la advance into Belgium after the Hun line had cracked.

Seems it was up in some dinky Belgian town where the Fritzies had been runnin' things for four years that Waddy meets this fair lady with the impulsive manners. His regiment had wandered in only a few hours after the Germans left and to say that the survivin' natives was glad to see 'em is drawin' it mild. This Miss Jedain was the gladdest of the glad, and when Waddy shows up at her front door with a billet ticket callin' for the best front room she just naturally falls on his neck. I take it he got kissed about four times in quick concussion. Also that the flavor lasted.

"To be received in that manner by a high born, charming young woman," says Waddy. "It—it was delightful. Perhaps you can imagine."

"No," says I. "I ain't got that kind of a mind. But go on. What's the rest?"

Well, him and the lovely Marcelle had three days of it. Not going to a fond clinch every time he came down to breakfast or drifted in for luncheon. She simmered down a bit, I under stand, after her first wild splurge. But she was very folksy all through his stay, insisted that Waddy was her heroic deliverer, and all that sort of thing.

"Of course," says Waddy, "I tried to tell her that I'd had very little to do personally with smashing the Hindenburg line. But she wouldn't listen to a word. Besides, my French was rather lame. So we—we—Well, we became very dear to each other. She was charming, utterly. And so full of gratitude to all America. She could not do enough for our boys. All day she was going among them, distributing little dainties she had cooked, giving them little keepsakes, smiling at them, singing to them. And every night she had half a dozen officers in to dinner. But to me—ah, I can't tell you how sweet she was."

"Don't try," says I. "I think I get a glimmer. All this lasted three days, eh! Then you moved on."

Waddy sighs deep. "I didn't know until then how dreadful war could be," says he. "I promised to come back to her just as soon as the awful mess was over. She declared that she would come to America if I didn't. She gave me one of her rings. 'It shall be as a token,' she told me, 'that I am yours.'"

"Sort of a trunk check, eh?" says I.

"Ah, that ring!" says Waddy. "You see, it was too large for my little finger too small for any of the others. And I was afraid of losing it if I kept it in my pocket. I was always losing things—shaving mirrors, socks, wrist watch. Going about like that one does. At least, I did. All over France I scattered my belongings. That's what you get by having had a valet for so long.

"So I called up Joe Bruzinski, my top sergeant. Best top in the army, Joe; systematic, methodical. I depended upon him for nearly everything; couldn't have gotten along without him, in fact. Not an educated fellow, you know. Rather crude. An Americanized Pole, I believe. But efficient, careful about little things. I gave him the ring to keep for me. Less than a week after that I was laid up with a beastly siege of influenza which came near finishing me. I was shipped back to a base hospital and it was more than a month before I was on my feet again. Meanwhile I'd gotten out of touch with my division, applied for a transfer to another branch, got stuck with an S. O. S. job, and landed home at the tail-end of everything after all the shouting was over."

"I see," says I. "Bruzinski lost in the shuffle."

"Precisely," says Waddy. "Mustered out months before I was. When I did get loose they wouldn't let me go back to Belgium. And then—"

"I remember," says I. "You side-tracked the lovely Marcelle for that little blonde from. Richmond, didn't you?"

"A mere passing fancy," says Waddy, flushin' up. "Nothing serious. She was really engaged all the time to Bent Hawley. They're to be married next month, I hear. But Marcelle! She has come. Just think, she has been in this country for weeks, came over with the King and Queen of Belgium and stayed on. Looking for me. I suppose. And I knew nothing at all about it until yesterday. She's in Washington. Jimmy Carson saw her driving down Pennsylvania avenue. He was captain of my company, you know. Rattle-brained chap, Jimmy. Hadn't kept track of Bruzinski at all. Knew he came back, but no more. So you see? In order to get that ring I must find Joe."

"I don't quite get you," says I. "Why not find the lovely Marcelle first and explain about the ring afterwards?"

Waddy shakes his head. "I was in uniform when she knew me," says he. "I—I looked rather well in it, I'm told. Anyway, different. But in civies, even a frock coat, I've an idea she wouldn't recognize me as a noble hero. Eh?"

"Might be something in that," I admits.

"But if I had the ring that she gave me—her token—well, you see?" goes on Waddy. "I must have it. So I must find Bruzinski."

"Yes, that's your play," I agrees. "Where did he hail from?"

"Why, from somewhere in Pennsylvania," says Waddy; "some weird little place that I never could remember the name of."

"Huh!" says I. "Quite a sizable state, you know. You couldn't ramble through it in an afternoon pagin' Joe Bruzinski."

"I suppose one couldn't," says Waddy. "But there must be some way of locating him. Couldn't I telegraph to the War Department?"

"You could," says I, "and about a year from next Yom Kippur you might get a notice that your wire had been received and placed on file. Why, they're still revisin' casualty lists from the summer of 1918. If you're in any hurry about gettin' in touch with Mr. Bruzinski—"

"Hurry!" gasps Waddy. "Why, I must find him by tonight."

"That's goin' to call for speed," says I. "I don't see how you could—Say, now! I just thought of something. We might tickle Uncle Sam in the W. R. I. B."

"Beg pardon!" says Waddy, gawpin'.

"War Risk Insurance Bureau," I explains. "That is, if Miss Callahan's still there. Used to be one of our stenogs until she went into war work. Last I knew she was still at it, had charge of one of the filing cases. They handle soldier's insurance there, you know, and if Bruzinski's kept his up—"

"By George!" breaks in Waddy. "Of course. Do you know, I never thought of that."

"No, you wouldn't," says I "May not work, at that. But we can try. She's a reg'lar person, Miss Callahan."

Anyway, she knew right where to put her fingers on Joe Bruzinski's card and shoots us back his mailin' address by lunch time. It's Coffee Creek, Pa.

"What an absurd place to live in!" says Waddy. "And how on earth can we ever find it."

"Eh?" says I. "We?"

"But I couldn't possibly get there by myself," says Waddy. "I've never been west of Philadelphia. Oh, yes, I've traveled a lot abroad, but that's different. One hires a courier. Really, I should be lost out of New York. Besides, you know Mr. Robert said you were to—oh, there he is now. I say, Bob, isn't Torchy to stay with me until I find Bruzinski?"

"Absolutely," says Mr. Robert, throwin' a grin over his

shoulder at me as he slips by.

"Maybe he thinks that's a life sentence," says I. "Chuck me that Pathfinder from the case behind you, will you? Now let's see. Here we are, page 937—Coffee Creek, Pa. Inhabitants 1,500. Flag station on the Lackawanna below Wilkes-Barre. That's in the Susquehanna valley. Must be a coal town. Chicago limited wouldn't stop there. But we can probably catch a jitney or something from Wilkes-Barre. Just got time to make the 1:15, too. Come on. Lunch on train."

I expect Waddy ain't been jumped around so rapid before in his whole career. I allows him only time enough to lay in a fresh supply of cigarettes on the way to the ferry and before he's caught his breath we are sittin' in the dinin' car zoomin' through the north end of New Jersey. I tried to get him interested in the scenery as we pounded through the Poconos and galloped past the Water Gap, but it couldn't be done. When he gets real set on anything it seems Waddy has a single track mind.

"I trust he still has that ring," he remarks.

"That'll ride until we've found your ex-top sergeant," says I. "What was his line before he went in the army—plumber, truck driver, or what?"

Waddy hadn't the least idea. Not having been mixed up in industry himself, he hadn't been curious. Now that I mentioned it he supposed Joe had done something for a living. Yes, he was almost sure. He had noticed that Joe's hands were rather rough and calloused.

"What would that indicate?" asks Waddy.

"Most anything," says I, "from the high cost of gloves to a

strike of lady manicures. Don't strain your intellect over it, though. If he's still in Coffee Creek there shouldn't be much trouble findin' him."

Which was where I took a lot for granted. When we piled off the express at Wilkes-Barre I charters a flivver taxi, and after a half hour's drive with a speed maniac who must have thought he was pilotin' a DeHaviland through the clouds we're landed in the middle of this forsaken, one horse dump, consistin' of a double row of punk tenement blocks and a sprinklin' of near-beer joints that was givin' their last gasp. I tried out three prominent citizens before I found one who savvied English.

"Sure!" says he. "Joe Bruzinski? He must be the mine boss by Judson's yet. First right hand turn you take and keep on the hill up."

"Until what?" says I.

"Why, Judson's operation—the mine," says he. "Can't miss. Road ends at Judson's."

Uh-huh. It did. High time, too. A road like that never should be allowed to start anywhere. But the flivver negotiated it and by luck we found the mine superin- tendent in the office—a grizzled, chunky little Welshman with a pair of shrewd eyes. Yes, he says Bruzinski is around somewhere. He thinks he's down on C level plotting out some new contracts for the night shift.

"What luck!" says Waddy. "I say, will you call him right up?"

"That I will, sir," says the superintendent, "if you'll tell me how."

"Why," says Waddy, "couldn't you—er—telephone to him, or send a messenger?"

It seems that can't be done. "You might try shouting down, the shaft though," says the Welshman, with a twinkle in his eyes.

Waddy would have gone hoarse doin' it, too, if I hadn't given him the nudge. "Wake up," says I. "You're being kidded."

"But see here, my man—" Waddy begins.

"Mr. Llanders is the name," says the superintendent a bit crisp.

"Ah, yes. Thanks," says Waddy. "It is quite important, Mr. Llanders, that I find Bruzinski at once."

"Mayhap he'll be up by midnight for a bite to eat," says Llanders.

"Then we'll just have to go down where he is," announces Waddy.

Llanders stares at him curious. "You'd have an interesting time doing that, young man," says he; "very interesting."

"But I say," starts in Waddy again, which was where I shut him off.

"Back up, Waddy," says I, "before you bug the case entirely. Let me ask Mr. Llanders where I can call up your good friend Judson."

"That I couldn't rightly say, sir," says Llanders. "It might be one place, and it might be another. Maybe they'd know better at the office of his estate in Scranton, but as he's been dead these eight years—"

"Check!" says I. "It would have been a swell bluff if it had worked though, wouldn't it?"

Llanders indulges in a grim smile. "But it didn't," says he.

"That's the sad part," says I, "for Mr. Fiske here is in a great stew to see this Bruzinski party right away. There's a lady in the case, as you might know; one they met while they were soldierin' abroad. So if there's any way you could fix it for them to get together—"

"Going down's the only way," says Llanders, "and that's strictly against orders."

"Except on a pass, eh?" says I. "Lucky we brought that along. Waddy, slip it to Mr. Llanders. No, don't look stupid. Feel in your right hand vest pocket. That's it, one of those yellow-backed ones with a double X in the corners. Ah, here! Don't you know how to present a government pass?" And I has to take it away from him and tuck it careless into the superintendent's coat pocket.

"Of course," says Llanders, "if you young gentlemen are on official business, it makes a difference."

"Then let's hurry along," says Waddy, startin' impatient.

"Dressed like that?" says Llanders, starin' at Waddy's Fifth Avenue costume. "I take it you've not been underground before, sir?"

"Only in the subway," says Waddy.

"You'll find a coal mine quite unlike the subway," says

Llanders. "I think we can fix you up for it, though."

They did. And when Waddy had swapped his frock coat for overalls and jumper, and added a pair of rubber boots and a greasy cap with an acetylene lamp stuck in the front of it he sure wouldn't have been recognized even by his favorite waiter at the club. I expect I looked about as tough, too. And I'll admit that all this preparation seemed kind of foolish there in the office. Ten minutes later I knew it wasn't. Not a bit.

"Do we go down in a car or something?" asks Waddy.

"Not if you go with me," says Llanders. "We'll walk down Slope 8. Before we start, however, it will be best for me to tell you that this was a drowned mine."

"Listens excitin'," says I. "Meanin' what?"

"Four years ago the creek came in on us," says Llanders, "flooded us to within ten feet of the shaft mouth. We lost only a dozen men, but it was two years before we had the lower levels clear. We manage to keep it down now with the pumps, Bruzinski is most likely at the further end of the lowest level."

"Is he?" says Waddy. "I must see him, you know."

Whether he took in all this about the creek's playful little habits or not I don't know. Anyway, he didn't hang back, and while I've started on evenin' walks that sounded a lot pleasanter I wasn't going to duck then. If Waddy could stand it I guessed I could.

So down we goes into a black hole that yawns in the middle of a muddy field. I hadn't gone far, either, before I discovers that being your own street light wasn't such an easy trick. I expect a miner has to wear his lamp on his head so's to have his hands free to swing a pick. But I'll be hanged if it's comfortable or easy. I unhooked mine and carried it in my hand, ready to throw the light where I needed it most.

And there was spots where I sure needed it bad, for this Slope 8 proposition was no garden pathway, I'll say. First off, it was mucky and slippery under foot, and in some places it dips down sharp, almost as steep as a church roof. Then again there was parts where they'd skimped on the ceilin', and you had to do a crouch or else bump your bean on unpadded rocks. On and down, down and on we went, slippin' and slidin', bracin' ourselves against the wet walls, duckin' where it was low and restin' our necks where they'd been more generous with the excavatin'.

There was one 'specially sharp pitch of a hundred feet or so and right in the worst of it we had to dodge a young waterfall that comes filterin' down through the rocks. It was doin' some roarin' and splashin', too. I was afraid Llanders might not have noticed it.

"How about it!" says I. "This ain't another visit from the creek, is it?"

"Only part of it," says he careless. "The pumps are going, you know."

"I hope they're workin' well," says I.

As for Waddy, not a yip out of him. He sticks close behind Llanders and plugs along just as if he was used to scramblin' through a muddy hole three hundred feet or so below the grass roots. That's what it is to be 100 per cent in love. All he could think of was gettin' that ring back and renewin' cordial relations with the lovely Marcelle.

But I was noticin' enough for two. I knew that we'd made so many twists and turns that we must be lost for keeps. I saw the saggy, rotten timbers that kept the State of Pennsylvania from cavin' in on us. And now and then I wondered how long it would be before they dug us out.

"Where's all the coal?" I asks Llanders, just by way of makin' talk.

"Why, here," says he, touchin' the side-wall.

Sure enough, there it was, the real black diamond stuff such as you shovel into the furnace—when you're lucky. I scaled off a piece and tested it with the lamp. And gradually I begun to revise my ideas of a coal mine. I'd always thought of it as a big cave sort of a place, with a lot of miners grouped around the sides pickin' away sociable. But here is nothing but a maze of little tunnels, criss-crossin' every which way, with nobody in sight except now and then, off in a dead-end, we'd get a glimpse of two or three kind of ghosty figures movin' about solemn. It's all so still, too. Except in places where we could hear the water roarin' there wasn't a sound. Only in one spot, off in what Llanders calls a chamber, we finds two men workin' a compressed air jack-hammer, drillin' holes.

"They'll be shooting a blast soon," says Llanders. "Want to wait?"

"No thanks," says I prompt. "Mr. Fiske is in a rush."

Maybe I missed something interestin', but with all that rock over my head I wasn't crazy to watch somebody monkey with dynamite. The jack-hammer crew gave us a line on where we might find Bruzinski, and I expect for a while there I led the way. After another ten-minute stroll, durin' which we dodged a string of coal cars being shunted down a grade, we comes across three miners chattin' quiet in a corner. One of 'em turns out to be the mine-boss.

"Hey, Joe!" says Llanders. "Somebody wants to see you."

At which Waddy pushes to the front. "Oh, I say, Bruzinski! Remember me, don't you?" he asks.

Joe looks him over casual and shakes his head.

"I'm Lieutenant Fiske, you know," says Waddy. "That is, I was."

"Well, I'll be damned!" says Joe earnest. "The Loot! What's up?"

"That ring I gave you in Belgium," goes on Waddy. "I—I hope you still have it?"

"Ye-e-es," says Joe draggy. "Fact is, I was goin' to use it tomorrow. I'm gettin' engaged. Nice girl, too. I was meanin' to—"

"But you can't, Joe," breaks in Waddy. "Not with that ring. Miss Jedain gave me that. Here, I'll give you another. How will this do?" And Waddy takes a low set spark off his finger.

"All right. Fine!" says Joe, and proceeds to unhook the other ring from his leather watch, guard. "But what's all the hurry about?"

"Because she's here," says Waddy. "In Washington, I mean. The lovely Marcelle. Came over looking for me, Joe, just as she promised. Perhaps you didn't know she did promise, though?"

"Sure," says Joe. "That's what she told all of us."

"Eh?" gasps Waddy.

"Some hugger, that one," says Joe. "Swell lady, too. A bear-cat for makin' love, I'll tell the world. Me, and the Cap., and the First Loot, and you, all the same day. She was goin' to marry us all. And the Cap., with a wife and two kids back in Binghamton, N. Y., he got almost nervous over it."

"I—I can't believe it," says Waddy gaspy. "Did—did she give you a—a token, as she did to me?"

"No," says Joe. "None of us fell quite so hard for her as you did. I guess we kinda suspected what was wrong with her."

"Wrong?" echoes Waddy.

"Why not?" asks Joe. "Four years of the Huns, and then we came blowin' in to lift the lid and let 'em come up out of the cellars. Just naturally went simple in the head, she did. Lots like her, only they took it out in different ways. Her line was marryin' us, singly and in squads; over-lookin' complete that she had one perfectly good hubby who was an aide or something to King Albert, as well as three nice youngsters. We heard about that later, after she'd come to a little."

For a minute or so Waddy stands there starin' at Joe with his mouth open and his shoulders sagged. Then he slumps on a log and lets his chin drop.

"Goin' to hunt her up and give back the ring?" asks Joe.

Sewell Ford

"That the idea?"

"Not—not precisely," says Waddy. "I—I shall send it by mail, I think."

And all the way out he walked like he was in a daze. He generally takes it hard for a day or so, I understand. So we had that underground excursion all for nothing. That is, unless you count my being able to give Mr. Robert the swift comeback next mornin' when he greets me with a chuckle.

"Well, Torchy," says he, "how did you leave Bruzinski?"

"Just where I found him," says I, "about three hundred feet underground."

CHAPTER VI

HOW TORCHY ANCHORED A COOK

It began with Stella Flynn, but it ended with the Hon. Sour Milk and Madam Zenobia. Which is one reason why my job as private sec. to Mr. Robert Ellins is one I wouldn't swap for Tumulty's—unless they came insistin' that I had to go to the White House to save the country. And up to date I ain't had any such call. There's no tellin' though. Mr. Robert's liable to sic 'em onto me any day.

You see, just because I've happened to pull a few winnin' acts where I had the breaks with me he's fond of playin' me up as a wizard performer in almost any line. Course, a good deal of it is just his josh, but somehow it ain't a habit I'm anxious to cure him of. Yet when he bats this domestic crisis up to me—this case of Stella Flynn—I did think it was pushin' the comedy a bit strong.

"No," says I, "I'm no miracle worker."

"Pooh, Torchy!" says Vee. "Who's saying you are? But at least you might try to suggest something. You think you're so clever at so many things, you know."

Trust the folks at home for gettin' in these little jabs.

"Oh, very well," says I. "What are the facts about Stella?"

While the bill of particulars is more or less lengthy all it amounts to is the usual kitchen tragedy. Stella has given notice. After havin' been a good and faithful cook for 'steen years; first for Mrs. Ellins's mother, and then being handed on to Mrs. Ellins herself after she and Mr. Robert hooked up; now Stella announces that she's about to resign the portfolio.

No, it ain't a higher wage scale she's strikin' for. She's been boosted three times durin' the last six months, until she's probably the best paid lady cook on Long Island. And she ain't demandin' an eight-hour day, or recognition as chairman of the downstairs soviet. Stella is a middle-aged, full-chested, kind of old-fashioned female who probably thinks a Bolshevik is a limb of the Old Boy himself and ought to be met with holy water in one hand and a red-hot poker in the other. She's satisfied with her quarters, havin' a room and bath to herself; she's got no active grouch against any of the other help; and being sent to mass every Sunday mornin' in the limousine suits her well enough.

But she's quittin', all the same. Why? Well, maybe Mr. Robert remembers that brother Dan of hers he helped set up as a steam fitter out in Altoona some six or seven years ago? Sure it was a kind act. And Danny has done well. He has fitted steam into some big plants and some elegant houses. And now Danny has a fine home of his own. Yes, with a piano that plays itself, and gilt chairs in the parlor, and a sedan top on the flivver, and beveled glass in the front door. Also he has a stylish wife who has "an evenin' wrap trimmed with vermin and is learnin' to play that auctioneer's bridge game." So why should his sister Stella be cookin' for other folks when she might be livin' swell and independent with them? Ain't there the four nieces and three nephews that hardly knows their aunt by sight? It's Danny's wife herself that wrote the letter urgin' her to come.

"And do all the cooking for that big family, I suppose?" suggests Mrs. Ellins.

"She wasn't after sayin' as much, ma'am," says Stella, "but would I be sittin' in the parlor with my hands folded, and her so stylish? And Danny always did like my cookin'."

"Why should he not?" asks Mrs. Ellins. "But who would go on adding to your savings account? Don't be foolish, Stella."

All of which hadn't gotten 'em anywhere. Stella was bent flittin' to Altoona. Ten days more and she would be gone. And as Mr. Robert finishes a piece of Stella's blue ribbon mince pies and drops a lump of sugar into a cup of Stella's unsurpassed after-dinner coffee he lets out a sigh.

"That means, I presume," says he, "hunting up a suite in some apartment hotel, moving into town, and facing a near-French menu three times a day. All because our domestic affairs are not managed on a business basis."

"I suppose you would find some way of inducing Stella to stay—if you were not too busy?" asks Mrs. Robert sarcastic.

"I would," says he.

"What a pity," says she, "that such diplomatic genius must be confined to mere business. If we could only have the benefit of some of it here; even the help of one of your bright young men assistants. They would know exactly how to go about persuading Stella to stay, I suppose?"

"They would find a way," says Mr. Robert. "They would bring a trained and acute mentality to the problem."

"Humph!" says Mrs. Robert, tossing her head. "We saw that worked out in a play the other night, you remember. Mr. Wise Business Man solves the domestic problem by hiring two private detectives, one to act as cook, the other as butler, and a nice mess he made of it. No, thank you."

"See here, Geraldine," says Mr. Robert. "I'll bet you a hundred Torchy could go on that case and have it all straightened out inside of a week."

"Done!" says Mrs. Robert.

And in spite of my protests, that's the way I was let in. But I might not have started so prompt if it hadn't been for Vee eggin' me on.

"If they do move into town, you know," she suggests, "it will be rather lonesome out here for the rest of the winter. We'll miss going there for an occasional Sunday dinner, too. Besides, Stella ought to be saved from that foolishness. She—she's too good a cook to be wasted on such a place as Altoona."

"I'll say she is," I agrees. "I wish I knew where to begin blockin' her off."

I expect some people would call it just some of my luck that I picks up a clue less'n ten minutes later. Maybe so. But I had to have my ear stretched to get it and even then I might have missed the connection if I'd been doin' a sleep walkin' act. As it is I'm pikin' past the servants' wing out toward the garage to bring around the little car for a start home, and Stella happens to be telephonin' from the butler's pantry with the window part open. And when

Stella 'phones she does it like she was callin' home the cows.

About all I caught was "Sure Maggie, dear—Madame Zenobia—two flights up over the agency—Thursday afternoon." But for me and Sherlock that's as good as a two-page description. And when I'd had my rapid-fire deducer workin' for a few minutes I'd doped out my big idea.

"Vee," says I, when we gets back to our own fireside, "what friend has Stella got that she calls Maggie, dear?"

"Why, that must be the Farlows' upstairs maid," says she. "Why, Torchy?"

"Oh, for instance," says I "And didn't you have a snapshot of Stella you took once last summer?"

Vee says she's sure she has one somewhere.

"Dig it out, will you?" says I.

It's a fairly good likeness, too, and I pockets it mysterious. And next day I spends most of my lunch hour prowlin' around on the Sixth Ave. hiring line rubberin' at the signs over the employment agencies. Must have been about the tenth hallway I'd scouted into before I ran across the right one. Sure enough, there's the blue lettered card announcin' that Madame Zenobia can be found in Room 19, third floor, ring bell. I rang.

I don't know when I've seen a more battered old battle-axe face, or a colder, more suspicious pair of lamps than belongs to this old dame with the henna-kissed hair and the gold hoops in her ears.

"Well, young feller," says she, "if you've come pussyfootin' up here from the District Attorney's office you can just sneak back and report nothing doing. Madame Zenobia has gone out of business. Besides, I ain't done any fortune tellin' in a month; only high grade trance work, and mighty little of that. So good day."

"Oh, come, lady," says I, slippin' her the confidential smile, "do I look like I did fourth-rate gumshoein' for a livin'? Honest, now? Besides, the trance stuff is just what I'm lookin' for. And I'm not expectin' any complimentary session, either. Here! There's a ten-spot on account. Now can we do business?"

You bet we could.

"If it's in the realm of Eros, young man," she begins, "I think—"

"But it ain't," says I. "No heart complications at all. This ain't even a matter of a missin' relative, a lost wrist watch, or gettin' advice on buyin' oil stocks. It's a case of a cook with a wilful disposition. Get me? I want her to hear the right kind of dope from the spirit world."

"Ah!" says she, her eyes brightenin'. "I think I follow you, child of the sun. Rather a clever idea, too. Your cook, is she?"

"No such luck," says I. "The boss's, or I wouldn't be so free with the expense money. And listen, Madame; there's another ten in it if the spirits do their job well."

"Grateful words, my son," says she. "But these high-class servants are hard to handle these days. They are no longer content to see the cards laid out and hear their past and future read. Even a simple trance sitting doesn't satisfy.

They must hear bells rung, see ghostly hands waved, and some of them demand a materialized control. But they are so few! And my faithful Al Nekkir has left me."

"Eh?" says I, gawpin'.

"One of the best side-kicks I ever worked with, Al Nekkir," says Madame Zenobia, sighin'. "He always slid out from behind the draperies at just the right time, and he had the patter down fine. But how could I keep a real artist like that with a movie firm offering him five times the money? I hear those whiskers of his screen lovely. Ah, such whiskers! Any cook, no matter how high born, would fall for a prophet's beard like that. And where can I find another?"

Well, I couldn't say. Whiskers are scarce in New York. And it seems Madame Zenobia wouldn't feel sure of tacklin' an A1 cook unless she had an assistant with luxurious face lamberquins. She might try to put it over alone, but she couldn't guarantee anything. Yes, she'd keep the snapshot of Stella, and remember what I said about the brother in Altoona. Also it might be that she could find a substitute for Al Nekkir between now and Thursday afternoon. But there wasn't much chance. I had to let it ride at that.

So Monday was crossed off, Tuesday slipped past into eternity with nothing much done, and half of Wednesday had gone the same way. Mr. Robert was gettin' anxious. He reports that Stella has set Saturday as her last day with them and that she's begun packin' her trunk. What was I doing about it?

"If you need more time off," says he, "take it."

"I always need some time off," says I, grabbin my hat.

Anyway, it was too fine an afternoon to miss a walk up Fifth Avenue. Besides, I can often think clearer when my rubber heels are busy. Did you ever try walkin' down an idea? It's a good hunch. The one I was tryin' to surround was how I could sub in for this Al Nekkir party myself without gettin' Stella suspicious. If I had to say the lines would she spot me by my voice? If she did it would be all up with the game.

Honest, I wasn't thinkin' of whiskers at all. In fact, I hadn't considered the proposition, but was workin' on an entirely different line, when all of a sudden, just as I'm passin' the stone lions in front of the public library, this freak looms up out of the crowd. Course you can see 'most anything on Fifth Avenue, if you trail up and down often enough—about anything or anybody you can see anywhere in the world, they say. And this sure was an odd specimen.

He was all of six feet high and most of him was draped in a brown raincoat effect that buttoned from his ankles to his chin. Besides that, he wore a green leather cap such as I've never seen the mate to, and he had a long, solemn face that was mostly obscured by the richest and rankest growth of bright chestnut whiskers ever in captivity.

I expect I must have grinned. I'm apt to. Probably it was a friendly grin. With hair as red as mine I can't be too critical. Besides, he was gazin' sort of folksy at people as he passed. Still, I didn't think he noticed me among so many and I hadn't thought of stoppin' him. I'd gone on, wonderin' where he had blown in from, and chucklin' over that fancy tinted beard, when the first thing I knew here he was at my elbow lookin' down on me.

"Forgive, sahib, but you have the face of a kindly one," says he.

"Well, I'm no consistent grouch, if that's what you mean," says I. "What'll it be?"

"Could you tell to a stranger in a strange land what one does who has great hunger and no rupees left in his purse?" says he.

"Just what you've done," says I. "He picks out an easy mark. I don't pass out the coin reckless, though. Generally I tow 'em to a hash house and watch 'em eat. Are you hungry enough for that?"

"Truly, I have great hunger," says he.

So, five minutes later I've led him into a side street and parked him opposite me at a chop house table. "How about a slice of roast beef rare, with mashed potatoes and turnips and a cup of coffee?" says I.

"Pardon," says he, "but it is forbidden me to eat the flesh of animals."

So we compromised on a double order of boiled rice and milk with a hunk of pumpkin pie on the side. And in spite of the beard he went to it business-like and graceful.

"Excuse my askin'," says I, "but are you going or coming?"

He looks a bit blank at that. "I am Burmese gentleman," says he. "I am named Sarrou Mollik kuhn Balla Ben."

"That's enough, such as it is," says I. "Suppose I use only the last of it, the Balla Ben part?"

"No," says he, "that is only my title, as you say Honorable Sir."

"Oh, very well," says I, "Sour Milk it is. And maybe you're willin' to tell how you get this way—great hunger and no rupees?"

He was willin'. It seems he'd first gone wanderin' from home a year or so back with a sporty young Englishman who'd hired him as guide and interpreter on a trip into the middle of Burmah. Then they'd gone on into India and the Hon. Sour Milk had qualified so well as all round valet that the young Englishman signed him up for a two-year jaunt around the world. His boss was some hot sport, though, I take it, and after a big spree coming over on a Pacific steamer from Japan he'd been taken sick with some kind of fever, typhoid probably, and was makin' a mad dash for home when he had to quit in New York and be carted to some hospital. Just what hospital Sour Milk didn't know, and as the Hon. Sahib was too sick to think about payin' his board in advance his valet had been turned loose by an unsympathizing hotel manager. And here he was.

"That sure is a hard luck tale," says I. "But it ought to be easy for a man of your size to land some kind of a job these days. What did you work at back in Burmah?"

"I was one of the attendants at the Temple," says he.

"Huh!" says I. "That does make it complicated. I'm afraid there ain't much call for temple hands in this burg. Now if you could run a button-holin' machine, or was a paper hanger, or could handle a delivery truck, or could make good as a floor walker in the men's furnishin' department, or had ever done any barberin'—Say! I've got it!" and I gazes fascinated at that crop of facial herbage.

"I ask pardon?" says he, starin' puzzled.

"They're genuine, ain't they?" I goes on. "Don't hook over the ears with a wire? The whiskers, I mean."

He assures me they grow on him.

"And you're game to tackle any light work with good pay?" I asks.

"I must not cause the death of dumb animals," says he, "or touch their dead bodies. And I may not serve at the altars of your people. But beyond that—"

"You're on, then," says I. "Come along while I stack you up against Madame Zenobia, the Mystic Queen."

We finds the old girl sittin' at a little table, her chin propped up in one hand and a cigarette danglin' despondent from her rouged lips. She's a picture of gloomy days.

"Look what I picked up on Fifth Ave.," says I.

And the minute she spots him and takes in the chestnut whiskers, them weary old eyes of hers lights up. "By the kind stars and the jack of spades!" says she. "A wise one from the East! Who is he?"

"Allow me, Madame Zenobia, to present the Hon. Sour Milk," says I.

"Pardon, Memsahib," he corrects. "I am Sarrou Mellik kuhn Balla Ben, from the Temple of Aj Wadda, in Burmah. I am far from home and without rupees."

"Allah be praised!" says Madame Zenobia.

"Ah!" echoes Sour Milk, in a deep boomin' voice that sounds like it came from the sub-cellar. "Allah il Allah!"

"Enough!" says Madame Zenobia. "The Sage of India is my favorite control and this one has the speech and bearing of him to the life. You may leave us, child of the sun, knowing that your wish shall come true. That is, provided the cook person appears."

"Oh, she'll be here, all right," says I. "They never miss a date like that. There'll be two of 'em, understand. The thin one will be Maggie, that I ain't got any dope on. You can stall her off with anything. The fat, waddly one with the two gold front teeth will be Stella. She's the party with the wilful disposition and the late case of wanderlust. You'll know her by the snapshot, and be sure and throw it into her strong if you want to collect that other ten."

"Trust Zenobia," says she, wavin' me away.

Say, I'd like to have been behind the curtains that Thursday afternoon when Stella Flynn squandered four dollars to get a message from the spirit world direct. I'd like to know just how it was done. Oh, she got it, all right. And it must have been mighty convincin', for when Vee and I drives up to the Ellinses that night after dinner to see if they'd noticed any difference in the cook, or if she'd dropped any encouragin' hints, I nearly got hugged by Mrs. Robert.

"Oh, you wonderful young person!" says she. "You did manage it, didn't you?"

"Eh?" says I.

"Stella is going to stay with us," says Mrs. Robert. "She is unpacking her trunk! However did you do it? What is this marvelous recipe of yours?"

"Why," says I, "I took Madame Zenobia and added

Sour Milk."

Yes, I had more or less fun kiddin' 'em along all the evenin'. But I couldn't tell 'em the whole story because I didn't have the details myself. As for Mr. Robert, he's just as pleased as anybody, only he lets on how he was dead sure all along that I'd put it over. And before I left he tows me one side and tucks a check into my pocket.

"Geraldine paid up," says he, "and I rather think the stakes belong to you. But sometime, Torchy, I'd like to have you outline your process to me. It should be worth copyrighting."

That bright little idea seemed to have hit Madame Zenobia, too, for when I drops around there next day to hand her the final instalment, she and the Hon. Sour Milk are just finishing a he-sized meal that had been sent in on a tray from a nearby restaurant. She's actin' gay and mirthful.

"Ah, I've always known there was luck in red hair," says she. "And when it comes don't think Zenobia doesn't know it by sight. Look!" and she hands me a mornin' paper unfolded to the "Help Wanted" page. The marked ad reads:

The domestic problem solved. If you would keep your servants consult Madame Zenobia, the Mystic Queen. Try her and your cook will never leave.

"Uh-huh!" says I. "That ought to bring in business these times. I expect that inside of a week you'll have the street lined with limousines and customers waitin' in line all up and down the stairs here."

"True words," says Madame Zenobia. "Already I have

made four appointments for this afternoon and I've raised my fee to $50."

"If you can cinch 'em all the way you did Stella," says I, "it'll be as good as ownin' a Texas gusher. But, by the way, just how did you feed it to her?"

"She wasn't a bit interested," says Madame Zenobia, "until I materialized Sarrou Mellik as the wise man of India. Give us that patter I worked up for you, Sarrou."

And in that boomin' voice of his the Hon. Sour Milk remarks: "Beware of change. Remain, woman, where thou art, for there and there only will some great good fortune come to you. The spirit of Ahmed the Wise hath spoken."

"Great stuff!" says I. "I don't blame Stella for changin' her mind. That's enough to make anybody a fixture anywhere. She may be the only one in the country, but I'll say she's a permanent cook."

And I sure did get a chuckle out of Mr. Robert when I sketches out how we anchored Stella to his happy home.

"Then that's why she looks at me in that peculiarly expectant way every time I see her," says he. "Some great good fortune, eh? Evidently she has decided that it will come through me."

"Well," says I, "unless she enters a prize beauty contest or something like that, you should worry. Even if she does get the idea that you're holdin' out on her, she won't dare quit. And you couldn't do better than that with an Act of Congress. Could you, now?"

At which Mr. Robert folds his hands over his vest and

indulges in a cat-and-canary grin. I expect he was thinkin' of them mince pies.

Sewell Ford

CHAPTER VII

HOW THE GARVEYS BROKE IN

Course, Vee gives me all the credit. Perfectly right, too. That's the way we have 'em trained. But, as a matter of fact, stated confidential and on the side, it was the little lady herself who pushed the starter button in this affair with the Garveys. If she hadn't I don't see where it would ever have got going.

Let's see, it must have been early in November. Anyway, it was some messy afternoon, with a young snow flurry that had finally concluded to turn to rain, and as I drops off the 5:18 I was glad enough to see the little roadster backed up with the other cars and Vee waitin' inside behind the side curtains.

"Good work!" says I, dashin' out and preparin' to climb in. "I might have got good and damp paddlin' home through this. Bright little thought of yours."

"Pooh!" says Vee. "Besides, there was an express package the driver forgot to deliver. It must be that new floor lamp. Bring it out, will you, Torchy?"

And by the time I'd retrieved this bulky package from the express agent and stowed it inside, all the other commuters had boarded their various limousines and flivver taxis and cleared out.

"Hello!" says I, glancin' down the platform where a large and elegant lady is pacin' up and down lonesome. "Looks like somebody has got left."

At which Vee takes a peek. "I believe it's that Mrs. Garvey," says she.

"Oh!" says I, slidin' behind the wheel and thrown' in the gear.

I was just shiftin' to second when Vee grabs my arm. "How utterly snobbish of us!" says she. "Let's ask if we can't take her home?"

"On the runnin' board?" says I.

"We can leave the lamp until tomorrow," says Vee. "Come on."

So I cuts a short circle and pulls up opposite this imposin' party in the big hat and the ruffled mink coat. She lets on not to notice until Vee leans out and asks:

"Mrs. Garvey, isn't it?"

All the reply she gives is a stiff nod and I notice her face is pinked up like she was peeved at something.

"If your car isn't here can't we take you home?" asks Vee.

She acts sort of stunned for a second, and then, after another look up the road through the sheets of rain, she steps up hesitatin'. "I suppose my stupid chauffeur forgot I'd gone to town," says she. "And as all the taxis have been taken I—I— But you haven't room."

"Oh, lots!" says Vee. "We will leave this ridiculous package in the express office and squeeze up a bit. You simply can't walk, you know."

"Well—" says she.

So I lugs the lamp back and the three of us wedges ourselves into the roadster seat. Believe me, with a party the size of Mrs. Garvey as the party of the third part, it was a tight fit. From the way Vee chatters on, though, you'd think it was some merry lark we was indulgin' in.

"This is what I call our piggy car," says she, "for we can never ask but one other person at a time. But it's heaps better than having no car at all. And it's so fortunate we happened to see you, wasn't it?"

Being more or less busy tryin' to shift gears without barkin' Mrs. Garvey's knees, and turn corners without skiddin' into the gutter, I didn't notice for a while that Vee was conductin' a perfectly good monologue. That's what it was, though. Hardly a word out of our stately passenger. She sits there as stiff as if she was crated, starin' cold and stony straight ahead, and that peevish flush still showin' on her cheekbones. Why, you'd most think we had her under arrest instead of doin' her a favor. And when I finally swings into the Garvey driveway and pulls up under the porte cochere she untangles herself from the brake lever and crawls out.

"Thank you," says she crisp, adjustin' her picture hat. "It isn't often that I am obliged to depend on—on strangers." And while Vee still has her mouth open, sort of gaspin' from the slam, the lady has marched up the steps and disappeared.

"Now I guess you know where you get off, eh, Vee?" says I chuckly. "You *will* pass up your new neighbors."

"How absurd of her!" says Vee. "Why, I never dreamed that I had offended her by not calling."

"Well, you've got the straight dope at last," says I. "She's as fond of us as a cat is of swimmin' with the ducks. Say, my right arm is numb from being so close to that cold shoulder she was givin' me. Catch me doin' the rescue act for her again."

"Still," says Vee, "they have been livin out here nearly a year, haven't they? But then—"

At which she proceeds to state an alibi which sounds reasonable enough. She'd rather understood that the Garveys didn't expect to be called on. Maybe you know how it is in one of these near-swell suburbs! Not that there's any reg'lar committee to pass on newcomers. Some are taken in right off, some after a while, and some are just left out. Anyway, that's how it seems to work out here in Harbor Hills.

I don't know who it was first passed around the word, or where we got it from, but we'd been tipped off somehow that the Garveys didn't belong. I don't expect either of us asked for details. Whether or not they did wasn't up to us. But everybody seems to take it that they don't, and act accordin'. Plenty of others had met the same deal. Some quit after the first six months, others stuck it out.

As for the Garveys, they'd appeared from nowhere in particular, bought this big square stucco house on the Shore road, rolled around in their showy limousine, subscribed liberal to all the local drives and charity funds, and made several stabs at bein' folksy. But there's no response. None of the bridge-playing set drop in of an afternoon to ask Mrs. Garvey if she won't fill in on Tuesday next, she ain't invited to join the Ladies' Improvement Society, or even the Garden Club; and when Garvey's application for membership gets to the Country Club committee he's notified that his name has been put on the waitin' list. I expect it's still there.

But it's kind of a jolt to find that Mrs. Garvey is sore on us for all this. "Where does she get that stuff?" I asks Vee, after we get home. "Who's been telling her we handle the social blacklist for the Roaring Rock district of Long Island?"

"I suppose she thinks we have done our share, or failed to do it," says Vee. "And perhaps we have. I'm rather sorry for the Garveys. I'm sure I don't know what's the matter with them."

I didn't, either. Hadn't given it a thought, in fact. But I sort of got to chewin' it over. Maybe it was the flashy way Mrs. Garvey dressed, and the noisy laugh I'd occasionally heard her spring on the station platform when she was talking to Garvey. Not that all the lady members of the Country Club set are shrinkin' violets who go around costumed in Quaker gray and whisper their remarks modest. Some are about as spiffy dressers as you'll see anywhere and a few are what I'd call speedy performers. But somehow you know who they are and where they came from, and make allowances. They're in the swim, anyway.

The trouble might be with Garvey. He's about the same type as the other half of the sketch—a big, two-fisted ruddy-faced husk, attired sporty in black and white checks, with gray gaiters and a soft hat to match the suit. Wore a diamond-set Shriners' watch fob, and an Elks' emblem in his buttonhole. Course, you wouldn't expect him to have any gentle, ladylike voice, and he don't. I heard he'd been sent on as an eastern agent of some big Kansas City packin' house. Must have been a good payin' line, for he certainly looks like ready money. But somehow he don't seem to be popular with our bunch of commuters, although at first I understand he tried to mix in free and easy.

Anyway, the verdict appears to be against lettin' the Garveys in, and we had about as much to do with it as we did about fixin' the price of coal, or endin' the sugar shortage. Yet here when we try to do one of 'em a good turn we get the cold eye.

"Next time," says I, "we'll remember we are strangers, and not give her an openin' to throw it at us."

So I'm a little surprised the followin' Sunday afternoon to see the Garvey limousine stoppin' out front. As I happens to be wanderin' around outside I steps up to the gate just as Garvey is gettin' out.

"Ah, Ballard!" he says, cordial. "I want to thank you and Mrs. Ballard for picking Mrs. Garvey up the other day when our fool chauffeur went to sleep at the switch. It—it was mighty decent of you."

"Not at all," says I "Couldn't do much less for a neighbor, could we?"

"Some could," says he. "A whole lot less. And if you don't mind my saying so, it's about the first sign we've had that we were counted as neighbors."

"Oh, well," says I, "maybe nobody's had a chance to show it before. Will you come in a minute and thaw out in front of the wood fire?"

"Why—er—I suppose it ain't reg'lar," says he, "but blamed if I don't."

And after I've towed him into the livin' room, planted him in a wing chair, and poked up the hickory logs, he springs this conundrum on me:

"Ballard," says he, "I'd like to ask you something and have you give me an answer straight from the shoulder."

"That's my specialty," says I. "Shoot."

"Just what's the matter with us—Mrs. Garvey and me?" he demands.

"Why—why—Who says there's anything the matter with either of you?" I asks, draggy.

"They don't have to say it," says he. "They act it. Everybody in this blessed town; that is, all except the storekeepers, the plumbers, the milkman, and so on. My money seems to be good enough for them. But as for the others—well, you know how we've been frozen out. As though we had something catching, or would blight the landscape. Now what's the big idea? What are some of the charges in the indictment?"

And I'll leave it to you if that wasn't enough to get me scrapin' my front hoof. How you goin' to break it to a gent sittin' by your own fireside that maybe he's a bit rough in the neck, or too much of a yawp to fit into the refined and exclusive circle that patronizes the 8:03 bankers' express? As I see it, the thing can't be done.

"Excuse me, Mr. Garvey," says I, "but if there's been any

true bill handed in by a pink tea grand jury it's been done without consultin' me. I ain't much on this codfish stuff myself."

"Shake, young man," says he grateful. "I thought you looked like the right sort. But without gettin' right down to brass tacks, or namin' any names, couldn't you slip me a few useful hints? There's no use denyin' we're in wrong here. I don't suppose it matters much just how; not now, anyway. But Tim Garvey is no quitter; at least, I've never had that name. And I've made up my mind to stay with this proposition until I'm dead sure I'm licked."

"That's the sportin' spirit," says I.

"What I want is a line on how to get in right," says he.

At which I scratches my head and stalls around.

"For instance," he goes on, "what is it these fine Harbor Hills folks do that I can't learn? Is it parlor etiquette? Then me for that. I'll take lessons. I'm willin' to be as refined and genteel as anybody if that's what I lack."

"That's fair enough," says I, still stallin'.

"You see," says Garvey, "this kind of a deal is a new one on us. I don't want to throw any bull, but out in Kansas City we thought we had just as good a bunch as you could find anywhere; and we were the ringleaders, as you might say. Mixed with the best people. All live wires, too. We had a new country club that would make this one of yours look like a freight shed. I helped organize it, was one of the directors. And the Madam took her part, too; first vice-president of the Woman's Club, charter member of the Holy Twelve bridge crowd, as some called it, and always a patroness at the big social affairs. A new

Sewell Ford

doormat wouldn't, last us a lifetime out there. But here—say, how do you break into this bunch, anyway?"

"Why ask me, who was smuggled in the back door?" says I, grinnin'.

"But you know a lot of these high-brows and aristocrats," he insists. "I don't. I don't get 'em at all. What brainy stunts or polite acts are they strongest for? How do they behave when they're among themselves?"

"Why, sort of natural, I guess," says I.

"Whaddye mean, natural?" demands Garvey. "For instance?"

"Well, let's see," says I. "There's Major Brooks Keating, the imposin' old boy with the gray goatee, who was minister to Greece or Turkey once. Married some plute's widow abroad and retired from the diplomatic game. Lives in that near-chateau affair just this side of the Country Club. His fad is paintin'."

"Pictures?" asks Garvey.

"No. Cow barns, fences, chicken houses," says I. "Anything around the place that will stand another coat."

"You don't mean he does it himself?" says Garvey.

"Sure he does," says I. "Gets on an old pair of overalls and jumper and goes to it like he belonged to the union. Last time I was up there he had all the blinds off one side of the house and was touchin' 'em up. Mrs. Keating was givin' a tea that afternoon and he crashes right in amongst 'em askin' his wife what she did with that can of turpentine. Nobody seems to mind, and they say he has a whale of a time doin' it. So that's his high-brow stunt."

Garvey shakes his head puzzled. "House painting, eh?" says he. "Some fad, I'll say."

"He ain't got anything on J. Kearney Rockwell, the potty-built old sport with the pink complexion and the grand duchess wife," I goes on. "You know?"

Garvey nods. "Of Rockwell, Griggs & Bland, the big brokerage house," says he. "What's his pet side line?"

"Cucumbers," says I. "Has a whole hothouse full of 'em. Don't allow the gardener to step inside the door, but does it all himself. Even lugs 'em down to the store in a suitcase and sells as high as $20 worth a week, they say. I hear he did start peddlin' 'em around the neighborhood once, but the grand duchess raised such a howl he had to quit. You're liable to see him wheelin' in a barrowful of manure any time, though."

"Ought to be some sight," says Garvey. "Cucumbers! Any more like him?"

"Oh, each one seems to have his own specialty," says I. "Take Austin Gordon, one of the Standard Oil crowd, who only shows up at 26 Broadway for the annual meetings now. You'd never guess what his hobby is. Puppet shows."

"Eh?" says Garvey, gawpin'.

"Sort of Punch and Judy stuff," says I. "Whittles little dummies out of wood, paints their faces, dresses 'em up, and makes 'em act by pullin' a lot of strings. Writes reg'lar plays for 'em. He's got a complete little theatre fitted up over his garage; stage, scenery, footlights, folding chairs and everything. Gives a show every now and then. Swell affairs. Everybody turns out. Course they snicker some in private, but he gets away with it."

Garvey stares at me sort of dazed. "And here I've been afraid to do anything but walk around my place wearing gloves and carrying a cane;" says he. "Afraid of doing something that wasn't genteel, or that would get the neighbors talking. While these aristocrats do what they please. They do, don't they!"

"That about states it," says I.

"Do—do you suppose I could do that, too?" he asks.

"Why not?" says I. "You don't stand to lose anything, do you, even if they do chatter? If I was you I'd act natural and tell 'em to go hang."

"You would?" says he, still starin'.

"To the limit," says I. "What's the fun of livin' if you can't?"

"Say, young man," says Garvey, slappin' his knee. "That listens sensible to me. Blamed if I don't. And I—I'm much obliged."

And after he's gone Vee comes down from upstairs and wants to know what on earth I've been talking so long to that Mr. Garvey about.

"Why," says I, "I've been givin' him some wise dope on how to live among plutes and be happy."

"Silly!" says Vee, rumplin' my red hair. "Do you know what I've made up my mind to do some day this week?

Have you take me for an evening call on the Garveys."

"Gosh!" says I. "You're some little Polar explorer, ain't you?"

It was no idle threat of Vee's. A few nights later we got under way right after dinner and drove over there. I expect we were about the first outsiders to push the bell button since they moved in. But we'd no sooner rung than Vee begins to hedge.

"Why, they must be giving a party!" says she. "Listen! There's an orchestra playing."

"Uh-huh!" says I. "Sounds like a jazz band."

A minute later, though, when the butler opens the door, there's no sound of music, and as we goes in we catches Garvey just strugglin' into his dinner coat. He seems glad to see us, mighty glad. Says so. Tows us right into the big drawin' room. But Mrs. Garvey ain't so enthusiastic. She warms up about as much as a cold storage turkey.

You can't feaze Vee, though, when she starts in to be folksy. "I'm just so sorry we've been so long getting over," says she. "And we came near not coming in this time. Didn't we hear music a moment ago. You're not having a dance or—or anything, are you?"

The Garveys look at each other sort of foolish for a second.

"Oh, no," says Mrs. Garvey. "Nothing of the sort. Perhaps some of the servants—"

"Now, Ducky," breaks in Garvey, "let's not lay it on the servants."

And Mrs. Garvey turns the color of a fire hydrant clear up into her permanent wave. "Very well, Tim," says she. "If you *will* let everybody know. I suppose it's bound to get out sooner or later, anyhow." And with that she turns to me. "Anyway, you're the young man who put him up to this nonsense. I hope you're satisfied."

"Me?" says I, doin' the gawp act.

"How delightfully mysterious!" says Vee. "What's it all about?"

"Yes, Garvey," says I. "What you been up to?"

"I'm being natural, that's all," says he.

"Natural!" snorts Mrs. Garvey. "Is that what you call it?"

"How does it break out?" says I.

"If you must know," says Mrs. Garvey, "he's making a fool of himself by playing a snare drum."

"Honest?" says I, grinnin' at Garvey.

"Here it is," says he, draggin' out from under a davenport a perfectly good drum.

"And you might as well exhibit the rest of the ridiculous things," says Mrs. Garvey.

"Sure!" says Garvey, swingin' back a Japanese screen and disclosin' a full trap outfit—base drum with cymbals, worked by a foot pedal, xylophone blocks, triangle, and sand boards—all rigged up next to a cabinet music machine.

"Well, well!" says I. "All you lack is a leader and Sophie Tucker to screech and you could go on at Reisenwebers."

"Isn't it all perfectly fascinating?" says Vee, testin' the drum pedal.

"But it's such a common, ordinary thing to do," protests Mrs. Garvey. "Drumming! Why, out in Kansas City I remember that the man who played the traps in our Country Club orchestra worked daytimes as a plumber. He was a poor plumber, at that."

"But he was a swell drummer," says Garvey. "I took lessons of him, on the sly. You see, as a boy, the one big ambition in my life was to play the snare drum. But I never had money enough to buy one. I couldn't have found time to play it anyway. And in Kansas City I was too busy trying to be a good sport. Here I've got more time than I know what to do with. More money, too. So I've got the drum, and the rest. I'm here to say, too, that knocking out an accompaniment to some of these new jazz records is more fun than I've ever had all the rest of my life."

"I'm sure it must be," says Vee. "Do play once for us, Mr. Garvey. Couldn't I come in on the piano? Let's try that 'Dardanella' thing?"

And say, inside of ten minutes they were at it so hard that you'd most thought Arthur Pryor and his whole aggregation had cut loose. Then they did some one-step pieces with lots of pep in 'em, and the way Garvey could roll the sticks, and tinkle the triangle, and keep the cymbals and base drum goin' with his foot was as good to watch as a jugglin' act, even if he does leak a lot on the face when he gets through.

"You're some jazz artist, I'll say," says I.

"So will the neighbors, I'm afraid," says Mrs. Garvey. "That will sound nice, won't it?"

"Oh, blow the neighbors!" says Garvey. "I'm going to do as I please from now on; and it pleases me to do this."

"Then we might as well nail up the front door and eat in the kitchen, like we used to," says she, sighin'.

But it don't work out that way for them. It was like this: Austin Gordon was pullin' off one of his puppet shows and comes around to ask Vee wouldn't she do some piano playin' for him between the acts and durin' parts of the performance. He'd hoped to have a violinist, too, but the party had backed out. So Vee tells him about Garvey's trap outfit, and how clever he is at it, and suggests askin' him in.

"Why, certainly!" says Gordon.

So Garvey pulls his act before the flower and chivalry of Harbor Hills. They went wild over it, too. And at the reception afterwards he was introduced all round, patted on the back by the men, and taffied up by the ladies. Even Mrs. Timothy Garvey, who'd been sittin' stiff and purple-faced all the evenin' in a back seat was rung in for a little of the glory.

"Say, Garvey," says Major Brooks Keating, "we must have you and Mrs. Ballard play for us at our next Country Club dinner dance after the fool musicians quit. Will you, eh? Not a member? Well, you ought to be. I'll see that you're made one, right away."

I don't know of anyone who was more pleased at the way

things had turned out than Vee. "There, Torchy!" says she. "I've always said you were a wonder at managing things."

"Why shouldn't I be?" says I, givin' her the side clinch. "Look at the swell assistant I've got."

CHAPTER VIII

NICKY AND THE SETTING HEN

Honest, the first line I got on this party with the steady gray eyes and the poker face was that he must be dead from the neck up. Or else he'd gone into a trance and couldn't get out.

Nice lookin' young chap, too. Oh, say thirty or better. I don't know as he'd qualify as a perfect male, but he has good lines and the kind of profile that had most of the lady typists stretchin' their necks. But there's no more expression on that map of his than there would be to a bar of soap. Just a blank. And yet after a second glance you wondered.

You see, I'd happened to drift out into the general offices in time to hear him ask Vincent, the fair-haired guardian of the brass gate, if Mr. Robert is in. And when Vincent tells him he ain't he makes no move to go, but stands there starin' straight through the wall out into Broadway. Looks like he might be one of Mr. Robert's club friends, so I steps up and asks if there's anything a perfectly good private sec. can do for him. He wakes up enough to shake his head.

"Any message?" says I.

Another shake. "Then maybe you'll leave your card?" says I.

Yes, he's willin' to do that, and hands it over.

"Oh!" says I. "Why didn't you say so? Mr. Nickerson Wells, eh? Why, you're the one who's going to handle that ore transportation deal for the Corrugated, ain't you?"

"I was, but I'm not," says the chatterbox.

"Eh?" says I, gawpin'.

"Can't take it on," says he. "Tell Ellins, will you?"

"Not much!" says I. "Guess you'll have to hand that to him yourself, Mr. Wells. He'll be here any minute. Right this way."

And a swell time I had keepin' him entertained in the private office for half an hour. Not that he's restless or fidgety, but when you get a party who only stares bored at a spot about ten feet behind the back of your head and answers most of your questions by blinkin' his eyes, it kind of gets on your nerves. Still, I couldn't let him get away. Why, Mr. Robert had been prospectin' for months to find the right man for that transportation muddle and when he finally got hold of this Nicky Wells he goes around grinnin' for three days.

Seems Nicky had built up quite a rep. by some work he did over in France on an engineerin' job. Ran some supply tracks where nobody thought they could be laid, bridged a river in a night under fire, and pulled a lot of stuff like that. I don't know just what. Anyway, they pinned all sorts of medals on him for it, made him a colonel, and when it was all over turned him loose as casual as any buck private. That's the army for you. And the railroad people he'd been with before had been shifted around so much that they'd forgotten all about him. He wasn't the kind to tell 'em what a whale of a guy he was, and nobody else did it for him. So there he was, floatin' around, when Mr. Robert happened to hear of him.

"Must have got you in some lively spots, runnin' a right of way smack up to the German lines?" I suggests.

"M-m-m-m!" says he, through his teeth.

"Wasn't it you laid the tracks that got up them big naval guns?" I asks.

"I may have helped," says he.

So I knew all about it, you see. Quite thrillin' if you had a high speed imagination. And you can bet I was some relieved when Mr. Robert blew in and took him off my hands. Must have been an hour later before he comes out and I goes into the private office to find Mr. Robert with his chin on his wishbone and his brow furrowed up.

"Well, I take it the one-syllable champion broke the sad news to you!" says I.

"Yes, he wants to quit," says Mr. Robert.

"Means to devote all his time to breakin' the long distance no-speech record, does he?" I asks.

"I'm sure I don't know what he means to do," says Mr. Robert, sighin'. "Anyway, he seems determined not to go to work for the Corrugated. I did discover one thing, though, Torchy; there's a girl mixed up in the affair. She's thrown him over."

"I don't wonder," says I. "Probably he tried to get through a whole evenin' with her on that yes-and-no stuff."

No, Mr. Robert says, it wasn't that. Not altogether. Nicky has done something that he's ashamed of, something she'd heard about. He'd renigged on takin' her to a dinner dance up in Boston a month or so back. He'd been on hand all right, was right on the spot while she was waitin' for him; but instead of callin' around with the taxi and the orchids he'd slipped off to another town without sayin' a word. The worst of it was that in this other place was the other woman, someone he'd had an affair with before. A Reno widow, too.

"Think of that!" says I, "Nicky the Silent! Say, you can't always tell, can you? What's his alibi?"

"That's the puzzling part of it," says Mr. Robert. "He hasn't the ghost of an excuse, although he claims he didn't see the other woman, had almost forgotten she lived there. But why he deserted his dinner partner and went to this place he doesn't explain, except to say that he doesn't know why he did it."

"Too fishy," says I. "Unless he can prove he was walkin' in his sleep."

"Just what I tell him," says Mr. Robert. "Anyway, he's taking it hard. Says if he's no more responsible than that he couldn't undertake an important piece of work. Besides, I believe he is very fond of the girl. She's Betty Burke, by the way."

"Z-z-zing!" says I. "Some combination, Miss Betty Burke and Nickerson Wells."

I'd seen her a few times at the Ellinses, and take it from

me she's some wild gazelle; you know, lots of curves and speed, but no control. No matter where you put her she's the life of the party, Betty is. Chatter! Say, she could make an afternoon tea at the Old Ladies' Home sound like a Rotary Club luncheon, all by herself. Shoots over the clever stuff, too. Oh, a reg'lar girl. About as much on Nicky Wells' type as a hummin' bird is like a pelican.

"Only another instance," says Mr. Robert, "to show that the law of opposites is still in good working condition. I've never known Betty to be as much cut up over anything as she's been since she found out about Nicky. Only we couldn't imagine what was the matter. She's not used to being forgotten and I suppose she lost no time in telling Nicky where he got off. She must have cared a lot for him. Perhaps she still does. The silly things! If they could only make it up perhaps Nicky would sign that contract and go to work."

"Looks like a case of Cupid throwin' a monkey wrench into the gears of commerce, eh?" says I. "How do you size up Nicky's plea of not guilty?"

"Oh, if he says he didn't see the other woman, he didn't, that's all," says Mr. Robert. "But until he explains why he went where she was when—"

"Maybe he would if he had a show," says I. "If you could plot out a get-together session for 'em somehow—"

"Exactly!" says Mr. Robert, slappin' his knee. "Thank you, Torchy. It shall be done. Get Mrs. Ellins on the long distance, will you?"

He's a quick performer, Mr. Robert, when he's got his program mapped out. He don't hesitate to step on the pedal. Before quittin' time that afternoon he's got it all fixed up.

"Tomorrow night," says he, "Nicky understands that we're having a dinner party out at the house. Betty'll be there. You and Vee are to be the party."

"A lot of help I'll be," says I. "But I expect I can fill a chair."

When you get a private sec. that can double in open face clothes, though, you've picked a winner. That's why I figure so heavy on the Corrugated pay roll. But say, when I finds myself planted next to Bubbling Betty at the table I begins to suspect that I've been miscast for the part.

She's some smart dresser, on and off, Betty is. Her idea of a perfectly good dinner gown is to make it as simple as possible. All she needs is a quart or so of glass beads and a little pink tulle and there she is. There's more or less of her, too. And me thinkin' that Theda Bara stood for the last word in bare. I hadn't seen Betty costumed for the dinin' room then. And I expect the blush roses in the flower bowl had nothing on my ears when it came to a vivid color scheme.

By that time, of course, she and Nicky had recovered from the shock of findin' themselves with their feet under the same table and they've settled down to bein' insultin'ly polite to each other. It's "Mr. Wells" and "Miss Burke" with them, Nicky with his eyes in his plate and Betty throwin' him frigid glances that should have chilled his soup. And the next thing I know she's turned to me and is cuttin' loose with her whole bag of tricks. Talk about bein' vamped! Say, inside of three minutes there she had me dizzy in the head. With them sparklin', roly-boly eyes of hers so near I didn't know whether I was butterin' a roll or spreadin' it on my thumb.

"Do you know," says she, "I simply adore red hair—your kind."

"Maybe that's why I picked out this particular shade," says I.

"Tchk!" says she, tappin' me on the arm. "Tell me, how do you get it to wave so cunningly in front?"

"Don't give it away," says I, "but I do demonstratin' at a male beauty parlor."

This seems to tickle Betty so much that she has to lean over and chuckle on my shoulder. "Bob calls you Torchy, doesn't he?" she goes on. "I'm going to, too."

"Well, I don't see how I can stop you," says I.

"What do you think of this new near-beer?" she demands.

"Why," says I, "it strikes me the bird who named it was a poor judge of distance." Which, almost causes Betty to swallow an olive pit.

"You're simply delightful!" says she. "Why haven't we met before?"

"Maybe they didn't think it was safe," says I. "They might be right, at that."

"Naughty, naughty!" says she. "But go on. Tell me a funny story while the fish is being served."

"I'd do better servin' the fish," says I.

"Pooh!" says she. "I don't believe it. Come!"

"How do you know I'm primed?" says I.

"I can tell by your eyes," says she. "There's a twinkle in them."

"S-s-s-sh!" says I. "Belladonna. Besides, I always forget the good ones I read in the comic section."

"Please!" insists Betty. "Every one else is being so stupid. And you're supposed to entertain me, you know."

"Well," says I, "I did hear kind of a rich one while I was waitin' at the club for Mr. Robert today only I don't know as—"

"Listen, everybody," announces Betty vivacious. "Torchy is going to tell a story."

Course, that gets me pinked up like the candle shades and I shakes my head vigorous.

"Hear, hear!" says Mr. Robert.

"Oh, do!" adds Mrs. Ellins.

As for Vee, she looks across at me doubtful. "I hope it isn't that one about a Mr. Cohen who played poker all night," says she.

"Wrong guess," says I. "It's one I overheard at Mr. Robert's club while a bunch of young sports was comparin' notes on settin' hens."

"How do you mean, setting hens?" asks Mr. Robert.

"It's the favorite indoor sport up in New England now, I understand," says I. "It's the pie-belt way of taking the sting out of the prohibition amendment. You know, building something with a kick to it. I didn't get the details, but they use corn-meal, sugar, water, raisins and the good old yeast cake, and let it set in a cask! for twenty-one days. Nearly everybody up there has a hen on, I judge, or one just coming off."

"Oh, I see!" says Mr. Robert. "And had any of the young men succeeded; that is, in producing something with—er—a kick to it?"

"Accordin' to their tale, they had," says I. "Seems they tried it out in Boston after the Harvard-Yale game. A bunch got together in some hotel room and opened a jug one of 'em had brought along in case Harvard should win, and after that 10-3 score—well, I expect they'd have celebrated on something, even if it was no more than lemon extract or Jamaica ginger."

"How about that, Nicky?" asks Mr. Robert, who's a Yale man.

"Quite possible," says Nicky, who for the first time seems to have his ears pricked up. "What then?"

"Well," says I, "there was one Harvard guy who wasn't much used to hitting anything of the sort, but he was so much cheered up over seeing his team win that he let 'em lead him to it. They say he shut his eyes and let four fingers in a water glass trickle down without stopping to taste it. From then on he was a different man. He forgot all about being a Delta Kappa, whatever that is; forgot that he had an aunt who still lived on Beacon Street; forgot most everything except that the birds were singin' 'Johnny Harvard' and that Casey was a great man. He climbed on a table and insisted on makin' a speech about it. You know how that home brew stuff works sometimes?"

"I've been told that it has a certain potency," says Mr. Robert, winkin' at Nicky.

"Anyway," I goes on, seein' that Nicky was still interested, "it seems to tie his tongue loose. He gets eloquent about the poor old Elis who had to stand around and watch the snake dance without lettin' out a yip. Then he has a bright idea, which he proceeds to state. Maybe they don't know anything about the glorious product of the settin' hen down in New Haven. And who needs it more at such a time as this? Ought to have some of 'em up there and lighten their load of gloom. Act of charity. Gotta be done. If nobody else'll do it, he will. Go out into highways and byways.

"And he does. Half an hour later he shows up at the home brew headquarters with an Eli that he's captured on the way to the South station. He's a solemn-faced, dignified party who don't seem to catch what it's all about and rather balks when he sees the bunch. But he's dragged in and introduced as Chester Beal, the Hittite."

"I beg pardon?" asks Nicky.

"I'm only giving you what I heard," says I. "Chester Beal might have been his right name, or it might not, and the Hittite part was some of his josh, I take it. Anyway, Chester was dealt a generous shot from the jug, followin' which he was one of 'em. Him and the Harvard guy got real chummy, and the oftener they sampled the home brew the more they thought of each other. They discovered they'd both served in the same division on the other side and had spent last Thanksgiving only a few miles from each other. It was real touchin'. When last seen they was driftin' up Tremont Street arm in arm singin'

'Madelon,' 'Boola-Boola,' 'Harvardiana' and other appropriate melodies."

"Just like the good old days, eh, Nicky?" suggests Mr. Robert.

But Nicky only shakes his head. "You say they were not seen again?" he demands.

"Not until about 1:30 a. m.," says I, "when they shows up in front of the Harvard Club on Commonwealth Avenue. One of the original bunch spots the pair and listens in. The Harvard man is as eloquent as ever. He's still going strong. But Chester, the Hittite, looks bored and weary. 'Oh, shut up!' says he. But the other one can't be choked off that way. He just starts in again. So Chester leads him out to the curb and hails a taxi driver. 'Take him away,' says Chester. 'He's been talking to me for hours and hours. Take him away.' 'Yes, sir,'says the driver. 'Where to, sir,' 'Oh, anywhere,' says Chester. 'Take him to—to Worcester.' 'Right,' says the driver, loadin' in his fare."

"But—but of course he didn't really take him all that distance?" puts in Betty.

"Uh-huh!" says I. "That's what I thought was so rich. And about 10:30 next mornin' a certain party wakes up in a strange room in a strange town. He's got a head on him like an observation balloon and a tongue that feels like a pussycat's back. And when he finally gets down to the desk he asks the clerk where he is. 'Bancroft House, Worcester, sir,' says the clerk. 'How odd!' says he. 'But—er—? what is this charge of $16.85 on my bill?' 'Taxi fare from Boston,' says the clerk. And they say he paid up like a good sport."

"In such a case," says Mr. Robert "one does."

"Worcester!" says Betty. "That's queer."

"The rough part of it was," I goes on, "that he was due to attend a big affair in Boston the night before, sort of a reunion of officers who'd been in the army of occupation—banquet and dance afterward—I think they call it the Society of the Rhine."

"What!" exclaims Betty.

"Oh, I say!" gasps Nicky. Then they look at each other queer.

I could see that I'd made some kind of a break but I couldn't figure out just what it was. "Anyway," says I, "he didn't get there. He got to Worcester instead. Course, though, you don't have to believe all you hear at a club."

"If only one could," says Betty.

And it wasn't until after dinner that I got a slant on this remark of hers.

"Torchy," says she, "where is Mr. Wells?"

"Why," says I, "I saw him drift out on the terrace a minute ago."

"Alone?" says she.

I nods.

"Then take me out to him, will you?" she asks.

"Sure thing," says I.

And she puts it up to him straight when we get him

cornered. "Was that the real reason why you were in Worcester?" she demands.

"I'm sorry," says he, hangin' his head, "but it must have been."

"Then, why didn't you say so, you silly boy!" she asks.

"How could I, Betty?" says he. "You see, I hadn't heard the rest of the story until just now."

"Oh, Nicky!" says she.

And the next thing I knew they'd gone to a clinch, which I takes as my cue to slide back into the house. Half an hour later they shows up smilin' and tells us all about it.

As we're leavin' for home Mr. Robert gets me one side and pats me on the back. "I say, Torchy," says he, "as a raconteur you're a great success. It worked. Nicky will sign up tomorrow."

"Good!" says I. "Only send him where they ain't got the settin' hen habit and the taxi drivers ain't so willin' to take a chance."

CHAPTER IX

BRINK DOES A SIDESLIP

Mostly it was a case of Old Hickory runnin' wild on the main track and Brink Hollis being in the way. What we really ought to have in the Corrugated general offices is one of these 'quake detectors, same as they have in Washington to register distant volcano antics, so all hands could tell by a glance at the dial what was coming and prepare to stand by for rough weather.

For you never can tell just when old Hickory Ellins is going to cut loose. Course, being on the inside, with my desk right next to the door of the private office, I can generally forecast an eruption an hour or so before it takes place. But it's apt to catch the rest of the force with their hands down and their mouths open.

Why, just by the way the old boy pads in at 9:15, plantin' his hoofs heavy and glarin' straight ahead from under them bushy eye dormers of his, I could guess that someone was goin' to get a call on the carpet before very long. And sure enough he'd hardly got settled in his big leather swing chair before he starts barkin' for Mr. Piddie.

I expect when it comes to keepin' track of the overhead, and gettin' a full day's work out of a bunch of lady typists,

Sewell Ford

and knowin' where to buy his supplies at cut-rates, Piddie is as good an office manager as you'll find anywhere along Broadway from the Woolworth tower to the Circle; but when it comes to soothin' down a 65-year-old boss who's been awake most of the night with sciatica, he's a flivver. He goes in with his brow wrinkled up and his knees shakin', and a few minutes later he comes out pale in the gills and with a wild look in his eyes.

"What's the scandal, Piddie?" says I. "Been sent to summon the firin' squad, or what?"

He don't stop to explain then, but pikes right on into the bond room and holds a half-hour session with that collection of giddy young near-sports who hold down the high stools. Finally, though, he tip-toes back to me, wipes the worry drops from his forehead, and gives me some of the awful details.

"Such incompetency!" says he husky. "You remember that yesterday Mr. Ellins called for a special report on outside holdings? And when it is submitted it is merely a jumble of figures. Why, the young man who prepared it couldn't have known the difference between a debenture 5 and a refunding 6!"

"Don't make me shudder, Piddie," says I. "Who was the brainless wretch?"

"Young Hollis, of course," whispers Piddie. "And it's not the first occasion, Torchy, on which he has been found failing. I am sending some of his books in for inspection."

"Oh, well," says I, "better Brink than some of the others. He won't take it serious. He's like a duck in a shower— sheds it easy."

At which Piddie goes off shakin' his head ominous. But then, Piddie has been waitin' for the word to fire Brink Hollis ever since this cheerful eyed young hick was wished on the Corrugated through a director's pull nearly a year ago, when he was fresh from college. You see, Piddie can't understand how anybody can draw down the princely salary of twenty-five a week without puttin' his whole soul into his work, or be able to look his boss in the face if there's any part of the business that he's vague about.

As for Brink, his idea of the game is to get through an eight-hour day somehow or other so he can have the other sixteen to enjoy himself in, and I expect he takes about as much interest in what he has to do as if he was countin' pennies in a mint. Besides that he's sort of a happy-go-lucky, rattle-brained youth who has been chucked into this high finance thing because his fam'ly thought he ought to be doing something that looks respectable; you know the type?

Nice, pleasant young chap. Keeps the bond room force chirked up on rainy days and always has a smile for everybody. It was him organized the Corrugated Baseball Nine that cleaned up with every other team in the building last summer. They say he was a star first baseman at Yale or Princeton or wherever it was he was turned loose from. Also he's some pool shark, I understand, and is runnin' off a progressive tournament that he got Mr. Robert to put up some cups for.

So I'm kind of sorry, when I answers the private office buzzer a little later, and finds Old Hickory purple in the face and starin' at something he's discovered between the pages of Brink's bond book.

"Young man," says he as he hands it over, "perhaps you

can fell me something about this?"

"Looks lite a program," says I, glancin' it over casual. "Oh, yes. For the first annual dinner of the Corrugated Crabs. That was last Saturday night."

"And who, may I ask," goes on Old Hickory, "are the Corrugated Crabs?"

"Why," says I, "I expect they're some of the young sports on the general office staff."

"Huh!" he grunts. "Why Crabs?"

I hunches my shoulders and lets it go at that.

"I notice," says Old Hickory, taking back the sheet, "that one feature of the entertainment was an impersonation by Mr. Brinkerhoff Hollis, of 'the Old He-Crab Himself unloading a morning grouch'. Now, just what does that mean?"

"Couldn't say exactly," says I. "I wasn't there."

"Oh, you were not, eh?" says he. "Didn't suppose you were. But you understand, Torchy, I am asking this information of you as my private secretary. I—er—it will be treated as confidential."

"Sorry, Mr. Ellins," says I, "but you know about as much of it as I do."

"Which is quite enough," says he, "for me to decide that the Corrugated can dispense with the services of this Hollis person at once. You will notify Mr. Piddie to that effect."

"Ye-e-es, sir," says I, sort of draggy.

He glances up at me quick. "You're not enthusiastic about it, eh?" says he.

"No," says I.

"Then for your satisfaction, and somewhat for my own," he goes on, "we will review the case against this young man. He was one of three who won a D minus rating in the report made by that efficiency expert called in by Mr. Piddie last fall."

"Yes, I know," says I. "That squint-eyed bird who sprung his brain tests on the force and let on he could card index the way your gray matter worked by askin' a lot of nutty questions. I remember. Brink Hollis was guyin' him all the while and he never caught on. Had the whole bunch chucklin'over it. One of Piddie's fads, he was."

Old Hickory waves one hand impatient. "Perhaps," says he. "I don't mean to say I value that book psychology rigamarole very highly myself. Cost us five hundred, too. But I've had an eye on that young man's work ever since, and it hasn't been brilliant. This bond summary is a sample. It's a mess."

"I don't doubt it!" says I. "But if I'd been Piddie I think I'd have hung the assignment for that on some other hook than Hollis's. He didn't know what a bond looked like until a year ago and that piece of work called for an old hand."

"Possibly, possibly," agrees Old Hickory. "It seems he is clever enough at this sort of thing, however," and he waves the program.

I couldn't help smotherin' a chuckle.

"Am I to infer," says Mr. Ellins, "that this He-Crab act of his was humorous?"

"That's what they tell me," says I. "You see, right after dinner Brink was missin' and everybody was wonderin' what had become of him, when all of a sudden he bobs up through a tin-foil lake in the middle of the table and proceeds to do this crab impersonation in costume. They say it was a scream."

"It was, eh?" grunts Old Hickory. "And the Old He-Crab referred to—who was that?"

"Who do you guess, Mr. Ellins?" says I, grinnin'.

"H-m-m-m," says he, rubbin' his chin. "I can't say I'm flattered. Thinks I'm an old crab, does he?"

"I expect he does," I admits.

"Do you?" demands Old Hickory, whirlin' on me sudden.

"I used to," says I, "until I got to know you better."

"Oh!" says he. "Well, I suppose the young man has a right to his own opinion. And my estimate of him makes us even. But perhaps you don't know with what utter contempt I regard such a worthless—"

"I got a general idea," says I. "And maybe that's because you don't know him very well."

For a second the old boy stares at me like he was goin' to blow a gasket. But he don't. "I will admit," says he, "that I may have failed to cultivate a close acquaintance with all the harum-scarum cut-ups in my employ. One doesn't always find the time. May I ask what course you would recommend?"

"Sure!" says I. "If it was me I wouldn't give him the chuck without a hearin'."

That sets him chewin' his cigar. "Very well," says he. "Bring him in."

I hadn't figured on gettin' so close to the affair as this, but as I had I couldn't do anything else but see it through. I finds Brink drummin' a jazz tune on his desk with his fingers and otherwise makin' the best of it.

"Well," says he, as I taps him on the shoulder, "is it all over?"

"Not yet," says I. "But the big boss is about to give you the third degree. So buck up."

"Wants to see me squirm, does he?" says Brink. "All right. But I don't see the use. What'll I feed him, Torchy?"

"Straight talk, nothing else," says I. "Come along."

And I expect when Brink Hollis found himself lined up in front of them chilled steel eyes he decided that this was a cold and cruel world.

"Let's see," opens Old Hickory, "you've been with us about a year, haven't you?"

Hollis nods.

"And how do you think you are getting on as a business man?" asks Mr. Ellins.

"Fairly rotten, thank you," says he.

"I must say that I agree with you," says Old Hickory. "How did you happen to honor us by making your start here?"

"Because the governor didn't want me in his office," says Hollis, "and could get me into the Corrugated."

"Hah!" snorts Old Hickory. "Think we're running a retreat for younger sons, do you!"

"If I started in with that idea," says Brink, "I'm rapidly getting over it. And if you want to know, Mr. Ellins, I'm just as sick of working in the bond room as you are of having me there."

"Then why in the name of the seven sins do you stick?" demands Old Hickory.

Brink shrugs his shoulders. "Dad thinks it's best for me," says he. "He imagines I'm making good. I suppose I've rather helped along the notion, and he's due to get some jolt when he finds I've nose-dived to a crash."

"Unfortunately," says Old Hickory, "we cannot provide shock absorbers for fond fathers. Any other reasons why you wished to remain on our pay roll?"

"One," says Brink, "but it will interest you less than the first. If I got a raise next month I was planning to be married."

Old Hickory sniffs. "That's optimism for you!" says he. "You expect us to put a premium on the sort of work you've been doing? Bah!"

"Oh, why drag out the agony?" says Brink. "I knew I'd put a crimp in my career when I remembered leaving that crab banquet program in the book. Let's get to that."

"As you like," says Old Hickory. "Not that I attach any great importance to such monkey shines, but we might as well take it up. So you think I'm an old crab, do you?"

"I had gathered that impression," says Brink. "Seemed to be rather general around the shop."

Old Hickory indulges in one of them grins that are just as humorous as a crack in the pavement. "I've no doubt," says he. "And you conceived the happy idea of dramatizing me as the leading comic feature for this dinner party of my employees? It was a success, I trust."

"Appeared to take fairly well," says Brink.

"Pardon me if I seem curious," goes on Old Hickory, "but just how did you—er—create the illusion?"

"Oh, I padded myself out in front," says Brink, "and stuck on a lot of cotton for eyebrows, and used the make-up box liberal, and gave them some red-hot patter on the line that—well, you know how you work off a grouch, sir. I may have caught some of your pet phrases. Anyway, they seemed to know who I meant."

"You're rather clever at that sort of thing, are you?" asks Old Hickory.

"Oh, that's no test," says Brink. "You can always get a hand with local gags. And then, I did quite a lot of that stuff at college; put on a couple of frat plays and managed the Mask Club two seasons."

"Too bad the Corrugated Trust offers such a limited field for your talents," says Old Hickory. "Only one annual dinner of the Crab Society. You organized that, I suppose?"

"Guilty," says Brink.

"And I understand you were responsible for the Corrugated baseball team, and are now conducting a pool tournament?" goes on Old Hickory.

"Oh, yes," says Brink, sort of weary. "I'm not denying a thing. I was even planning a little noonday dancing club for the stenographers. You may put that in the indictment if you like."

"H-m-m-m!" says Old Hickory, scratchin' his ear. "I think that will be all, young man."

Brink starts for the door but comes back. "Not that I mind being fired, Mr. Ellins," says he. "I don't blame you a bit for that, for I suppose I'm about the worst bond clerk in the business. I did try at first to get into the work, but it was no good. Guess I wasn't cut out for that particular line. So we'll both be better off. But about that He-Crab act of mine. Sounds a bit raw, doesn't it? I expect it was, too. I'd like to say, though, that all I meant by it was to make a little fun for the boys. No personal animosity behind it, sir, even if—"

Old Hickory waves his hand careless. "I'm beginning to get your point of view, Hollis," says he. "The boss is always fair game, eh?"

"Something like that," says Brink. "Still, I hate to leave with you thinking—"

"You haven't been asked to leave—as yet," says Old Hickory. "I did have you slated for dismissal a half hour ago, and I may stick to it. Only my private secretary seemed to think I didn't know what I was doing. Perhaps he was right. I'm going to let your case simmer for a day or so. Now clear out, both of you."

We slid through the door. "Much obliged for making the try, Torchy," says Brink. "You had your nerve with you, I'll say."

"Easiest thing I do, old son," says I. "Besides, his ain't a case of ingrowin' grouch, you know."

"I was just getting that hunch myself," says Brink. "Shouldn't wonder but he was quite a decent old boy when you got under the crust. If I was only of some use around the place I'll bet we'd get along fine. As it is—" He spreads out his hands.

"Trust Old Hickory Ellins to find out whether you're any use or not," says I. "He don't miss many tricks. If you do get canned, though, you can make up your mind that finance is your short suit."

Nearly a week goes by without another word from Mr. Ellins. And every night as Brink streamed out with the advance guard at 5 o'clock he'd stop long enough at my desk to swap a grin with me and whisper: "Well, I won't have to break the news to Dad tonight, anyway."

"Nor to the young lady, either," says I.

"Oh, I had to spill it to Marjorie, first crack," says he. "She's helping me hold my breath."

And then here yesterday mornin', as I'm helping Old

Hickory sort the mail, he picks out a letter from our Western manager and slits it open.

"Hah!" says he, through his cigar. "I think this solves our problem, Torchy."

"Yes, sir?" says I, gawpin'.

"Call in that young humorist of yours from the bond room," says he.

And I yanks Brink Hollis off the high stool impetuous.

"Know anything about industrial welfare work, young man?" demands Old Hickory of him.

"I've seen it mentioned in magazine articles," says Brink, "but that's about all. Don't think I ever read one."

"So much the better," says Mr. Ellins. "You'll have a chance to start in fresh, with your own ideas."

"I—I beg pardon?" says Brink, starin' puzzled.

"You're good at play organizing, aren't you," goes on Old Hickory. "Well, here's an opportunity to spread yourself. One of the manufacturing units we control out in Ohio. Three thousand men, in a little one-horse town where there's nothing better to do in their spare time than go to cheap movies and listen to cheaper walking delegates. I guess they need you more than we do in the bond room. Organize 'em as much as you like. Show 'em how to play. Give that He-Crab act if you wish. We'll start you in at a dollar a man. That satisfactory?"

I believe Brink tried to say it was, only what he got out was so choky you could hardly tell. But he goes out beamin'.

"Well!" says Old Hickory, turnin' to me. "I suppose he'll call that coming safely out of a nose dive, eh?"

"Or side-slippin' into success," says I. "I think you've picked another winner, Mr. Ellins."

"Huh!" he grunts. "You mean you think you helped me do it. But I want you to understand, young man, that I learned to be tolerant of other people's failings long before you were born. Toleration. It's the keystone of every big career. I've practiced it, too, except—well, except after a bad night."

And then, seein' that rare flicker in Old Hickory's eyes, I gives him the grin. Oh, sure you can. It's all in knowin' when.

CHAPTER X

'IKKY-BOY COMES ALONG

Being a parent grows on you, don't it? Course, at first, when it's sprung on you so kind of sudden, you hardly know how to act. That is, if you're makin' your debut in the part. And I expect for a few months there, after young Richard Hemmingway Ballard came and settled down with Vee and me, I put up kind of a ragged amateur performance as a fond father. All I can say about it now is I hope I didn't look as foolish as I felt.

As for Vee, she seemed to get her lines and business perfect from the start. Somehow young mothers do. She knew how to handle the youngster right off; how to hold him and what to say to him when he screwed up his face and made remarks to her that meant nothing at all to me. And she wasn't fussed or anything when company came in and caught her at it. Also young Master Richard seemed to be right at home from the very first. Didn't seem surprised or strange or nervous in the presence of a pair of parents that he found wished on him without much warnin'. Just gazed at us as calm and matter-of-fact as if he'd known us a long time. While me, well it must have been weeks before I got over feelin' kind of panicky whenever I was left alone with him.

But are we acquainted now? I'll say we are. In fact, as Harry Lander used to put it, vurra well acquainted. Chummy, I might say. Why not, after we've stood two years of each other without any serious dispute? Not that I'm claimin' any long-distance record as a model parent. No. I expect I do most of the things I shouldn't and only a few of them that I should. But 'Ikky-boy ain't a critical youngster. That's his own way of sayin' his name and mostly we call him that. Course, he answers to others, too; such as Old Scout, and Snoodlekins, and young Rough-houser. I mean, he does when he ain't too busy with important enterprises; such as haulin' Buddy, the Airedale pup, around by the ears; or spoonin' in milk and cereal, with Buddy watchin' hopeful for sideslips; or pullin' out the spool drawer of Vee's work table.

It's been hinted to us by thoughtful friends who have all the scientific dope on bringin' up children, although most of 'em never had any of their own, that this is all wrong. Accordin' to them we ought to start right in makin' him drop whatever he's doin' and come to us the minute we call. Maybe we should, too. But that ain't the way it works out, for generally, we don't want anything special, and he seems so wrapped up in his private little affairs that it don't seem worth while breakin' in on his program. Course, maulin' Buddy around may seem to us like a frivolous pastime, but how can you tell if it ain't the serious business in life to 'Ikky-boy just then? Besides, Buddy seems to like it. So as a rule we let 'em finish the game.

But there is one time each day when he's always ready to quit any kind of fun and come toddlin' with his hands stretched out and a wide grin on his chubby little face. That's along about 6:15 when I blow in from town. Then he's right there with the merry greetin' and the friendly motions. Also his way of addressin' his male parent would give another jolt to a lot of people, I suppose.

"Hi, Torchy!" That's his favorite hail.

"Reddy yourself, you young freshy," I'm apt to come back at him.

Followin' which I scooch to meet his flyin' tackle and we roll on the rug in a clinch, with Buddy yappin' delighted and mixin' in promiscuously. Finally we end up on the big davenport in front of the fireplace and indulge in a few minutes of lively chat.

"Well, 'Ikky-boy, how you and Buddy been behavin' yourselves, eh?" I'll ask. "Which has been the worst cut-up today, eh?"

"Buddy bad dog," he'll say, battin' him over the head with a pink fist. "See?" And he'll exhibit a tear in his rompers or a chewed sleeve.

"Huh! I'll bet it's been fifty-fifty, you young rough-houser," I'll say. "Who do you like best around this joint, anyway?"

"Buddy," is always the answer.

"And next?" I'll demand.

"Mamma," he'll say.

"Hey, where do I come in?" I'll ask, shakin' him.

Then he'll screw up his mouth mischievous and say: "Torchy come in door. Torchy, Torchy!"

I'll admit Vee ain't so strong for all this. His callin' me

Torchy, I mean. She does her best, too, to get him to change it to Daddy. But that word don't seem to be on 'Ikky-boy's list at all. He picked up the Torchy all by himself and he seems to want to stick to it. I don't mind. Maybe it ain't just the thing for a son and heir to spring on a perfectly good father, chucklin' over it besides, but it sounds quite all right to me. Don't hurt my sense of dignity a bit.

And it looks like he'll soon come to be called young Torchy himself. Uh-huh. For a while there Vee was sure his first crop of hair, which was wheat colored like hers, was goin' to be the color scheme of his permanent thatch. But when the second growth begun to show up red she had to revise her forecast. Now there's no doubt of his achievin' a pink-plus set of wavy locks that'll make a fresh-painted fire hydrant look faded. They're gettin' brighter and brighter and I expect in time they'll show the same new copper kettle tints that mine do.

"I don't care," says Vee "I rather like it."

"That's the brave talk, Vee!" says I. "It may be all he'll inherit from me, but it ain't so worse at that. With that hair in evidence there won't be much danger of his being lost in a crowd. Folks will remember him after one good look. Besides, it's always sort of cheerin' on a rainy day. He'll be able to brighten up the corner where he is without any dope from Billy Sunday. Course, he'll be joshed a lot about it, but that'll mean he'll either have to be a good scrapper or develop an easy-grin disposition, so he wins both ways."

The only really disappointed member of the fam'ly is Vee's Auntie. Last time she was out here she notices the change in 'Ikky-boy's curls and sighs over it.

"I had hoped," says she, "that the little fellow's hair would be—well, of a different shade."

"Sort of a limousine body-black, eh?" says I. "Funny it ain't, too."

"But he will be so—so conspicuous," she goes on.

"There are advantages," says I, "in carryin' your own spotlight with you. Now take me."

But Auntie only sniffs and changes the subject.

She's a grand old girl, though. A little hard to please, I'll admit. I've been at it quite some time, but it's only now and then I can do anything that seems to strike her just right. Mostly she disapproves of me, and she's the kind that ain't a bit backward about lettin' you know. Her remarks here the other day when she arrives to help celebrate Master Richard's second birthday will give you an idea.

You see, she happens to be in the living room when me and 'Ikky-boy has our reg'lar afternoon reunion. Might be we went at it a little stronger and rougher than usual, on account of the youngster's havin' been held quiet in her lap for a half hour or so.

"Hi, hi, ol' Torchy, Torchy!" he shouts, grippin' both hands into my hair gleeful.

"Burny burn!" says I makin' a hissin' noise.

"Yah, yah! 'Ikky-boy wanna ride hossy," says he.

"And me with my trousers just pressed!" says I. "Say, where do you get that stuff?"

"I must say," comes in Auntie, "that I don't consider that the proper way to talk to a child."

"Oh, he don't mind," says I.

"But he is so apt to learn such expressions and use them himself," says she.

"Yes, he picks up a lot," says I. "He's clever that way. Aren't you, you young tarrier?"

"Whe-e-e!" says 'Ikky-boy, slidin' off my knee to make a dive at Buddy and roll him on the floor.

"One should speak gently to a child," says Auntie, "and use only the best English."

"I might be polite to him," says I, "if he'd be polite to me, but that don't seem to be his line."

Auntie shrugs her shoulders and gives us up as hopeless. We're in bad with her, both of us, and I expect if there'd been a lawyer handy she'd revised her will on the spot. Honest, it's lucky the times she's decided to cross me off as one of her heirs don't show on me anywhere or I'd be notched up like a yardstick, and if I'd done any worryin' over these spells of hers I'd be an albino from the ears up. But when she starts castin' the cold eye at Richard Hemmingway I almost works up that guilty feelin' and wonders if maybe I ain't some to blame.

"You ain't overlookin, the fact, are you, Auntie," I suggests, "that he's about 100 per cent. boy? He's full of pep and jump and go, same as Buddy, and he's just naturally got to let it out."

"I fail to see," says Auntie, "how teaching him to use

slang is at all necessary. As you know, that is something of which I distinctly disapprove."

"Now that you remind me," says I, "seems I have heard you say something of the kind before. And take it from me I'm going to make a stab at trainin' him different. Right now. Richard, approach your father."

'Ikky-boy lets loose of Buddy's collar and stares at me impish.

"Young man," says I severe, "I want you to lay off that slang stuff. Ditch it. It ain't lady like or refined. And in future when you converse with your parents see that you do it respectful and proper. Get me?"

At which 'Ikky-boy looks bored. "Whee!" he remarks boisterous, makin' a grab for Buddy's stubby tail and missin' it.

"Perfectly absurd!" snorts Auntie, retirin' haughty to the bay window.

"Disqualified!" says I, under my breath. "Might as well go the limit, Snoodlekins. We'll have to grow up in our own crude way."

That was the state of affairs when this Mrs. Proctor Butt comes crashin' in on the scene of our strained domestic relations. Trust her to appear at just the wrong time. Mrs. Buttinski I call her, and she lives up to the name.

She's a dumpy built blond party, Mrs. Proctor Butt, with projectin' front teeth, bulgy blue eyes and a hurried, trottin' walk like a duck makin' for a pond. Her chief aim in life seems to be to be better posted on your affairs than you are yourself, and, of course, that keeps her reasonably busy. Also she's a lady gusher from Gushville. Now, I don't object to havin' a conversational gum drop tossed at me once in a while, sort of offhand and casual. But that ain't Mrs. Buttinski's method. She feeds you raw molasses with a mixin' spoon. Just smears you with it.

"Isn't it perfectly wonderful," says she, waddlin' in fussy, "that your dear darling little son should be two years old? Do you know, Mrs. Robert Ellins just told me of what an important day it was in the lives of you two charming young people, so I came right over to congratulate you. And here I discover you all together in your beautiful little home, proud father and all. How fortunate!"

As she's beamin' straight at me I has to give her some comeback. "Yes, you're lucky, all right," says I. "Another minute and you wouldn't found me here, for I was just—"

Which is where I gets a frown and a back-up signal from Vee. She don't like Mrs. Proctor Butt a bit more'n I do but she ain't so frank about lettin' her know it.

"Oh, please don't run away," begs Mrs. Butt. "You make such an ideal young couple. As I tell Mr. Butt, I just can't keep my eyes off you two whenever I see you out together."

"I'm sure that's nice of you to say so," says Vee, blushin'.

"Oh, every one thinks the same of you, my dear," says the lady. "Only I simply can't keep such things to myself. I have such an impulsive nature. And I adore young people and children, positively adore them. And now where is the darling little baby that I haven't seen for months and months? You'll forgive my running in at this unseasonable hour, I know, but I just couldn't wait another day to—oh, there he is, the darling cherub! And isn't that a picture for an artist?"

He'd have to be some rapid-fire paint slinger if he was to use 'Ikky-boy as a model just then for him and Buddy was havin' a free-for-all mix-up behind the davenport that nothing short of a movie camera would have done justice to.

"Oh, you darling little fellow!" she gurgles on. "I must hold you in my arms just a moment. Please, mother mayn't I?"

"I—I'm afraid you would find him rather a lively armful just now," warns Vee. "You see, when he gets to playing with Buddy he's apt to—"

"Oh, I sha'n't mind a bit," says Mrs. Butt. "Besides, the little dears always seem to take to me. Do let me have him for a moment?"

"You get him, Torchy," says Vee.

So after more or less maneuverin' I untangles the two, shuts Buddy in another room, and deposits 'Ikky-boy, still kickin' and strugglin' indignant, in whatever lap Mrs. Butt has to offer.

Then she proceeds to rave over him. It's enough to make you seasick. Positively. "Oh, what exquisite silky curls of spun gold!" she gushes. "And such heavenly big blue eyes with the long lashes, and his 'ittle rosebud mousie. O-o-o-o-o!"

From that on all she spouts is baby talk, while she mauls and paws him around like he was a sack of meal. I couldn't help glancin' at Auntie, for that's one thing she and Vee have agreed on, that strangers wasn't to be allowed to take any such liberties with baby. Besides, Auntie never did have any use for this Mrs. Butt anyway and hardly speaks to her civil when she meets her. Now Auntie is squirmin' in her chair and I can guess how her fingers are itchin' to rescue the youngster.

"Um precious 'ittle sweetums, ain't oo?" gurgles Mrs. Butt, rootin' him in the stomach with her nose. "Won't um let me tiss um's tweet 'ittle pinky winky toes?"

She's just tryin' to haul off one of his shoes when 'Ikky-boy cuts loose with the rough motions, fists and feet both in action, until she has to straighten up to save her hat and her hair.

"Dess one 'ittle toe-tiss?" she begs.

"Say," demands 'Ikky-boy, pushin' her face away fretful, "where oo get 'at stuff?"

"Wha-a-at?" gasps Mrs. Butt.

"Lay off 'at, tant you?" says he "Oo—oo give 'Ikky-boy a big pain, Oo does. G'way!"

"Why, how rude!" says Mrs. Butt, gazin' around bewildered; and then, as she spots that approvin' smile on Auntie's face, she turns red in the ears.

Say, I don't know when I've seen the old girl look so tickled over anything. What she's worked up is almost a grin. And there's no doubt that Mrs. Butt knows why it's there.

"Of course," says she, "if you approve of such language— " and handin' the youngster over to Vee she straightens her lid and makes a quick exit.

"Bing!" says I. "I guess we got a slap on the wrist that time."

"I don't care a bit," says Vee, holdin' her chin well up. "She had no business mauling baby in that fashion."

"I ain't worryin' if she never comes back," says I, "only I'd just promised Auntie to train 'Ikky-boy to talk different and—"

"Under similar provocation," says Auntie, "I might use the same expressions—if I knew how."

"Hip, hip, for Auntie!" I sings out. "And as for your not knowin' how, that's easy fixed. 'Ikky-boy and I will give you lessons."

And say, after he'd finished his play and was about ready to be tucked into his crib, what does the young jollier do but climb up in Auntie's lap and cuddle down folksy, all on his own motion.

"Do you like your old Auntie, Richard?" she asks, smoothin' his red curls gentle.

"Uh-huh," says 'Ikky-boy, blinkin' up at her mushy. "Oo's a swell Auntie."

Are we back in the will again? I'll guess we are.

CHAPTER XI

LOUISE REVERSES THE CLOCK

It was one of Mr. Robert's cute little ideas, you might know. He's an easy boss in a good many ways and I have still to run across a job that I'd swap mine for, the pay envelopes being fifty-fifty. But say, when it comes to usin' a private sec. free and careless he sure is an ace of aces.

Maybe you don't remember, but I almost picked out his wife for him, and when she'd set the date he turns over all the rest of the details to me, even to providin' a minister and arrangin' his bridal tour. Honest I expect when the time comes for him to step up and be measured for a set of wings and a halo he'll look around for me to hold his place in the line until his turn comes. And he won't be quite satisfied with the arrangements unless I'm on hand.

So I ought to be prepared for 'most any old assignment to be hung on the hook. I must say, though, that in the case of this domestic mix-up of Mrs. Bruce Mackey's I was caught gawpin' on and unsuspectin'. In fact, I was smotherin' a mild snicker at the situation, not dreamin' that I'd ever get any nearer to it than you would to some fool movie plot you might be watchin' worked out on the screen.

We happens to crash right into the middle of it, Vee and me, when we drops in for our usual Sunday afternoon call on the Ellinses and finds these week-end guests of theirs puttin' it up to Mr. and Mrs. Robert to tell 'em what they ought to do. Course, this Mrs. Mackey is an old friend of Mrs. Robert's and we'd seen 'em both out there before; in fact, we'd met 'em when she was Mrs. Richard Harrington and Bruce was just a sympathetic bachelor sort of danglin' around and makin' himself useful. So it wasn't quite as if they'd sprung the thing on total strangers.

And, anyway, it don't rate very rank as a scandal. Not as scandals run. This No. 1 hubby, Harrington, had simply got what was coming to him, only a little late. Never was cut out to play the lead in a quiet domestic sketch. Not with his temperament and habits. Hardly. Besides, he was well along in his sporty career when he discovered this 19-year-old pippin with the trustin' blue eyes and the fascinatin' cheek dimples. But you can't tell a bad egg just by glancin' at the shell, and she didn't stop to hold him in front of a candle. Lucky for the suspender wearin' sex there ain't any such pre-nuptial test as that, eh? She simply tucked her head down just above the top pearl stud, I suppose, and said she would be his'n without inquirin' if that cocktail breath of his was a regular thing or just an accident.

But she wasn't long in findin' out that it was chronic. Oh yes. He wasn't known along Broadway as Dick Harry for nothing. He might be more or less of a success as a corporation lawyer between 10:30 and 5 p. m. in the daytime, but after the shades of night was well tied down and the cabarets begun takin' the lid off he was apt to be missin' from the fam'ly fireside. Wine, women and the deuces wild was his specialties, and when little wifie tried to read the riot act to him at 3 a. m. he just naturally told her where she got off. And on occasions, when the deuces hadn't been runnin' his way, or the night had been wilder than usual, he was quite rough about it.

Yet she'd stood for that sort of thing nine long years before applyin' for a decree. She got it, of course, with the custody of the little girl and a moderate alimony allowance. He didn't even file an answer, so it was all done quiet with no stories in the newspapers. And then for eight or ten years she'd lived by herself, just devotin' all her time to little Polly, sendin' her to school, chummin' with her durin' vacations, and tryin' to make her forget that she had a daddy in the discards.

Must have been several tender-hearted male parties who was sorry for a lonely grass widow who was a perfect 36 and showed dimples when she laughed, but none of 'em seemed to have the stayin' qualities of Bruce Mackey. He had a little the edge on the others, too, because he was an old fam'ly friend, havin' known Dick Harry both before and after he got the domestic dump. At that, though, he didn't win out until he'd almost broken the long distance record as a patient waiter, and I understand it was only when little Miss Polly got old enough to hint to Mommer that Uncle Bruce would suit her first rate as a stepdaddy that the match was finally pulled off.

And now Polly, who's barely finished at boardin' school, has announced that she intends to get married herself. Mommer has begged her weepy not to take the high dive so young, and pointed out where she made her own big mistake in that line. But Polly comes back at her by declarin' that her Billy is a nice boy. There's no denyin' that. Young Mr. Curtis seems to be as good as they come. He'd missed out on his last year at college, but he'd spent it in an aviation camp and he was just workin' up quite a rep. as pilot of a bombin' plane when the closed season on Hun towns was declared one eleventh of November. Then he'd come back modest to help his father run the zinc and tinplate trust, or something like that, and was payin' strict attention to business until he met Polly at a football game. After that he had only one aim in life, which was leadin' Polly up the middle aisle with the organ playin' that breath of Eden piece.

Well, what was a fond mommer to do in a case like that? Polly admits being a young person, but she insists that she knows what she wants. And one really couldn't find any fault with Billy. She had had Bruce look up his record and, barrin' a few little 9 a. m. police court dates made for him by grouchy traffic cops, it was as clean as a new shirt front. True, he had been born in Brooklyn, but his family had moved to Madison Avenue before he was old enough to feel the effects.

So at last Mrs. Mackey had given in. Things had gone so far as settlin' the date for the weddin'. It was to be some whale of an affair, too, for both the young folks had a lot of friends and on the Curtis side especially there was a big callin' list to get invitations. Nothing but a good-sized church would hold 'em all.

Which was where Bruce Mackey, usually a mild sort of party and kind of retirin', had come forward with the balky behavior.

"What do you think?" says Mrs. Bruce. "He says he won't go near the church."

"Eh?" demands Mr. Robert, turnin' to him. "What do you mean by that, Bruce?"

Mr. Mackey shakes his head stubborn. "Think I can stand up there before a thousand or more people and give Polly away?" says he. "No. I—I simply can't do it."

"But why not?" insists Mrs. Robert.

"Well, she isn't my daughter," says he, "and it isn't my place to be there. Dick should do it."

"But don't you see, Bruce," protests Mrs. Mackey, "that if he did I—I should have to—to meet him again?"

"What of it?" says Bruce. "It isn't likely he'd beat you in church. And as he is Polly's father he ought to be the one to give her away. That's only right and proper, as I see it."

And there was no arguin' him out of that notion. He came from an old Scotch Presbyterian family. Bruce Mackey did, and while he was easy goin' about most things now and then he'd bob up with some hard-shell ideas like this. Principles, he called 'em. Couldn't get away from 'em.

"But just think, Bruce," goes on Mrs. Mackey, "we haven't seen each other for ever so many years. I—I wouldn't like it at all."

"Hope you wouldn't," says Bruce. "But I see no other way. You ought to go to the church with him, and he ought to bring you home afterwards. He needn't stay for the reception unless he wants to. But as Polly's father—"

"Oh, don't go over all that again," she breaks in. "I suppose I must do it. That is, if he's willing. I'll write him and ask if he is."

"No," says Bruce. "I don't think you ought to write. This is such a personal matter and a letter might seem—well, too formal."

"What shall I do, then?" demands Mrs. Mackey. "Telephone?"

"I hardly think one should telephone a message of that sort," says Bruce. "Someone ought to see him, explain the situation, and get his reply directly."

"Then you go, Bruce, dear," suggests Mrs. Mackey.

No, he shies at that. "Dick would resent my coming on such an errand," says Bruce. "Besides, I should feel obliged to urge him that it was his duty to go, and if he feels inclined to refuse—Well, of course, we have done our part."

"Then you rather hope he'll refuse to come?" she asks.

"I don't allow myself to think any such thing," says Bruce. "It wouldn't be right. But if he should decide not to it would be rather a relief, wouldn't it? In that ease I suppose I should be obliged to act in his stead. He ought to be asked, though."

Mr. Robert chuckles. "I wish I had an acrobatic conscience such as yours, Bruce," says he. "I could amuse myself for hours watching it turn flip-flops."

"Too bad yours died so young," Bruce raps back at him.

"Oh, I don't know," says Mr. Robert. "There are compensations. I don't grow dizzy trying to follow it when it gets frisky. To get back to the main argument, however; just how do you think the news should be broken to Dick Harrington?"

"Someone ought to go to see him," says Bruce; "a—a person who could state the circumstances fairly and sound him out to see how he felt about it. You know? Someone who would—er—"

"Do the job like a Turkish diplomat inviting an Armenian revolutionist to come and dine with him in some secluded mosque at daybreak, eh?" asks Mr. Robert. "Polite, but not insistent, I suppose?"

"Oh, something like that," says Bruce.

"He's right here," says Mr. Robert.

"I beg pardon?" says Bruce, starin'.

"Torchy," says Mr. Robert. "He'll do it with finesse and finish, and if there's any way of getting Dick to hang back by pretending to push him ahead our young friend who cerebrates in high speed will discover the same."

"Ah, come, Mr. Robert!" says I.

"Oh, we shall demand no miracles," says he. "But you understand the situation. Mr. Mackey's conscience is on the rampage and he's making this sacrifice as a peace offering. If the altar fires consume it, that's his look out. You get me, I presume?"

"Oh, sure!" says I. "Sayin' a piece, wasn't you?"

Just the same, I'm started out at 2:30 Monday afternoon to interview Mr. Dick Harrington on something intimate and personal. Mr. Robert has been 'phonin' his law offices and found that Mr. Harrington can probably be located best up in the Empire Theatre building, where they're havin' a rehearsal of a new musical show that he's interested in financially.

"With a sentimental interest, no doubt, in some sweet young thing who dances or sings, or thinks she does," comments Mr. Robert. "Anyway, look him up."

And by pushin' through a lot of doors that had "Keep Out" signs on 'em, and givin' the quick back up to a few fresh office boys, I trails Mr. Dick Harrington into the dark front of a theatre where he's sittin' with the producer and four of the seven authors of the piece watchin' a stage full of more or less young ladies in street clothes who are listenin' sort of bored while a bald-headed party in his shirt sleeves asks 'em for the love of Mike can't they move a little less like they was all spavined.

Don't strike me as just the place to ask a man will he stand up in church and help his daughter get married, but I had my orders. I slips into a seat back of him, taps him on the shoulder, and whispers how I have a message for him from his wife as was.

"From Louise?" says he. "The devil you say!"

"I could put it better," I suggests, "if we could find a place where there wasn't quite so much competition."

"Very well," says he. "Let's go back to the office. And by the way, Marston, when you get to that song of Mabel's hold it until I'm through with this young man."

And when he's towed me to the manager's sanctum he demands: "Well, what's gone wrong with Louise?"

"Nothing much," says I, "except that Miss Polly is plannin' to be married soon."

"Married!" he gasps. "Polly? Why, she's only a child!"

"Not at half past nineteen," says I. "I should call her considerable young lady."

"Well, I'll be blanked!" says he. "Little Polly grown up

and wanting to be married! She ought to be spanked instead. What are they after; my consent, eh?"

"Oh, no," says I. "It's all settled. Twenty-fifth of next month at St. Luke's. You're cast for the giving away act."

"Wh-a-at?" says he, his heavy under jaw saggin' astonished. "Me?"

"Fathers usually do," says I, "when they're handy."

"And in good standing," he adds. "You—er—know the circumstances, I presume?"

"Uh-huh," says I. "Don't seem to make any difference to them, though. They've got you down for the part. Church weddin', you know; big mob, swell affair. I expect that's why they think everything ought to be accordin' to Hoyle."

"Just a moment, young man," says he, breathin' a bit heavy. "I—I confess this is all rather disturbing."

It was easy to see that. He's fumblin' nervous with a gold cigarette case and his hand trembles so he can hardly hold a match. Maybe some of that was due to his long record as a whiteway rounder. The puffy bags under the eyes and the deep face lines couldn't have been worked up sudden, though.

"Can you guess how long it has been since I have appeared in a church?" he goes on. "Not since Louise and I were married. And I imagine I wasn't a particularly appropriate figure to be there even then. I fear I've changed some, too. Frankly now, young man, how do you think I would look before the altar?"

"Oh, I'm no judge," says I. "And I expect that with a clean shave and in a frock coat—"

"No," he breaks in, "I can't see myself doing it. Not before all that mob. How many guests did you say?"

"Only a thousand or so," says I.

He shudders. "How nice!" says he. "I can hear 'em whispering to each other: 'Yes that's her father—Dick Harry, you know. She divorced him, and they say—' No, no, I—I couldn't do it. You tell Louise that—Oh, by the way! What about her? She must have changed, too. Rather stout by this time, I suppose?"

"I shouldn't say so," says I. "Course I don't know what she used to be, but I'd call her more or less classy."

"But she is—let me see—almost forty," he insists.

"You don't mean it?" says I, openin' my mouth to register surprise. This looked like a good line to me and I thought I'd push it. "Course," I goes on, "with a daughter old enough to wear orange blossoms, I might have figured that for myself. But I'll be hanged if she looks it. Why, lots of folks take her and Polly for sisters."

He's eatin' that up, you can see. "Hm-m-m!" says he, rubbin' his chin. "I suppose I would be expected to—er— meet her there?"

"I believe the program is for you to take her to the church and bring her back for the reception," says I. "Yes, you'd have a chance for quite a reunion."

"I wonder how it would seem, talking to Louise again," says he.

"Might be a little awkward at first," says I, "but—"

"Do you know," he breaks in, "I believe I should like it. If you think she's good looking now, young man, you should have seen her at 19, at 22, or at 25. What an ass I was! And now I suppose she's like a full blown rose, perfect, exquisite?"

"Oh, I don't mean she's any ravin' beauty," says I, hedgin'.

"You don't, eh?" says he. "Well, I'd just like to see. You may tell her that I will—No, I'll 'phone her myself. Where is she?"

And all the stallin' around I could do didn't jar him away from that idea. He seems to have forgotten all about this Mabel person who was going to sing. He wanted to call up Louise right away. And he did.

So I don't have any chesty bulletin to hand Mr. Robert when I gets back.

"Well?" says he. "Did you induce him to give the right answer?"

"Almost," says I. "Had him panicky inside of three minutes."

"And then?" asks Mr. Robert.

"I overdid the act," says I. "Talked too much. He's coming."

Mr. Robert shrugs his shoulders. "Serves Bruce right," says he. "I wonder, though, how Louise will take it."

For a couple of days she took it hard. Just talking over the

Sewell Ford

'phone with Dick Harrington left her weak and nervous. Said she couldn't sleep all that night for thinking what it would be like to meet an ex-hubby that she hadn't seen for so long. She tried to picture how he would look, and how she would look to him. Then she braced up.

"If I must go through it," she confides to Mrs. Robert, "I mean to look my best."

Isn't that the female instinct for you?

As a matter of fact I'd kind of thrown it into him a bit strong about what a stunner she was. Oh, kind of nice lookin', fair figure, and traces of a peaches and cream complexion. There was still quite a high voltage sparkle in the trustin' blue eyes and the cheek dimples was still doin' business. But she was carryin' more or less excess weight for her height and there was the beginnings of a double chin. Besides, she always dressed quiet and sort of matronly.

From the remarks I heard Vee make, though, just before the weddin', I judge that Louise intended to go the limit. While she was outfittin' Polly with the snappiest stuff to be found in the Fifth Avenue shops she picked some for herself. I understand, too, that she was makin' reg'lar trips to a beauty parlor, and all that.

"How foolish!" I says to Vee. "I hope when you get to be forty you won't try to buy your way back to 25. It simply can't be done."

"Really?" says Vee, givin' me one of them quizzin' looks.

And, say, that's my last stab at givin' off the wise stuff about the nose powderin' sex. Pos-itively. For I've seen Louise turn the clock back. Uh-huh! I can't tell how it was done, or go into details of the results, but when she sails into that front pew on the big day, with Dick Harrington trailin' behind, I takes one glance at her and goes bug-eyed. Was she a stunner? I'll gurgle so. What had become of that extra 20 pounds I wouldn't even try to guess. But she's right there with the svelte figure, the school girly flush, and the sparklin' eyes. Maybe it was the way the gown was built. Fits like the peel on a banana. Or the pert way she holds her head, or the general excitement of the occasion. Anyway, mighty few 20-year-old screen favorites would have had anything on her.

As for Dick Harry—Well, he's spruced up quite a bit himself, but you'd never mistake him for anything but an old rounder who's had a clean shave and a face massage. And he just can't seem to see anything but Louise. Even when he has to leave and join the bridal procession his eyes wander back to that front pew where she was waitin'. And after it's all over I sees him watchin' her fascinated while she chatters along lively.

I wasn't lookin' to get his verdict at all, but later on, as I'm makin' myself useful at the reception, I runs across him just as he's slippin' away.

"I say, young man," says he, grabbin' me by the elbow. "Wasn't I right about Louise?"

"You had the dope," says I. "Some queen, even if she is near the forty mark."

"And only imagine," he adds, "within a year or so she may be a grandmother!"

"That don't count these days," says I. "It's gettin' so you can hardly tell the grandmothers from the vamps."

And when I said that I expect I unloaded my whole stock of wisdom about women.

.

CHAPTER XII

WHEN THE CURB GOT GYPPED

It was what you might call a session of the big four. Anyway, that's the way I'd put it; for besides Old Hickory, planted solid in his mahogany swing chair with his face lookin' more'n ever like a two-tone cut of the Rock of Gibraltar, there was Mr. Robert, and Piddie and me. Some aggregation, I'll say. And it didn't need any jiggly message from the ouija board to tell that something important in the affairs of the Corrugated Trust might happen within the next few minutes. You could almost feel it in the air. Piddie did. You could see that by the nervous way he was twitchin' his lips.

Course it was natural the big boss should turn first to me. "Torchy," he growls, "shut that door."

And as I steps around to close the only exit from the private office I could watch Piddie's face turn the color of a piece of cheese. Mr. Robert looks kind of serious, too.

"Gentlemen," goes on Old Hickory, tossin' the last three inches of a double Corona reckless into a copper bowl, "there's a leak somewhere in this office."

That gets a muffled gasp out of Piddie which puts him

under the spotlight at once, and when he finds we're all lookin' at him he goes through all the motions of a cabaret patron tryin' to sneak past one of Mr. Palmer's agents with something on the hip. If he'd been caught in the act of borin' into the bond safe he couldn't have looked any guiltier.

"I—er—I assure you, Mr. Ellins," he begins spluttery, "that I—ah—I—"

"Bah!" snorts Old Hickory impatient. "Who is implying that you do? If you were under suspicion in the least you wouldn't have been called in here, Mr. Piddie. So your panic is quite unnecessary."

"Of course," puts in Mr. Robert. "Don't be absurd, Piddie. Anything new this morning, Governor?"

"Rather," says Old Hickory, pointin' to a Wall Street daily that has broke loose on its front page with a three-column headline. "See what the Curb crowd did to G. L. T. common yesterday? Traded nearly one hundred thousand shares and hammered the opening quotations for a twenty-point loss. All on a rumor of a passed dividend. Well, you know that at three o'clock the day before we tabled a motion to pass that dividend and that an hour later, with a full board present, we decided to pay the regular four per cent semi-annual. But the announcement was not to be made until next Monday. Yet during that hour someone from this office must have carried out news of that first motion. True, it was a false tip; but I propose, gentlemen, to find out where that leak came from."

There's only one bet I'd be willin' to make on a proposition of that kind. If Old Hickory had set himself to trail down anything he'd do it. And we'd have to help.

Course, this Great Lakes Transportation is only one of our side lines that we carry on a separate set of books just to please the Attorney General. And compared to other submerged subsidiaries, as Mr. Robert calls 'em, it don't amount to much. But why its outstanding stock should be booted around Broad Street was an interestin' question. Also who the party was that was handin' out advance dope on such confidential details as board meetin' motions— Well, that was more so. Next time it might be a tip on something important. Mr. Robert suggests this.

"There is to be no next time," says Old Hickory, settin' his jaw.

So we starts the drag-net. First we went over the directors who had been present. Only five, includin' Old Hickory and Mr. Robert. And of the other three there was two that it would have been foolish to ask. Close-mouthed as sea clams after being shipped to Kansas City. The third was Oggie Kendall, a club friend of Mr. Robert's, who'd been dragged down from luncheon to make up a quorum.

"Oggie might have chattered something through sheer carelessness," says Mr. Robert. "I'll see if I can get him on the 'phone."

He could. But it takes Mr. Robert nearly five minutes to explain to Oggie what he's being queried about. Finally he gives it up.

"Oh, never mind," says he, hangin' up. Then, turnin' to us, he shrugs his shoulders. "It wasn't Oggie. Why, he doesn't even know which board he was acting on, and says he doesn't remember what we were talking about. Thought it was some sort of committee meeting."

"Then that eliminates all but some member of the office

staff," says Old Hickory. "Torchy, you acted as secretary. Do you remember that anyone came into the directors' room during our session?"

"Not a soul," says I.

"Except the boy Vincent," suggests Piddie.

"Ah, he wasn't in," says I. "Only came to the door with some telegrams; I took 'em myself."

"But was not a letter sent to our Western manager," Piddie goes on, "hinting that the G. L. T. dividend might be passed, and doesn't the boy have access to the private letter book?"

"Carried it from my desk to the safe, that's all," says I.

"Still," insists Piddie, "that would give him time enough to look."

"Oh, sure!" says I. "And since he's been here he's had a chance to snitch, off a barrel full of securities, or drop bombs down the elevator well; but somehow he hasn't."

"Well, we might as well have him in," says Old Hickory, pushin' the buzzer.

Seemed kind of silly to me, givin' fair-haired Vincent the third degree on sketchy hunch like that. Vincent! Why, he's been with the Corrugated four or five years, ever since they took me off the gate. And when he went on the job he was about the most innocent-eyed office boy, I expect, that you could find along Broadway. Reg'lar mommer's boy. Was just that, in fact. Used to tell me how worried his mother was for fear he'd get to smokin' cigarettes, or shootin' craps, or indulgin' in other big-town vices. Havin' seen mother, I could well believe it. Nice, refined old girl, still wearin' a widow's bonnet. Shows up occasionally on a half-holiday and lets Vincent take her to the Metropolitan Museum, or to a concert.

Course, Vincent hadn't stayed as green as when he first came. Couldn't. For it's more or less of a liberal education, being on the gate in the Corrugated General Offices, as I used to tell him. You simply gotta get wise to things or you don't last. And Vincent has wised up. Oh, yes.

Why, here only this last week, for instance, he makes a few plays that I couldn't have done any better myself. One was when I turns over to him the job of gettin' Pullman reservations on the Florida Limited for Freddie, the chump brother-in-law of Mr. Robert. Marjorie—that's the sister—had complained how all she could get was uppers, although they'd had an application in for six weeks. And as she and Freddie was taking both youngsters and two maids along they were on the point of givin' up the trip.

"Bah!" says Mr. Robert. "Freddie doesn't know how to do it, that's all. We'll get your reservations for you."

So he passes it on to me, and as I'm too busy just then to monkey with Pullman agents I shoots it on to Vincent. And inside of an hour he's back with a drawin' room and a section.

"Have to buy somebody; eh, Vincent?" I asks.

"Oh, yes, sir," says he cheerful.

"Just how did you work it?" says I.

"Well," says Vincent, "there was the usual line, of course. And the agent told three people ahead of me the same thing. 'Only uppers on the Limited.' So when it came my turn I simply shoved a five through the grill work and remarked casual: 'I believe you are holding a drawing-room and a section for me, aren't you?' 'Why, yes,' says he. 'You're just in time, too.' And a couple of years ago he would have done it for a dollar. Not now, though. It takes a five to pull a drawing-room these days."

"A swell bunch of grafters Uncle Sam turned back when he let go of the roads, eh?" says I.

"It's the same in the freight department," says Vincent. "You know that carload of mill machinery that had been missing for so long? Well, last week Mr. Robert sent me to the terminal offices for a report on their tracer. I told him to let me try a ten on some assistant general freight agent. It worked. He went right out with a switch engine and cut that car out of the middle of a half-mile long train on a siding, and before midnight it was being loaded on the steamer."

Also it was Vincent who did the rescue act when we was entertainin' that bunch of government inspectors who come around once a year to see that we ain't carryin' any wildcat stocks on our securities list, or haven't scuttled our sinking fund, or anything like that. Course, our books are always in such shape that they're welcome to paw 'em over all they like. That's easy enough. But, still, there's no sense in lettin' 'em nose around too free. Might dig up something they could ask awkward questions about. So Old Hickory sees to it that them inspectors has a good time, which means a suite of rooms at the Plutoria for a week, with dinners and theatre parties every night. And now with this Volstead act being pushed so hard it's kind of inconvenient gettin' a crowd of men into the right frame of mind. Has to be done though, no matter what may have happened to the constitution.

But this time it seems someone tip at the Ellins home had forgot to transfer part of the private cellar stock down to the hotel and when Old Hickory calls up here we has to chase Vincent out there and have him load two heavy suitcases into a taxi and see that the same are delivered without being touched by any bellhops or porters. Knew what he was carryin', Vincent did, and the chance he was taking; but he put over the act off hand, as if he was cartin' in a case of malted milk to a foundling hospital. They do say it was some party Old Hickory gave 'em.

I expect if a lot of folks out in the church sociable belt knew of that they'd put up a big howl. But what do they think? As I was tellin' Vincent: "You can't run big business on grape juice." That is, not our end of it. Oh, it's all right to keep the men in the plants down to one and a half per cent stuff. Good for 'em. We got the statistics to prove it. But when it comes to workin' up friendly relations with federal agents you gotta uncork something with a kick to it. Uh-huh. What would them Rubes have us do—say it with flowers? Or pass around silk socks, or scented toilet soap?

And Vincent, for all his innocent big eyes and parlor manners, has come to know the Corrugated way of doing things. Like a book. Yet when he walks in there on the carpet in front of Old Hickory and the cross-questionin' starts he answers up as straight and free as if he was being asked to name the subway stations between Wall Street and the Grand Central. You wouldn't think he'd ever gypped anybody in all his young career.

Oh, yes, he'd known about the G. L. T. board meetin'. Surely. He'd been sent up to Mr. Robert's club with the message for Oggie Kendall to come down and do his director stunt. The private letter book? Yes, he remembered putting that away in the safe. Had he taken a look at it? Why should he? Vincent seems kind of hurt that anyone should suggest such a thing. He stares at Old Hickory surprised and pained. Well, then, did he happen to have any outside friends connected with the Curb; anybody that he'd be apt to let slip little things about Corrugated affairs to?

"I should hope, sir, that if I did have such friends I would know enough to keep business secrets to myself," says Vincent, his lips quiverin' indignant.

"Yes, yes, to be sure," says Old Hickory, "but—"

Honest, he was almost on the point of apologizin' to Vincent when there comes this knock on the private office door and I'm signalled to see who it is. I finds one of the youths from the filin' room who's subbin' in on the gate for Vincent. He grins and whispers the message and I tells-him to stay there a minute.

"It's a lady to see you, Mr. Ellins," says I. "Mrs. Jerome St Claire."

"Eh?" grunts Old Hickory. "Mrs. St. Claire? Who the syncopated Sissyphus is she?"

"Vincent's mother, sir," says I.

This time he lets out a snort like a freight startin' up a grade. "Well, what does she want with—?" Here he breaks off and fixes them chilled steel eyes of his on Vincent.

No wonder. The pink flush has faded out of Vincent's fair young cheeks, his big blue eyes are rolled anxious at the door, and he seems to be tryin' to swallow something like a hard-boiled egg.

"Your mother, eh?" says Old Hickory. "Perhaps we'd better have her in."

"Oh, no, sir! Please. I—I'd rather see her first," says Vincent choky.

"Would you?" says Old Hickory. "Sorry, son, but as I understand it she has called to see me. Torchy, show the lady in."

I hated to do it, but there was no duckin'. Such a nice, modest little old girl, too. She has the same innocent blue eyes as Vincent, traces of the same pink flush in her cheeks, and her hair is frosted up genteel and artistic.

She don't make any false motions, either. After one glance around the group she picks out Old Hickory, makes straight for him, and grabs one of his big paws in both hands.

"Mr. Ellins, is it not?" says she. "Please forgive my coming in like this, but I did want to tell you how grateful I am for all that you have done for dear Vincent and me. It was so generous and kind of you?"

"Ye-e-es?" says Old Hickory, sort of draggy and encouragin'.

"You see," she goes on, "I had been so worried over that dreadful mortgage on our little home, and when Vincent came home last night with that wonderful check and told me how you had helped him invest his savings so wisely it seemed perfectly miraculous. Just think! Twelve hundred dollars! Exactly what we needed to free our home from debt. I know Vincent has told you how happy you have made us both, but I simply could not resist adding my own poor words of gratitude."

She sure was a weak describer. Poor words! If she hadn't said a whole mouthful then my ears are no good. Less'n a minute and a half by the clock she'd been in there, but she certainly had decanted the beans. She had me tinted up like a display of Soviet neckwear, Piddie gawpin' at her with his face ajar, and Vincent diggin' his toes into the rug. Lucky she had her eyes fixed on Old Hickory, whose hand-hewn face reveals just as much emotion as if he was bettin' the limit on a four-card flush.

"It is always a great pleasure, madam, to be able to do things so opportunely," says he; "and, I may add, unconsciously."

"But you cannot know," she rushes on, "how proud you have made me of my dear boy." With that she turns to Vincent and kisses him impetuous. "He does give promise of being a brilliant business man, doesn't he?" she demands.

"Yes, madam," says Old Hickory, indulgin' in one of them grim smiles of his, "I rather think he does."

"Ah-h-h!" says she. Another quick hug for Vincent, a happy smile tossed at Old Hickory, and she has tripped out.

For a minute or so all you could hear in the private office was Piddie's heart beatin' on his ribs, or maybe it was his knees knockin' together. He hasn't the temperament to sit in on deep emotional scenes, Piddie. As for Old Hickory, he clips the end off a six-inch brunette cigar, lights up careful, and then turns slow to Vincent.

"Well, young man," says he, "so you did know about that motion to pass the dividend, after all, eh!"

Vincent nods, his head still down.

"Took a look at the letter book, did you!" asks Old Hickory.

Another weak nod.

"And 'phoned a code message to someone in Broad Street, I suppose?" suggests Old Hickory.

"No, sir," says Vincent. "He—he was waiting in the Arcade. I slipped out and handed him a copy of the motion—as carried. But not until after the full board had reversed it."

"Oh!" says Old Hickory. "Gave your friend the double cross, as I believe you would state it?"

"He wasn't a friend," protests Vincent. "It was Izzy Goldheimer, who used to work in the bond room before I came. He's with a Curb firm now and has been trying for months to work me for tips on Corrugated holdings. Promised me a percentage. But he was a welcher, and I knew it. So when I did give him a tip it—it was that kind."

"Hm-m-m!" says Old Hickory, wrinklin' his bushy eyebrows. "Still, I fail to see just where you would have time to take advantage of such conditions."

"I had put up my margins on G. L. T. the day before," explains Vincent. "Taking the short end, sir. If the dividend had gone through at first I would have 'phoned in to change my trade to a buying order before Izzy could get down with the news. As it didn't, I let it stand. Of course, I knew the market would break next morning and I closed out the deal for a 15-point gain."

"Fairly clever manipulation," comments Old Hickory. "Then you cleared about—"

"Fifteen hundred," says Vincent. "I could have made more by pyramiding, but I thought it best to pull out while I was sure."

"What every plunger knows—but forgets," says Old Hickory. "And you still have a capital of three hundred for future operations, eh?"

"I'm through, sir," says Vincent. "'I—I don't like lying to mother. Besides after next Monday I don't think Izzy will bother me for any more tips. I—I suppose I'm fired, sir?"

"Eh?" says Old Hickory, scowlin' at him fierce. "Fired? No. Boys who have a dislike for lying to mother are too scarce. Besides, anyone who can beat a curb broker at his own game ought to be valuable to the Corrugated some day. Mr. Piddie, see that this young man is promoted as soon as there's an opening. And—er—I believe that is all, gentlemen."

As me and Piddie trickle out into the general offices Piddie whispers awed: "Wonderful man, Mr. Ellins! Wonderful!"

"How clever of you to find it out, Piddie," says I. "Did you get the hunch from Vincent's mother?"

CHAPTER XIII

THE MANTLE OF SANDY THE GREAT

"Vincent," says I, as I blows in through the brass gate from lunch, "who's the poddy old party you got parked on the bench out in the anteroom?"

"He's waiting to see Mr. Ellins," says Vincent. "This is his third try. Looks to me like some up-state stockholder who wants to know when Corrugated common will strike 110."

"Well, that wouldn't be my guess exactly," says I. "What's the name?"

"Dowd," says Vincent, reachin' for a card. "Matthew K"

"Eh," says I. "Mesaba Matt. Dowd? Say, son, your guesser is way out of gear. You ought to get better posted on the Order of Who-Who's."

"I'm sorry," says Vincent, pinkin' up in the ears. "Is—is he somebody in particular?"

"Only one of the biggest iron ore men in the game," says I. "That is, he was until he unloaded that Pittsburgh syndicate a few years ago. Also he must be a special crony of Old Hickory's. Anyway, he was playin' around with him down South last month. And here we let him warm a seat out in the book-agent pen! Social error, Vincent."

"Stupid of me," admits Vincent. "I will—"

"Better let me soothe him down now," says I. "Then I'll get Old Hickory on the 'phone and tell him who's here."

I will say that I did it in my best private sec. style, too, urgin' him into the private office while I explains how the boy on the gate couldn't have read the name right and assurin' him I'd get word to Mr. Ellins at once.

"He's only having a conference with his attorneys," says I. "I think he'll be up very, soon. Just a moment while I get him on the wire, Mr. Dowd."

"Thank you, young man," says Matthew K. "I—I rather would like to see Ellins today, if I could."

"Why, sure!" says I, easin' him into Old Hickory's swing chair.

But somehow when I'd slipped out to the 'phone booth and got in touch with the boss he don't seem so anxious to rush up and meet his old side kick. No. He's more or less calm about it.

"Eh?" says he. "Dowd? Oh, yes! Well, you just tell him, Torchy, that I'm tied up here and can't say when I'll be through. He'd better not wait."

"Excuse me, Mr. Ellins," says I, "but he's been here twice before. Seems to have something on his mind that—well, might be important, you know."

"Yes, it might be," says Old Hickory, and I couldn't tell whether he threw in a snort or a chuckle right there. "And since you think it is, Torchy, perhaps you'd better get him to sketch it out to you."

"All right," says I. "That is, if he'll loosen up."

"Oh, I rather think he will," says Old Hickory.

It was a good guess. For when I tells Dowd how sorry Mr. Ellins is that he can't come just then, and suggests that I've got power of attorney to take care of anything confidential he might spill into my nigh ear, he opens right up.

Course, what I'm lookin' for is some big business stuff; maybe a straight tip on how this new shift in Europe is going to affect foreign exchange, or a hunch as to what the administration means to put over in regard to the railroad muddle. He's a solemn-faced, owl-eyed old party, this Mesaba Matt. Looks like he was thinkin' wise and deep about weighty matters. You know. One of these slow-movin', heavy-lidded, double-chinned old pelicans who never mention any sum less than seven figures. So I'm putting up a serious secretarial front myself when he starts clearin' his throat.

"Young man," says he, "I suppose you know something about golf!"

"Eh?" says I. "Golf? Oh, yes. That is. I've seen it played some. I was on a trip with Mr. Ellins down at Pinehurst, five or six years back, when he broke into the game, and I read Grant Rice's dope on it more or less reg'lar."

"But you haven't played golf yourself, have you?" he goes on.

"No," says I, "I've never indulged in the Scottish rite to any extent. Just a few swipes with a club."

"Then I'm afraid," he begins, "that you will hardly—"

"Oh, I'm a great little understander," says I, "unless you mean to go into the fine points, or ask me to settle which is the best course. I've heard some of them golf addicts talk about Shawnee or Apawamis or Ekwanok like—well, like Billy Sunday would talk about heaven. But I've stretched a willing ear for Mr. Ellins often enough so I can—"

"I see," breaks in Dowd. "Possibly you will do. At any rate, I must tell this to someone."

"I know," says I. "I've seen 'em like that. Shoot."

"As you are probably aware," says he, "Ellins was in Florida with me last month. In fact, we played the same course together, day in and day out, for four weeks. He was my partner in our foursome. Rather a helpful partner at times, I must admit, although he hasn't been at the game long enough to be a really experienced golfer. Fairly long off the tee, but erratic with the brassie, and not all dependable when it came to short iron work. However, as a rule we held them. Our opponents, I mean."

I nods like I'd taken it all in.

"A quartette of bogey hounds, I expect," says I.

Dowd shakes his head modest. No, he confesses that wasn't an exact description of their ratin'. "We usually qualified, when we got in at all," says he, "in the fourth flight for the Seniors' tournament. But as a rule we did not attempt the general competitions. We stuck to our daily foursome. Staples and Rutter were the other two. Rutter's in steel, you know; Staples in copper. Seasoned golfers, both of them. Especially Rutter. Claims to have turned in a card of 89 once at Short Hills. That was years ago, of course, but he has never forgotten it. Rather an irritating opponent, Rutter. Patronizing. Fond of telling you what you did when you've dubbed a shot. And if he happens to win—" Dowd shrugs his shoulders expressive.

"Chesty, eh?" says I.

"Extremely so," says Dowd. "Even though his own medal score wasn't better than 115. Mine was a little worse, particularly when I chanced to be off my drive. Yes, might as well be honest. I was the lame duck of the foursome. They usually gave my ball about four strokes. Thought they could do it, anyway. And I accepted."

"Uh-huh," says I, grinnin' intelligent—I hope. I sure was gettin' an earful of this golf stuff, but I was still awake.

Dowd goes on to tell how reg'lar the old foursome got under way every afternoon at 2:30. That is, every day but Sunday.

"Oh, yes," says I. "Church?"

"No," says Dowd. "Sandy the Great."

"Eh?" says I, gawpin'.

"Meaning," says Dowd, "Alexander McQuade, to my mind the best all around golf professional who ever came out of Scotland. He was at our Agapoosett course in summer, you know, and down there in the winter. And Sunday afternoons he always played an exhibition match with visiting pro's, or some of the crack amateurs. I never missed joining the gallery for those matches. I was following the day he broke the course record with a 69. Just one perfect shot after another. It was an inspiration. Always was to watch Sandy the Great play. Such a genial, democratic fellow, too. Why, he has actually talked to me on the tee just before taking his stand for one of those 275-yard drives of his. 'Watch this one, me laddie buck,' he'd say, or 'Weel, mon, stand a bit back while I gie th' gutty a fair cr-r-rack.' He was always like that with me. Do you wonder that I bought all my clubs of him, had a collection of his best scores, and kept a large 'photo of him in my room? I've never been much of a hero worshiper, but when it came to Sandy the Great—well, that was different. You've heard of him, of course?"

"I expect I have," says I, "but just how does he fit into this—"

"I am coming to that," says Dowd. "It was a remarkable experience. Weird, you might say. You see, it was the last day of our stay in Florida; our last foursome of the season. We had been losing steadily for several days, Ellins and I. Not that the stakes were high. Trivial. Dollar Nassau, with side bets. I'd been off my drive again and Ellins had been putting atrociously. Anyway, we had settled regularly.

"And Rutter had been particularly obnoxious in his manner. Offered to increase my handicap to five bisque, advised me to get my wrists into the stroke and keep my body out. That sort of thing. And from a man who lunges at every shot and makes a 75-yard approach with a brassie—Well, it was nothing short of maddening. I kept my temper, though. Can't say that my friend Ellins did. He had sliced into a trap on his drive, while I had topped mine short. We started the first hole with our heads down. Rutter and Staples were a trifle ostentatious with their cheerfulness.

"I will admit that I played the first four holes very badly. A ten on the long third. Wretched golf, even for a duffer. Ellins managed to hold low ball on the short fourth, but we were seven points down. I could have bitten a piece out of my niblick. Perhaps you don't know, young man, but there is no deeper humiliation than that which comes to a dub golfer who is playing his worst. I was in the depths.

"At the fifth tee I was last up. I'd begun waggling as usual, body swaying, shoulders rigid, muscles tense, dreading to swing and wondering whether the result would be a schlaff or a top, when—well, I simply cannot describe the sensation. Something came over me; I don't know what. As if someone had waved a magic wand above my head. I stopped swaying, relaxed, felt the weight of the club head in my fingers, knew the rhythm of the swing, heard the sharp crack as the ivory facing met the ball. If you'll believe it, I put out such a drive as I'd never before made in all my 12 years of golf. Straight and clean and true past the direction flag and on and on.

"The others didn't seem to notice. Rutter had hooked into the scrub palmettos, Staples had sliced into a pit, Ellins had topped short somewhere in the rough. I waited until they were all out on the fairway. Some had played three, some four shots. 'How many do you lie?' asked Rutter. I told him that was my drive. He just stared skeptical. I could scarcely blame him. As a rule I need a fair drive and two screaming brassies on this long fifth before I am in position to approach across the ravine. But this time, with a carry of some 160 yards ahead of me, I picked my mid-iron from the bag, took a three-quarter swing, bit a small divot from the turf as I went through, and landed the ball fairly on the green with a back-spin that held it as though I'd had a string tied to it. And when the others had climbed out of the ravine or otherwise reached the green I putted in my four. A par four, mind you, on a 420-yard hole that I'd never had better than a lucky 5 on, and usually a 7 or an 8!

"Rutter asked me to count my strokes for him and then had the insolence to ask how I got that way. I couldn't tell him. I did feel queer. As if I was in some sort of trance. But my next drive was even better. A screamer with a slight hook on the end that gave the ball an added roll. For my second I played a jigger to the green. Another par four. Rutter hadn't a word to say.

"Well, that's the way it went. Never had any one in our foursome played such golf as I did for nine consecutive holes. Nothing over 5 and one birdie 3. I think that Staples and Rutter were too stunned to make any comment. As for Ellins, he failed to appreciate what I was doing. Somewhat self-centered, Ellins. He's always counting his own score and seldom notices what others are making.

"Not until we had finished the 12th, which I won with an easy 3, did Staples, who was keeping score, seem to realize what had happened. 'Hello!' he calls to Rutter. 'They've got us beaten.' 'No,' says Rutter. 'Can't be possible!' 'But we are,'insists Staples. 'Thirteen points down and twelve to go. It's all over. Dowd, here, is playing like a crazy man.'"

"And then the spell, or whatever it was, broke. I flubbed my drive, smothered my brassie shot, and heeled my third into the woods. I finished the round in my usual style, mostly sevens and eights. But there was the score to prove that for nine straight holes I had played par golf; professional golf, if you please. Do you think either Rutter or Staples gave me credit for that? No. They paid up and walked off to the shower baths.

"I couldn't account for my performance. It was little short of a miracle. Actually it was so unusual that I hardly felt like talking about it. I know that may sound improbable to a golfer, but it is a fact. Except that I did want to tell Alexander McQuade. But I couldn't find him. They said at the shop he was laid up with a cold and hadn't been around for several days. So I took the train north that night without having said a word to a soul about those wonderful nine holes. But I've thought a lot about 'em since. I've tried to figure out just what happened to me that I could make such a record. No use. It was all beginning to be as unreal as if it was something I had dreamed of doing.

"And then yesterday, while reading a recent golf magazine, I ran across this item of news which gave me such a shock. It told of the sudden death from pneumonia of Alexander McQuade. At first I was simply grieved over this loss to myself and to the golfing profession in general. Then I noticed the date. McQuade died the very morning of the day of our last match. Do you see?"

I shook my head. All I could see was a moonfaced, owl-eyed old party who was starin' at me with an eager, batty look. "No," says I. "I don't get the connection. McQuade had checked out and you won your foursome."

"Precisely," says Dowd. "The mantle of Elijah."

"Who?" says I.

"To make it plainer," says Dowd, "the mantle of Sandy the Great. It fell on my shoulders."

"That may be clear enough to you, Mr. Dowd," says I, "but I'll have to pass it up."

He sighs disappointed. "I wish Ellins would have the patience to let me tell him about it myself," says he. "He'll not, though, so I must make you understand in order that you may give him the facts. I want him to know. Of course, I can't pretend to explain the thing. It was psychic, that's all; supernatural, if you please. Must have been. For there I was, a confirmed duffer, playing that course exactly as Alexander McQuade would have played it had he been in my shoes. And he was, for the time being. At least, I claim that I was being controlled, or whatever you want to call it, by the recently departed spirit of Sandy the Great."

I expect I was gawpin' at him with a full open-face expression. Say, I thought I'd heard these golf nuts ravin' before, but I'd never been up against anything quite like this. Honest, it gave me a creepy feelin' along the spine. And yet, come to look him over close, he's just a wide-beamed old party with bags under his eyes and heavy common-place features.

"You grasp the idea now, don't you?" he asks.

"I think so," says I. "Ghost stuff, eh?"

"I'm merely suggesting that as the only explanation which occurs to me," says he. "I would like to have it put before Ellins and get his opinion. That is, if you think you can make it clear."

"I'll make a stab at it, Mr. Dowd," says I.

And of course I did, though Old Hickory aint such an easy listener. He comes in with snorts and grunts all through the tale, and when I finishes he simply shrugs his shoulders.

"There's a warning for you, young man," says he. "Keep away from the fool game. Anyway, if you ever do play, don't let it get to be a disease with you. Look at Dowd. Five years ago he was a sane, normal person; the best iron ore expert in the country. He could sniff a handful of red earth and tell you how much it would run to a ton within a dime's worth. Knew the game from A to Izzard—deep mining, open pit, low grade washing, transportation, smelting. He lived with it. Never happier than when he was in his mining rig following a chief engineer through new cross-cuts on the twenty-sixth level trying to locate a fault in the deposit or testing some modern method of hoisting. Those were things he understood. Then he retired. Said he'd made money enough. And now look at him. Getting cracked over a sport that must have been invented by some Scotchman who had a grudge against the whole human race. As though any game could be a substitute for business. Bah!"

"Then you don't think, Mr. Ellins," says I, "that we ought to have the boy page Sir Oliver Lodge?"

"Eh?" says he.

"I mean," says I, "that you don't take any stock in that mantle of Sandy the Great yarn?"

"Tommyrot!" says he. "For once in his life the old fool played his head off, that's all. Nine holes in par. Huh! I'm liable to do that myself one of these days, and without the aid of any departed spirits. Yes, sir. The fact is, Torchy, I am practicing a new swing that ought to have me playing in the low 90's before the middle of the next season. You see, it all depends on taking an open stance and keeping a stiff right knee. Here' pass me that umbrella and I'll show you."

And for the next ten minutes he kept a bank president, two directors and a general manager waiting while he swats a ball of paper around the private office with me for an audience. Uh-huh. And being a high ace private sec. I aint even supposed to grin. Say, why don't some genius get up an anti-golf serum so that when one of these old plutes found himself slippin' he could rush to a clinic and get a shot in the arm?

CHAPTER XIV

TORCHY SHUNTS A WIZARD

I'd hardly noticed when Mr. Robert blew in late from lunch until I hears him chuckle. Then I glances over my shoulder and sees that he's lookin' my way. Course, that gets me curious, for Mr. Robert ain't the kind of boss that goes around chucklin' casual, 'specially at a busy private sec.

"Yes, sir?" says I, shoving back a tray full of correspondence I'm sortin'.

"I heard something rather good, at luncheon, Torchy," says he.

"On red hair, I expect," says I.

"It wasn't quite so personal as that," says he. "Still, I think you'll be interested."

"It's part of my job to look so, anyway," says I, givin' him the grin.

"And another item on which you specialize, I believe," he goes on, "is the detection of book agents. At least, you used to do so when you were head office boy. Held a record, didn't you?"

"Oh, I don't know," says I tryin' to register modesty. "One got past the gate; one in five years. That was durin' my first month."

"Almost an unblemished career," says Mr. Robert. "What about your successor, Vincent?"

"Oh, he's doing fairly well," says I. "Gets stung now and then. Like last week when that flossy blonde with the Southern accent had him buffaloed with a tale about having met dear Mr. Ellins at French Lick and wantin' to show him something she knew he'd be just crazy about. She did, too. 'Lordly Homes of England,' four volumes, full morocco, at fifty a volume. And I must say she was nearly right. He wasn't far from being crazy for the next hour or so. Vincent got it, and then I got it, although I was downtown at the time it happened. But I'm coachin' Vincent, and I don't think another one of 'em will get by very soon."

"You don't eh?" says Mr. Robert, indulgin' in another chuckle.

Then he spills what he overheard at lunch. Seems he was out with a friend who took him to the Papyrus Club, which is where a lot of these young hicks from the different book publishin' houses get together noon-times; not Mr. Harper, or Mr. Scribner, or Mr. Dutton, but the heads of departments, assistant editors, floor salesmen and so on.

And at the next table to Mr. Robert the guest of honor was a loud talkin' young gent who'd just come in from a tour of the Middle West with a bunch of orders big enough, if you let him tell it, to keep his firm's presses on night shifts for a year. He was some hero, I take it, and for the benefit of the rest of the bunch he was sketchin' out his methods.

"As I understood the young man," says Mr. Robert, "his plan was to go after the big ones; the difficult proposition, men of wealth and prominence whom other agents had either failed to reach or had not dared to approach. 'The bigger the better,' was his motto, and he referred to himself, I think, as 'the wizard of the dotted line.'"

"Not what you'd exactly call a shrinkin' violet, eh?" I suggests.

"Rather a shrieking sunflower," says Mr. Robert. "And he concluded by announcing that nothing would suit him better than to be told the name of the most difficult subject in the metropolitan district—'the hardest nut' was his phrase, I believe. He guaranteed to land the said person within a week. In fact, he was willing to bet $100 that he could."

"Huh," says I.

"Precisely the remark of one of his hearers," says Mr. Robert. "The wager was promptly made. And who do you suppose, Torchy, was named as the most aloof and difficult man in New York for a book agent to—"

"Mr. Ellins," says I.

Mr. Robert nods. "My respected governor, none other," says he. "I fancy he would be rather amused to know that he had achieved such a reputation, although he would undoubtedly give you most of the credit."

"Or the blame," says I.

"Yes," admits Mr. Robert, "if he happened to be in the blaming mood. Anyway, young man, there you have a direct challenge. Within the next week the inner sanctum of the Corrugated Trust is to be assailed by one who claims that he can penetrate the impenetrable, know the unknowable, and unscrew the inscrutable."

"Well, that's cute of him," says I. "I'm bettin', though, he never gets to his man."

"That's the spirit!" says Mr. Robert. "As the French said at Verdun, 'Ils ne passeront pas.' Eh?"

"Meaning 'No Gangway', I expect!" says I.

"That's the idea," says he.

"But say, Mr. Robert, what's he look like, this king of the dotted line!" says I.

Mr. Robert shakes his head. "I was sitting back to him," says he. "Besides, to give you his description would be taking rather an unfair advantage. That would tend to spoil what now stands as quite a neat sporting proposition. Of course, if you insist—"

"No," says I. "He don't know me and I don't know him. It's fifty-fifty. Let him come."

I never have asked any odds of book agents, so why begin now? But, you can bet I didn't lose any time havin' a heart to heart talk with Vincent.

"Listen, son," says I, "from this on you want to watch this gate like you was a terrier standin' over a rat hole. It's up to you to see that no stranger gets through, no matter who he says he is; and that goes for anybody, from first cousins of the boss to the Angel Gabriel himself. Also, it includes stray window cleaners, buildin' inspectors and parties who come to test the burglar alarm system. They might be in disguise. If their faces ain't as familiar to you as the back of your hand give 'em the sudden snub and tell 'em 'Boom boom, outside!' In case of doubt keep 'em there until you can send for me. Do you get it?"

Vincent says he does. "I shouldn't care to let in another book agent," says he.

"You might just as well resign your portfolio if you do," says I. "Remember the callin' down, you got from Old Hickory last week."

Vincent shudders. "I'll do my best, sir," says he.

And he's a thorough goin', conscientious youth. Within the next few hours I had to rescue one of our directors, our first assistant Western manager, and a personal friend of Mr. Robert's, all of whom Vincent had parked on the bench in the anteroom and was eyein' cold, and suspicious. He even holds up the Greek who came luggin' in the fresh towels, and Tony the spring water boy.

"I feel like old Horatius," says Vincent.

"Never met him," says I, "but whoever he was I'll bet you got him lookin' like one of the seven sleepers. That's the stuff, though. Keep it up."

I expect I was some wakeful myself, too. I worked with my eyes ready to roll over my shoulder and my right ear stretched. I was playin' the part of right worthy inside guard, and nobody came within ten feet of the private office door but what I'd sized 'em up before they could reach the knob. Still, two whole days passed without any attack on the first line trenches. The third day Vincent and I had a little skirmish with a mild-eyed young gent who claimed he wanted to see Mr. Ellins urgent, but he turns out to be only a law clerk from the office of our general solicitors bringin' up some private papers to be signed.

Then here Friday—and it was Friday the 13th, too—Vincent comes sleuthin' in to my desk and shows me a card.

"Well," says I, "who does this H. Munson Schott party say he is?"

"That's just it," says Vincent. "He doesn't say. But he has a letter of introduction to Mr. Ellins from the Belgian Consul General. Rather an important looking person, too."

"H-m-m-m!" says I, runnin' my fingers through my red hair thoughtful.

You see, we'd been figurin' on some big reconstruction contracts with the Belgian government, and while I hadn't heard how far the deal had gone, there was a chance that this might be an agent from the royal commission.

"If it is," says I, "we can't afford to treat him rough. Let's see, the Hon. Matt. Dowd, the golf addict, is still in the private office givin' Old Hickory another earful about the Scotch plague, ain't he?"

"No, sir," says Vincent. "Mr. Ellins asked him to wait half an hour or so. He's in the director's room."

"Maybe I'd better take a look at your Mr. Schott first then," says I.

But after I'd gone out and given him the north and south careful I was right where I started. I didn't quite agree with Vincent that he looked important, but he acted it. He's pacin' up and down outside the brass rail kind of impatient, and as I appears he's just consultin' his watch. A nifty tailored young gent with slick putty-colored hair and Maeterlinck blue eyes. Nothing suspicious in the way of packages about him. Not even a pigskin document case or an overcoat with bulgy pockets. He's grippin' a French line steamship pamphlet in one hand, a letter in the other, and from the crook of his right elbow hangs a heavy silver-mounted walkin' stick. Also he's wearin' gray spats. Nothing book agency about any of them signs.

"Mr. Schott?" says I, springin' my official smile. "To see Mr. Ellins, I understand. I'm his private secretary. Could I—"

"I wish to see Mr. Ellins personally," breaks in Mr. Schott, wavin' me off with a yellow-gloved hand.

"Of course," says I. "One moment, please. I'll find out if he's in. And if you have any letters, or anything like that—"

"I prefer to present my credentials in person," says he.

"Sorry," says I. "Rules of the office. Saves time, you know. If you don't mind—" and I holds out my hand for the letter.

He gives it up reluctant and I backs out. Another minute and I've shoved in where Old Hickory is chewin' a cigar butt savage while he pencils a joker clause into a million-dollar contract.

"Excuse me, sir," says I, "but you were expectin' a party

from the Belgian Commission, were you?"

"No," snaps Old Hickory. "Nor from the Persian Shah, or the Sultan of Sulu, or the Ahkoond of Swat. All I'm expecting, young man, is a half hour of comparative peace, and I don't get it. There's Matt. Dowd in the next room waiting like the Ancient Mariner to grip me by the sleeve and pour out a long tale about what he calls his discovery of psychic golf. Say, son, couldn't you—"

"I've heard it, you know, sir," says I.

Old Hickory groans. "That's so," says he. "Well then, why don't you find me a substitute? Suffering Cicero, has that inventive brain of yours gone into a coma!"

"Not quite, sir," says I. "You don't happen to know a Mr. Schott, do you?"

"Gr-r-r!" says Old Hickory, as gentle as a grizzly with a sore ear. "Get out!"

I took the hint and trickled through the door. I was just framin' up something polite to feed Mr. Schott when it strikes me I might take a peek at this little note from the Belgian consul. It wasn't much, merely suggests that he hopes Mr. Ellins will be interested in what Mr. Schott has to say. There's the consul general's signature at the bottom, too. Yes. And I was foldin' it up to tuck it back into the envelope when—well, that's what comes of my early trainin' on the Sunday edition when the proof readers used to work me in now and then to hold copy. It's a funny thing, but I notice that the Consul General doesn't spell his name when he writes it the way he has it printed at the top of his letterhead.

"Might be a slip by the fool engraver," thinks I. "I'll look it up in the directory."

And the directory agreed with the letterhead.

"Oh, ho!" says I. "Pullin' the old stuff, eh? Easy enough to drop into the Consul's office and dash off a note to anybody. Say, lemme at this Schott person."

No, I didn't call in Pat, the porter, and have him give Mr. Schott a flyin' start down the stairs. No finesse about that. Besides, I needed a party about his size just then. I steps back into the directors' room and rouses Mr. Dowd from his trance by tappin' him on the shoulder.

"Maybe you'd be willin', Mr. Dowd," says I, "to sketch out some of that psychic golf experience of yours to a young gent who claims to be something of a wizard himself."

Would he? Say, I had to push him back in the chair to keep him from followin' me right out.

"Just a minute," says I, "and I'll bring him in. There's only one thing. He's quite a talker himself. Might want to unload a line of his own first, but after that—"

"Yes, yes," says Dowd. "I shall be delighted to meet him."

"It's goin' to be mutual," says I.

Why, I kind of enjoyed my little part, which consists in hurryin' out to the gate with my right forefinger up and a confidential smirk wreathin' my more or less classic features.

"Right this way, Mr. Schott," says I.

He shrugs his shoulders, shoots over a glance of scornful contempt, like a room clerk in a tourist hotel would give to a guest who's payin' only $20 or $30 a day, and shoves past Vincent with his chin up. Judgin' by the name and complexion and all there must have been a lot of noble Prussian blood in this Schott person, for the Clown Prince himself couldn't have done the triumphal entry any better. And I expect I put considerable flourish into the business when I announces him to Dowd, omittin' careful to call the Hon. Matt, by name.

Schott aint wastin' any precious minutes. Before Dowd can say a word he's started in on his spiel. As I'm makin' a slow exit I manages to get the openin' lines. They was good, too.

"As you may know," begins Schott, "I represent the International Historical Committee. Owing to the recent death of prominent members we have decided to fill those vacancies by appointment and your name has been mentioned as—"

Well, you know how it goes. Only this was smooth stuff. It was a shame to have it all spilled for the benefit of Matthew Dowd, who can only think of one thing these days—250-yard tee shots and marvelous mid-iron pokes that always sail toward the pin. Besides, I kind of wanted to see how a super-book agent would work.

Openin' the private office door easy I finds Old Hickory has settled back in his swing chair and is lightin' a fresh Fumadora satisfied. So I slips in, salutes respectful and jerks my thumb toward the directors' room.

"I've put a sub. on the job, sir," says I.

"Eh?" says he. "Oh, yes. Who did you find?"

"A suspicious young stranger," says I. "I sicced him and Mr. Dowd on each other. They're at it now. It's likely to be entertainin'."

Old Hickory nods approvin' and a humorous flicker flashes under them bushy eyebrows of his. "Let's hear how they're getting along," says he.

So I steps over sleuthy and swings the connectin' door half way open, which not only gives us a good view but brings within hearin' range this throaty conversation which Mr. Schott is unreelin' at high speed.

"You see, sir," he's sayin', "this monumental work covers all the great crises of history, from the tragedy on Calvary to the signing of the peace treaty at Versailles. Each epoch is handled by an acknowledged master of that period, as you may see by this table of contents."

Here Mr. Schott produces from somewhere inside his coat a half pound or so of printed pages and shoves them on Dowd.

"The illustrations," he goes on, "are all reproduced in colors by our new process, and are copies of famous paintings by the world's greatest artists. There are to be more than three hundred, but I have here a few prints of these priceless works of art which will give you an idea."

At that he reaches into the port side of his coat, unbuttons the lining, and hauls out another sheaf of leaves.

"Then we are able to offer you," says Schott, "a choice of bindings which includes samples of work from the most skilful artisans in that line. At tremendous expense we have reproduced twelve celebrated bindings. I have them here."

And blamed if he don't unscrew the thick walkin' stick and pull out a dozen imitation leather bindings which he piles on Mr. Dowd's knee.

"Here we have," says he, "the famous Broissard binding, made for the library of Louis XIV. Note the fleur de lis and the bee, and the exquisite hand-tooling on the doublures. Here is one that was done by the Rivieres of London for the collection of the late Czar Nicholas, and so on. There are to be thirty-six volumes in all and to new members of the Historical Committee we are offering these at practically the cost of production, which is $28 the volume. In return for this sacrifice all we ask of you, my dear sir, is that we may use your indorsement in our advertising matter, which will soon appear in all the leading daily papers of this country. We ask you to pay no money down. All you need to do, sir, to become a member of the International Historical Committee and receive this magnificent addition to your library, is to sign your name here and—"

"Is—is that all?" breaks in Dowd, openin' his mouth for the first time.

"Absolutely," says Schott, unlimberin' his ready fountain pen.

"Then perhaps you would be interested to hear of a little experience of mine," says Dowd, "on the golf course."

"Charmed," says Schott.

He didn't know what was comin'. As a book agent he had quite a flow of language, but I doubt if he ever ran up against a real golf nut before. Inside of half a minute Dowd was off in high gear, tellin' him about that wonderful game he played with Old Hickory when he was under the control of the spirit of the great Sandy McQuade. At first Schott looks kind of dazed, like a kid who's been foolin' with a fire hydrant wrench and suddenly finds he's turned on the high pressure and can't turn it off. Three or four times he makes a stab at breakin' in and urgin' the fountain pen on Dowd, but he don't have any success. Dowd is in full swing, describin' his new theory of how all the great golfers who have passed on come back and reincarnate themselves once more; sometimes pickin' out a promisin' caddie, as in the case of Ouimet, or now and again a hopeless duffer, same as he was himself. Schott can't get a word in edgewise, and is squirmin' in his chair while Old Hickory leans back and chuckles.

Finally, after about half an hour of this, Schott gets desperate. "Yes, sir," says he, shoutin' above Dowd's monologue, "but what about this magnificent set of—"

"Bah!" says Dowd. "Books! Never buy 'em."

"But—but are you sure, sir," Schott goes on, "that you understand what an opportunity you are offered for—"

"Wouldn't have the junk about the house," says Dowd. "But later on, young man, if you are interested in the development of my psychic golf, I shall be glad to tell you—"

"Not if I see you first," growls Schott, gatherin' up his pile of samples and backin out hasty.

He's in such a hurry to get away that he bumps into Mr. Robert, who's just strollin' toward the private office, and the famous bindings, art masterpieces, contents pages and so on are scattered all over the floor.

"Who was our young friend with all the literature?" asks

Mr. Robert.

"That's Mr. Schott," says I, "your wizard of the dotted line, who was due to break in on Mr. Ellins and get him to sign up."

"Eh?" says Old Hickory, starin'. "And you played him off against Matt. Dowd? You impertinent young rascal! But I say, Robert, you should have seen and heard 'em. It was rich. They nearly talked each other to a standstill."

"Then I gather, Torchy," says Mr. Robert, grinnin', "that the king of book agents now sits on a tottering throne. In other words, the wizard met a master mind, eh?"

"I dunno," says I. "Guess I gave him the shunt, all right. Just by luck, though. He had a clever act, I'll say, even if he didn't get it across."

CHAPTER XV

STANLEY TAKES THE JAZZ CURE

I remember how thrilled Vee gets when she first discovers that these new people in Honeysuckle Lodge are old friends of hers. I expect some poetical real estater wished that name on it. Anyway, it's the proper thing out here in Harbor Hills to call your place after some sort of shrubbery or tree. And maybe this little stone cottage effect with the green tiled roof and the fieldstone gate posts did have some honeysuckle growin' around somewhere. It's a nice enough shack, what there is of it, though if I'd been layin' out the floor plan I'd have had less cut-under front porch and more elbow room inside. However, as there are only two of the Rawsons it looked like it would do. That is, it did at first.

"Just think, Torchy," says Vee. "I haven't seen Marge since we were at boarding school together. Why, I didn't even know she was married, although I suppose she must be by this time."

"Well, she seems to have found a male of the species without your help," says I. "Looks like a perfectly good man, too."

"Oh, I'm sure he must be," says Vee, "or Marge wouldn't

Sewell Ford

have had him. In fact, I know he is, for I used to hear more or less about Stanley Rawson, even when we were juniors. I believe they were half engaged then. Such a jolly, lively fellow, and so full of fun. Won't it be nice having them so near?"

"Uh-huh!" says I.

Not that we've been lonesome since we moved out on our four-acre Long Island estate, but I will say that young married couples of about our own age haven't been so plenty. Not the real folksy kind. Course, there are the Cecil Rands, but they don't do much but run a day and night nursery for those twins of theirs. They're reg'lar Class A twins, too, and I expect some day they'll be more or less interestin'; but after they've been officially exhibited to you four or five times, and you've heard all about the system they're being brought up on, and how many ounces of Pasteurized cow extract they sop up a day, and at what temperature they get it, and how often they take their naps and so on—Well, sometimes I'm thankful the Rands didn't have triplets. When I've worked up enthusiasm for twins about four times, and remarked how cunnin' of them to look so much alike, and confessed that I couldn't tell which was Cecillia and which Cecil, Jr., I feel that I've sort of exhausted the subject.

So whenever Vee suggests that we really ought to go over and see the Rands again I can generally think up an alibi. Honest, I aint jealous of their twins. I'm glad they've got 'em. Considerin' Cecil, Sr., and all I'll say it was real noble of 'em. But until I can think up something new to shoot about twins I'm strong for keepin' away.

Then there are Mr. and Mrs. Jerry Kipp, but they're ouija board addicts and count it a dull evening when they can't gather a few serious thinkers around the dinin' room table under a dim light and spell out a message from Little Bright Wings, who checked out from croup at the age of six and still wants her Uncle Jerry to know that she thinks of him out there in the great beyond. I wouldn't mind hearin' from the spirit land now and then if the folks there had anything worth sayin', but when they confine their chat to fam'ly gossip it seems to me like a waste of time. Besides, I always come home from the Kipps feelin' creepy down the back.

So you could hardly blame Vee for welcomin' some new arrivals in the neighborhood, or for bein' so chummy right from the start. She asks the Rawsons over for dinner, tips Mrs. Rawson off where she can get a wash-lady who'll come in by the day and otherwise extends the glad hand.

Seems to be a nice enough party, young Mrs. Rawson. Kind of easy to look at and with an eye twinkle that suggests a disposition to cut up occasionally. Stanley is a good runnin' mate, so far as looks go. He could almost pose for a collar ad, with that straight nose and clean cut chin of his. But he's a bit stiff and stand-offish, at first.

"Oh, he'll get over that," says Vee. "You see, he comes from some little place down in Georgia where the social set is limited to three families and he isn't quite sure whether we know who our grandfathers were."

"It'll be all off then if he asks about mine," says I.

But he don't. He wants to know what I think of the recent slump in July cotton deliveries and if I believe the foreign credits situation looks any better.

"Why, I hadn't thought much about either," says I, "but I've had a good hunch handed me that the Yanks are goin' to show strong for the pennant this season."

Stanley just stares at me and after that confines his remarks to statin' that he don't care for mint sauce on roast lamb and that he never takes coffee at night.

"Huh!" says I to Vee afterward. "When does he spring that jolly stuff? Or was that conundrum about July cotton a vaudeville gag that got past me?"

No, I hadn't missed any cues. Vee explains that young Mr. Rawson has been sent up to New York as assistant manager of a Savannah firm of cotton brokers and is taking his job serious.

"That's good," says I, "but he don't need to lug it to the dinner table, does he?"

We gave the Rawsons a week to get settled before droppin' in on 'em for an evenin' call, and I'd prepared for it by readin' up on the cotton market. Lucky I did, too, for we discovers Stanley at his desk with a green eye-shade draped over his classic brow and a lot of crop reports spread out before him. Durin' the next hour, while the girls were chattin' merry in the other corner of the livin' room, Stanley gave me the straight dope on boll weevils, the labor conditions in Manchester, and the poor prospects for long staple. I finished, as you might say, with both ears full of cotton.

"Stanley's going to be a great help—I don't think," says I to Vee. "Why, he's got cotton on the brain."

"Now let's not be critical, Torchy," says Vee. "Marge told me all about it, how Stanley is a good deal worried over his business and so on. He's really doing very well, you know, but he can't seem to leave his office troubles behind, the way you do. He wants to make a big success, but he's so afraid something will go wrong—"

"There's no surer way of pullin' down trouble," says I. "Next thing he knows he'll be tryin' to sell cotton in his sleep, and from that stage to a nerve sanitarium is only a hop."

Not that I tries to reform Stanley. Nay, nay, Natalia. I may go through some foolish motions now and then, but regulatin' the neighbors ain't one of my secret vices. We allows the Rawsons to map out their own program, which seems to consist in stickin' close to their own fireside, with Marge on one side readin' letters about the gay doin's of her old friends at home, and Stanley on the other workin' up furrows in his brow over what might not happen to spot cotton day after tomorrow. They'd passed up a chance to join the Country Club, had declined with thanks when Vee asked 'em to go in on a series of dinner dances with some of the young married set, and had even shied at taking an evening off for one of Mrs. Robert Ellins' musical affairs.

"Thanks awfully," says Stanley, "but I have no time for social frivolities."

"Gosh!" says I. "I hope you don't call two hours of Greig frivolous."

That seems to be his idea, though. Anything that ain't connected with quotations on carload lots or domestic demands for middlings he looks at scornful. He tells me he's on the trail of a big foreign contract, but is afraid its going to get away from him.

"Maybe you'd linger on for a year or so if it did," I suggests.

"Perhaps," says he, "but I intend to let nothing distract me from my work."

And then here a few days later I runs across him making for the 5:03 with two giggly young sub-debs in tow. After he's planted 'em in a seat and stowed their hand luggage and wraps on the rack I slips into the vacant space with him behind the pair.

"Where'd you collect the sweet young things, Stanley?" says I.

He shakes his head and groans. "Think of it!" says he. "Marge's folks had to chase off to Bermuda for the Easter holidays and so they wish Polly, the kid sister, onto us for two whole weeks. Not only that, but Polly has the nerve to bring along this Dot person, her roommate at boarding school. What on earth we're ever going to do with them I'm sure I don't know."

"Is Polly the one with the pointed chin and the I-dare-you pout?" I asks.

"No, that's Dot," says he. "Polly's the one with the cheek dimples and the disturbing eyes. She's a case, too."

"They both look like they might be live wires," says I. "I see they've brought their mandolins, also. And what's so precious in the bundle you have on your knees?"

"Jazz records," says Stanley. "I've a mind to shove them under the seat and forget they're there."

He don't though, for that's the only bundle Polly asks about when we unload at our home station. I left Stanley negotiatin' with the expressman to deliver two wardrobe trunks and went along chucklin' to myself.

"My guess is that Dot and Polly are in for kind of a pokey vacation," I tells Vee. "Unless they can get as excited over the cotton market as Stanley does."

"The poor youngsters!" says Vee. "They might as well be visiting on a desert island, for Marge knows hardly anyone in the place but us."

She's a great one for spillin' sympathy, and for followin' it up when she can with the helpin' hand. So a couple of nights later I'm dragged out on a little missionary expedition over to Honeysuckle Lodge, the object being to bring a little cheer into the dull gray lives of the Rawsons' young visitors. Vee makes me doll up in an open face vest and dinner coat, too.

"The girls will like it, I'm sure," says she.

"Very well," says I. "If the sight of me in a back number Tuck will lift the gloom from any young hearts, here goes. I hope the excitement don't prove too much for 'em, though."

I'd kind of doped it out that we'd find the girls sittin' around awed and hushed; while Stanley indulged in his usual silent struggle with some great business problem; or maybe they'd be over in a far corner yawnin' through a game of Lotto. But you never can tell. From two blocks away we could see that the house was all lit up, from cellar to sleepin' porch.

"Huh!" says I. "Stanley must be huntin' a burglar, or something."

"No," says Vee. "Hear the music. If I didn't know I should think they were giving a party."

"Who would they give it to?" I asks.

And yet when the maid lets us in hanged if the place ain't full of people, mostly young hicks in evenin' clothes, but with a fair sprinklin' of girls in flossy party dresses. All the livin' room furniture had been shoved into the dinin' room, the rugs rolled into the corners, and the music machine is grindin' out the Blitzen Blues, accompanied by the two mandolins.

In the midst of all this merry scene I finds Stanley wanderin' about sort of dazed and unhappy.

"Excuse us for crashin' in on a party," says I. "We came over with the idea that maybe Polly and Dot would be kind of lonesome."

"Lonesome!" says Stanley. "Say, I ask you, do they look it?"

"Not at the present writing," says I.

That was statin' the case mild, too. Over by the music machine Dot and a youth who's sportin' his first aviation mustache—one of them clipped eyebrow affairs—are tinklin' away on the mandolins with their heads close together, while in the middle of the floor Polly and a blond young gent who seems to be fairly well contented with himslf are practicin' some new foxtrot steps, with two other youngsters waitin' to cut in.

"Where did you round up all the perfectly good men?" I asks.

"I didn't," says Stanley. "That's what amazes me. Where did they all come from? Why, I supposed the girls didn't know a soul in the place. Said they didn't on the way out. Yet before we'd left the station two youths appeared who claimed they'd met Polly somewhere and asked if they couldn't come up that evening. The next morning they brought around two others, and some girls, for a motor trip. By afternoon the crowd had increased to a dozen, and they were all calling each other by their first names and speaking of the aggregation as 'the bunch.' I came home tonight to find a dinner party of six and this dance scheduled. Now tell me, how do they do it?"

"It's by me," says I. "But maybe this kid sister-in-law of yours and her chum are the kind who don't have to send out S. O. S. signals. And if this keeps up I judge you're let in for a merry two weeks."

"Merry!" says Stanley. "I should hardly call it that. How am I going to think in a bedlam like this?"

"Must you think?" says I.

"Of course," says he. "But if this keeps up we shall go crazy."

"Oh, I don't know," says I. "You may, but I judge that Mrs. Rawson will survive. She seems to be endurin' it all right," and I glances over where Marge is allowin' a youngster of 19 or so to lead her out for the next dance.

"Oh, Marge!" says Stanley. "She's always game for anything. But she hasn't the business worries and responsibilities that I have. Do you know, Torchy, the cotton situation is about to reach a crisis and if I cannot put through a—"

"Come on, Torchy," breaks in Vee. "Let's try this one."

"Sure!" says I. "Although I'm missin' some mighty thrillin' information about what's going to happen to cotton."

"Oh, bother cotton!" says Vee. "It would do Stanley good to forget about his silly old business for a little while. Look at him! Why, you would thing he was a funeral."

"Or that he was just reportin' as chairman of the grand jury," says I.

"And little Polly is having such a good time, isn't she?" goes on Vee.

"I expect she is," says I. "She's goin' through the motions, anyway."

Couldn't have been more than 16 or so, Polly. But she has a face like a flower, the disposition of a butterfly, and a pair of eyes that shouldn't be used away from home without dimmers on. I expect she don't know how high voltage they are or she wouldn't roll 'em around so reckless. It's entertainin' just to sit on the side lines and watch her pull this baby-vamp act of hers and then see the victims squirm. Say, at the end of a dance some of them youths didn't know whether they was leadin' Polly to a corner or walkin' over a pink cloud with snowshoes on. And friend Dot ain't such a poor performer herself. Her strong line seems to be to listen to 'em patient while they tells her all they know, and remark enthusiastic at intervals: "Oh, I think that's simp-ly won-n-n-nderful!" After they'd hear her say it about five times most of 'em seemed to agree with her that they were wonderful, and I heard one young hick confide to another: "She's a good pal, Dot. Understands a fellow, y'know."

Honest, I was havin' so much fun minglin' with the younger set that way, and gettin' my dancin' toes limbered up once more, that it's quite a shock to glance at the livin' room clock and find it pointin' to 1:30. As we were leavin', though, friend Dot has just persuaded Stanley to try a one-step with her and I had to snicker when he goes whirlin' off. I expect either she or Polly had figured out that the only way to keep him from turnin' off the lights was to get him into the game.

From all the reports we had Polly and Dot got through their vacation without being very lonesome. Somehow or other Honeysuckle Lodge seems to have been established as the permanent headquarters of "the bunch," and most any time of day or night you could hear jazz tunes comin' from there, or see two or three cars parked outside. And, although the cotton market was doing flip-flops about that time I don't see any signs of nervous breakdown about Stanley. In fact, he seems to have bucked up a lot.

"Well, how about that foreign contract?" I asks reckless one mornin' as we meets on the train.

"Oh, I have that all sewed up," says Stanley. "One of those young chaps who came to see Polly so much gave me a straight tip on who to see—someone who had visited at his home. Odd way to get it, eh? But I got a lot out of those boys. Rather miss them, you know."

"Eh?" says I, gawpin' at him.

"Been brushing up on my dancing, too," goes on Stanley. "And say, if there's still a vacancy in that dinner dance club I think Marge and I would like to go in."

"But I thought you said you didn't dance any more?" says I.

"I didn't think I could," says Stanley, "until Dot got me at it again the other night. Why, do you know, she quite encouraged me. She said—"

"Uh-huh!" says I. "I know. She said, 'Oh, I think you're a wonderful dancer, simp-ly won-n-n-derful!' Didn't she now?"

First off Stanley stiffens up like he was goin' to be peeved. But then he remembers and lets out chuckle. "Yes," says he, "I believe those were her exact words. Perhaps she was right, too. And if I have such an unsuspected talent as that shouldn't I exercise it occasionally? I leave it to you."

"You've said it, Stanley," says I. "And after all, I guess you're goin' to be a help. You had a narrow call, though."

"From what?" asks Stanley.

"Premature old age," says I, givin' him the friendly grin.

CHAPTER XVI

THE MYSTERY OF THE THIRTY-ONE

If I knew how, you ought to be worked up to the proper pitch for this scene. You know—lights dimmed, throbby music from the bull fiddle and kettle drums, and the ushers seatin' nobody durin' the act. Belasco stuff. The stage showin' the private office of the Corrugated Trust. It's a case of the big four in solemn conclave.

Maybe you can guess the other three. Uh-huh! Old Hickory Ellins, Mr. Robert, and Piddie. I forget just what important problem we was settlin'. But it must have been something weighty and serious. Millions at stake, most likely. Thousands anyway. Or it might have been when we should start the Saturday half-holidays.

All I remember is that we was grouped around the big mahogany desk; Old Hickory in the middle chewin' away at the last three inches of a Cassadora; Mr. Robert at right center, studyin' the documents in the case; Piddie standin' respectful at his side weavin' his fingers in and out nervous; and me balanced on the edge of the desk at the left, one shoe toe on the floor, the other foot wavin' easy and graceful. Cool and calm, that's me. But not sayin' a word. Nobody was. We'd had our turn. It was up to Old Hickory to give the final decision. We was waitin', almost breathless. He'd let out a grunt or two, cleared his throat, and was about to open in his usual style when—

Cr-r-rash! Bumpety-bump!

Not that this describes it adequate. If I had a mouth that could imitate the smashin' of a 4x6 foot plate glass window I'd be on my way out to stampede the national convention for some favorite son. For that's exactly what happens. One of them big panes through which Old Hickory can view the whole southern half of Manhattan Island, not to mention part of New Jersey, has been shattered as neat as if someone had thrown a hammer through it. And havin' that occur not more'n ten feet from your right ear is some test of nerves, I'll say. I didn't even fall off the desk. All Old Hickory does is set his teeth into the cigar a little firmer and roll his eyes over one shoulder. Piddie's the only one who shows signs of shell shock. When he finally lets out a breath it's like openin' a bottle of home brew to see if the yeast cake is gettin' in its work.

The bumpety-bump noise comes from something white that follows the crash and rolls along the floor toward the desk. Naturally I makes a grab for it.

"Don't!" gasps Piddie. "It—it might be a bomb."

"Yes," says I, "it might. But it looks to me more like a golf ball."

"What?" says Old Hickory. "Golf ball! How could it be?"

"I don't know, sir," says I, modest as usual.

"Let's see," says he. I hands it over. He takes a glance at it and snorts out: "Impossible, but quite true. It is a golf ball.

A Spalldop 31."

"You're right, Governor," says Mr. Robert. "That's just what it is."

Piddie takes a cautious squint and nods his head. So we made it unanimous.

"But I don't quite see, sir," goes on Piddie, "how a—"

"Don't you?" breaks in Old Hickory. "Well, that's strange. Neither do I."

"Might it not, sir," adds Piddie, "have been dropped from an airplane?"

"Dropped how?" demands Old Hickory. "Sideways? The law of gravity doesn't work that way. At least, it didn't when I met it last."

"Certainly!" says Piddie. "I had not thought of that. It couldn't have been dropped. Then it must have been driven by some careless golfer."

He's some grand little suggester, Piddie is. Old Hickory glares at him and snorts. "An amazingly careless golfer," he adds, "considering that the nearest course is in Englewood, N. J., fully six miles away. No, Mr. Piddie, I fear that even Jim Barnes at his best, relayed by Gil Nichols and Walter Hagen, couldn't have made that drive."

"They—they never use a—a rifle for such purposes, do they?" asks Piddie.

"Not in the best sporting circles," says Old Hickory.

"I suppose," puts in Mr. Robert, "that some golf enthusiast might have taken it into his head to practice a shot from somewhere in the neighborhood."

"That's logical," admits Old Hickory, "but from where did he shoot? We are nineteen stories above the sidewalk, remember. I never saw a player who could loft a ball to that height."

Which gives me an idea. "What if it was some golf nut who'd gone out on a roof?" I asks.

"Thank you, Torchy," says Old Hickory. "From a roof, of course. I should have made that deduction myself within the next half hour. The fellow must be swinging away on the top of some nearby building. Let's see if we can locate him."

Nobody could, though. Plenty of roofs in sight, from five to ten stories lower than the Corrugated buildin', but no mashie maniac in evidence. And while they're scoutin' around I takes another squint at the ball.

"Say, Mr. Ellins," I calls out, "if it was shot from a roof how do you dope out this grass stain on it?"

"Eh?" says Old Hickory. "Grass stain! Must be an old one. No, by the green turban of Hafiz, it's perfectly fresh! Even a bit of moist earth where the fellow took a divot. Young man, that knocks out your roof practice theory. Now how in the name of the Secret Seven could this happen? The nearest turf is in the park, across Broadway. But no golfer would be reckless enough to try out a shot from there. Besides, this came from a southerly direction. Well, son, what have you to offer?"

"Me?" says I, stallin' around a bit and lookin' surprised.

"Oh, I didn't know I'd been assigned to the case of the mysterious golf ball."

"You have," says Old Hickory. "You seem to be so clever in deducing things and the rest of us so stupid. Here take another look at the ball. I presume that if you had a magnifying glass you could tell where it came from and what the man looked like who hit it. Eh?"

"Oh, sure!" says I, grinnin'. "That is, in an hour or so."

That's the only way to get along with Old Hickory; when he starts kiddin' you shoot the josh right back at him. I lets on to be examinin' the ball careful.

"I expect you didn't notice the marks on it?" says I.

"Where?" says he, gettin' out his glasses. "Oh, yes! The fellow has used an indelible pencil to put his initials on it. I often do that myself, so the caddies can't sell me my own balls. He's made 'em rather faint, but I can make out the letters. H. A. And to be sure, he's put 'em on twice."

"Yes," says I, "they might be initials, and then again they might be meant to spell out something. My guess would be 'Ha, ha!'"

"What!" says Old Hickory. "By the Sizzling Sisters, you're right! A message! But from whom?"

"Why not from Minnie?" I asks winkin' at Mr. Robert.

"Minnie who?" demands Old Hickory.

"Why, from Minnehaha?" says I, and I can hear Piddie gasp at my pullin' anything like that on the president of the Corrugated Trust.

Old Hickory must have heard him, too, for he shrugs his shoulders and remarks to Piddie solemn: "Even brilliant intellects have their dull spots, you see. But wait. Presently this spasm of third rate comedy will pass and he will evolve some apt conclusion. He will tell us who sent me a Ha, ha! message on a golf ball, and why. Eh, Torchy?"

"Guess I'll have to sir," says I. "How much time off do I get, a couple of hours?"

"The whole afternoon, if you'll solve the mystery," says he. "I am going out to luncheon now. When I come back—"

"That ought to be time enough," says I.

Course nine-tenths of that was pure bluff. All I had mapped out then was just a hunch for startin' to work. When they'd all left the private office I wanders over for another look from the punctured window. The lower sash had been pushed half-way up when the golf ball hit it, and the shade had been pulled about two-thirds down. It was while I was runnin' the shade clear to the top that I discovers this square of red cardboard hung in the middle of the top sash.

"Hah!" says I. "Had the window marked, did he?"

Simple enough to see that a trick of that kind called for an inside confederate. Who? Next minute I'm dashin' out to catch Tony, who runs express elevator No. 3.

"Were the window washers at work on our floor this mornin'?" says I.

"Sure!" says Tony, "What you miss?"

"It was a case of direct hit," says I. "Where are they now?"

"On twenty-two," says Tony.

"I'll ride up with you," says I.

And three minutes later I've corralled a Greek glass polisher who's eatin' his bread and sausage at the end of one of the corridors.

"You lobster!" says I. "Why didn't you hang that blue card in the right window?"

"Red card!" he protests, sputterin' crumbs. "I hang him right, me."

"Oh, very well," says I, displayin' half a dollar temptin'. "Then you got some more comin' to you, haven't you?"

He nods eager and holds out his hand.

"Just a minute," says I, "until I'm sure you're the right one. What was the party's name who gave you the job?"

"No can say him name," says the Greek. "He just tell me hang card and give me dollar."

"I see," says I. "A tall, thin man with red whiskers, eh?"

"No, no!" says he. "Short thick ol' guy, fat in middle, no whiskers."

"Correct so far," says I. "And if you can tell where he hangs out—"

"That's all," says the Greek. "Gimme half dollar."

"You win," says I, tossin' it to him.

But that's makin' fair progress for the first five minutes, eh? So far I knew that a smooth faced, poddy party had shot a golf ball with "Ha, ha!" written on it into Old Hickory's private office. Must have been done deliberate, too, for he'd taken pains to have the window marked plain for him with the red card. And at that it was some shot, I'll say. Couldn't have come from the street, on account of the distance. Then there was the grass stain. Grass? Now where—

By this time I'm leanin' out over the sill down at the roofs of the adjoinin' buildings. And after I'd stretched my neck for a while I happens to look directly underneath. There it was. Uh-huh. A little green square of lawn alongside the janitor's roof quarters. You know you'll find 'em here and there on office building roofs, even down in Wall Street. And this being right next door and six or seven stories below had been so close that we'd overlooked it at first.

So now I knew what he looked like, and where he stood. But who was he, and what was the grand idea? It don't take me long to chase down to the ground floor and into the next building. And, of course, I tackles the elevator starter. They're the wise boys. Always. I don't know why it is, but you'll generally find that the most important lookin' and actin' bird around a big buildin' is the starter. And what he don't know about the tenants and their business ain't worth findin' out.

On my way through the arcade I'd stopped at the cigar counter and invested in a couple of Fumadoras with fancy bands on 'em. Tuckin' the smokes casual into the starter's outside coat pocket I establishes friendly relations almost from the start.

"Well, son," says he, "is it the natural blond on the seventh, or the brunette vamp who pounds keys on the third that you want to meet?"

"Ah, come, Captain!" says I. "Do I look like a Gladyshound? Nay, nay! I'm simply takin' a sport census."

"Eh!" says he. "That's a new one on me."

"Got any golf bugs in your buildin', Cap?" I goes on.

"Any?" says he. "Nothing but. Say, you'll see more shiny hardware lugged out of here on a Saturday than—"

"But did you notice any being lugged in today?" I breaks in.

"No," says he. "It's a little early for 'em to start the season, and too near the first of the week. Don't remember a single bag goin' in today."

"Nor a club, either?" I asks.

He takes off his cap and rubs his right ear. Seems to help, too. "Oh, yes," says he. "I remember now. There was an old boy carried one in along about 10 o'clock. A new one that he'd just bought, I expect."

"Sort of a poddy, heavy set old party with a smooth face?" I suggests.

"That was him," says the starter. "He's a reg'lar fiend at it. But, then, he can afford to be. Owns a half interest in the buildin', I understand."

"Must be on good terms with the janitor, then," says I. "He could practice swings on the roof if he felt like it,

I expect."

"You've said it," says the starter. "He could do about what he likes around this buildin', Mr. Dowd could."

"Eh?" says I. "The Hon. Matt?"

"Good guess!" says the starter. "You must know him."

"Rather," says I. "Him and my boss are old chums. Golf cronies, too. Thanks. I guess that'll be all."

"But how about that sport census?" asks the starter.

"It's finished," says I, makin' a quick exit.

And by the time I'm back in the private office once more I've untangled all the essential points. Why, it was only two or three days ago that the Hon. Matt broke in on Old Hickory and gave him an earful about his latest discovery in the golf line. I'd heard part of it, too, while I was stickin' around waitin' to edge in with some papers for Mr. Ellins to sign.

Now what was the big argument? Say, I'll be driven to take up this Hoot-Mon pastime myself some of these days. Got to if I want to keep in the swim. It was about some particular club Dowd claimed he had just learned how to play. A mashie-niblick, that was it. Said it was revealed to him in a dream—something about gripping with the left hand so the knuckles showed on top, and taking the turf after he'd hit the ball. That gave him a wonderful loft and a back-spin.

And I remember how Old Hickory, who was more or less busy at the time, had tried to shunt him off. "Go on, you old fossil," he told him. "You never could play a mashie-niblick, and I'll bet twenty-five you can't now. You always top 'em. Couldn't loft over a bow-legged turtle, much less a six foot bunker. Yes, it's a bet. Twenty-five even. But you'll have to prove it, Matt."

And Mr. Dowd, chucklin' easy to himself, had allowed how he would. "To your complete satisfaction, Ellins," says he, "or no money passes. And within the week."

As I takes another look down at the little grass plot on the roof I has to admit that the Hon. Matt knew what he was talkin' about. He sure had turned the trick. Kind of clever of him, too, havin' the window marked and all that. And puttin' the "Ha, ha!" message on the ball.

I was still over by the window, sort of smilin' to myself, when Old Hickory walks in, havin' concluded to absorb only a sandwich and a glass of milk at the arcade cafeteria instead of goin' to his club.

"Well, young man," says he. "Have you any more wise deductions to submit?"

"I've got all the dope, if that's what you mean, sir," says I.

"Eh?" says he. "Not who and what and why?"

I nods easy.

"I don't believe it, son," says he. "It's uncanny. To begin with, who was the man?"

"Don't you remember havin' a debate not long ago with someone who claimed he could pull some wonderful stunt with a mashie-niblick?" says I.

"Why," says Old Hickory, "with no one but Dowd."

"You bet him he couldn't, didn't you?" I asks.

"Certainly," says he.

"Well, he can," says I. "And he has."

"Wha-a-at!" gasps Old Hickory.

"Uh-huh!" says I. "It was him that shot in the ball with the Ha, ha! message on it."

"But—but from where?" he demands.

"Look!" says I, leadin' him to the window.

"The old sinner!" says Mr. Ellins. "Why, that must be nearly one hundred feet, and almost straight up! Some shot! I didn't think it was in him. Hagen could do no better. And think of putting it through a window. That's accuracy for you. Say, if he can do that in a game I shall be proud to know him. Anyway, I shall not regret handing over that twenty-five."

"It'll cost him nearly that to set another pane of plate glass," I suggests.

"No, Torchy, no," says Old Hickory, wavin' his hand. "Any person who can show such marksmanship with a golf ball is quite welcome to—Ah, just answer that 'phone call, will you, son?"

So I steps over and takes down the receiver. "It's the buildin' superintendent," says I "He wants to speak to you, sir."

"See what he wants," says Old Hickory

And I expect I was grinnin' some when I turns around after gettin' the message. "He says somebody has been shootin' golf balls at the south side of the buildin' all the forenoon," says I, "and that seventeen panes of glass have, been smashed. He wants to know what he shall do."

"Do?" says Old Hickory. "Tell him to send for a glazier."

CHAPTER XVII

NO LUCK WITH AUNTIE

Well, I expect I've gone and done it again. Queered myself with Auntie. Vee's, of course. You'd most think I'd know how to handle the old girl by this time, for we've been rubbin' elbows, as you might say, for quite a few years now. But somehow we seldom hit it off just right.

Not that I don't try. Say, one of the big ambitions of my young life has been to do something that would please Auntie so much that no matter what breaks I made later on she'd be bound to remember it. Up to date, though, I haven't pulled anything of the kind. No. In fact, just the reverse.

I've often wished there was some bureau I could go to and get the correct dope on managin' an in-law aunt with a hair-trigger disposition. Like the Department of Agriculture. You know if it was boll-weevils, or cattle tick, or black rust, all I'd have to do would be to drop a postcard to Washington and in a month or so I'd have all kinds of pamphlets, with colored plates and diagrams, tellin' me just what to do. But balky aunts on your wife's side seem to have been overlooked.

Somebody ought to write a book on the subject. You can

get 'em that will tell you how to play bridge, or golf, or read palms, or raise chickens, or bring up babies. But nothin' on aunts who give you the cold eye and work up suspicions. And it's more or less important, 'specially if they're will-makin' aunts, with something to make wills about.

Not that I'm any legacy hound. She can do what she wants with her money, for all of me. Course, there's Vee to be considered. I wouldn't want to think, when the time comes, if it ever does, that her Auntie is with us no more, that it was on account of something I'd said or done that the Society for the Suppression of Jazz Orchestras was handed an unexpected bale of securities instead of the same being put where Vee could cash in on the coupons. Also there's Master Richard Hemmingway. I want to be able to look sonny in the face, years from now, without having to explain that if I'd been a little more diplomatic towards his mother's female relations he might he startin' for college on an income of his own instead of havin' to depend on my financin' his football career.

Besides, our family is so small that it seems to me the least I can do to be on good terms with all of 'em. 'Specially I'd like to please Auntie now and then just for the sake of—well, I don't go so far as to say I could be fond of Auntie for herself alone, but you know what I mean. It's the proper thing.

At the same time, I wouldn't want to seem to be overdoin' the act. No. So when it's a question of whether Auntie should be allowed to settle down for the spring in an apartment hotel in town, or be urged to stop with us until Bar Harbor opened for the season, I was all for the modest, retirin' stuff.

"She might think she had to come if she was asked," I

suggests to Vee. "And if she turned us down we'd have to look disappointed and that might make her feel bad."

"I hadn't considered that, Torchy," says Vee. "How thoughtful of you!"

"Oh, not at all," says I, wavin' my hand careless. "I simply want to do what is best for Auntie. Besides, you know how sort of uneasy she is in the country, with so little going on. And later, if we can persuade her to make us a little visit, for over night maybe, why—" I shrugs my shoulders enthusiastic. Anyway, that's what I tried to register.

It went with Vee, all right. One of the last things she does is to get suspicious of my moves. And that's a great help. So we agrees to let Auntie enjoy her four rooms and bath on East Sixty-umpt Street without tryin' to drag her out on Long Island where she might be annoyed by the robins singin' too early in the mornin' or havin' the scent of lilacs driftin' too heavy into the windows.

"Besides," I adds, just to clinch the case, "if she stays in town she won't be bothered by Buddy barkin' around, and she won't have to worry about how we're bringin' up 'Ikky boy. Yep. It's the best thing for her."

If Auntie had been in on the argument I expect she'd differed with me. She generally does. It's almost a habit with her. But not being present maybe she had a hunch herself that she'd like the city better. Anyway, that's where she camps down, only runnin' out once or twice for luncheon, while I'm at the office, and havin' nice little chatty visits with Vee over the long distance.

Honest, I can enjoy an Auntie who does her droppin' in by 'phone. I almost got so fond of her that I was on the point of suggestin' to Vee that she tell Auntie to reverse the charges. No, I didn't quite go that far. I'd hate to have her think I was gettin' slushy or sentimental. But it sure was comfortin', when I came home after a busy day at the Corrugated Trust, to reflect that Auntie was settled nice and cozy on the ninth floor about twenty-five miles due west from us.

I should have knocked on wood, though. Uh-huh. Or kept my fingers crossed, or something. For here the other night, as I strolls up from the station I spots an express truck movin' on ahead in the general direction of our house. I felt kind of a sinkin' sensation the minute I saw that truck. I can't say why. Psychic, I expect. You know. Ouija stuff.

And sure enough, the blamed truck turns into our driveway. By the time I arrives the man has just unloaded two wardrobe trunks and a hat box. And in the livin' room I finds Auntie.

"Eh?" says I, starin'. "Why, I—I thought you was—"

"How cordial!" says Auntie.

"Yes," says I, catchin' my breath quick. "Isn't it perfectly bully that you could come? We was afraid you'd be havin' such a good time in town that we couldn't—"

"And so I was, until last night," says Auntie. "Verona, will tell you all about it, I've no doubt."

Oh yes, Vee does. She unloads it durin' a little stroll we took out towards the garden. New York hadn't been behavin' well towards Auntie. Not at all well. Just got on one of its cantankerous streaks. First off there was a waiters' strike on the roof-garden restaurant where most of the tenants took their dinners. It happened between soup and fish. In fact, the fish never got there at all. Nor the roast, nor the rest of the meal. And the head waiter and the house manager had a rough-and-tumble scrap right in plain sight of everybody and some perfectly awful language was used. Also the striking waiters marched out in a body and shouted things at the manager as they went. So Auntie had to put on her things and call a taxi and drive eight blocks before she could finish her dinner.

Then about 9 o'clock, as she was settling down for a quiet evening in her rooms, New York pulled another playful little stunt on her. Nothing unusual. A leaky gas main and a poorly insulated electric light cable made connection with the well-known results. For half a mile up and down the avenue that Auntie's apartment faced on the manhole covers were blown off. They go off with a roar and a bang, you know. One of 'em sailed neatly up within ten feet of Auntie's back hair, crashed through the window of the apartment just above her and landed on the floor so impetuous that about a yard of plaster came rattlin' down on Auntie's head. Some fell in her lap and some went down the back of her neck.

All of which was more or less disturbin' to an old girl who was tryin' to read Amy Lowell's poems and had had her nerves jarred only a couple of hours before. However, she came out of it noble, with the aid of her smellin' salts and the assurance of the manager that it wouldn't happen again. Not that same evenin', anyway. He was almost positive it wouldn't. At least, it seldom did.

But being in on a strike, and a free-for-all fight, and a conduit explosion hadn't prepared Auntie to hit the feathers early. So at 1:30 A. M. she was still wide awake and wanderin' around in her nightie with the shades up and the lights out. That's how she happened to be stretchin' her neck out of the window when this offensive broke loose on the roof of the buildin' across the way.

Auntie was just wondering why those two men were skylarking around on the roof so late at night when two more popped out of skylights and began to bang away at them with revolvers. Then the first two started to shoot back, and the first thing Auntie knew there was a crash right over her head where a stray bullet had wandered through the upper pane. Upon which Auntie screamed and fainted. Of course, she had read about loft robbers, but she hadn't seen 'em in action. And she didn't want to see 'em at such close range any more. Not her. She'd had enough, thank you. So when she came to from her faintin' spell she begun packin' her trunks. After breakfast she'd called Vee on the 'phone, sketched out some of her troubles, and been invited to come straight to Harbor Hills.

"It was the only thing to be done," says Vee.

"Well, maybe," says I. "Course, she might have tried another apartment hotel. They don't all have strikes and explosions and burglar hunts goin' on. Not every night. She might have taken a chance or one or two more."

"But with her nerves all upset like that," protests Vee, "I don't see why she should, when here we are with—"

"Yes, I expect there was no dodgin' it," I agrees.

At dinner Auntie is still sort of jumpy but she says it's a great satisfaction to know that she is out here in the calm, peaceful country. "It's dull, of course," she goes on, "but at the same time it is all so restful and soothing. One knows that nothing whatever is going to happen."

"Ye-e-es," says I, draggy. "And yet, you can't always tell."

"Can't always tell what?" demands Auntie.

"About things not happenin' out here," says I.

"But, Torchy," says Vee, "what could possibly happen here; that is, like those things in town?"

I shrugs my shoulders and shakes my head.

"How absurd!" says Vee.

Auntie gives me one of them cold storage looks of hers. "I have usually noticed," says she, "that things do not happen of themselves. Usually some one is responsible for their happening."

What she meant by that I couldn't quite make out. Oh yes, takin' a little rap at me, no doubt. But just how or what for I passed up. I might have forgotten it altogether if she hadn't reminded me now and then by favorin' me with a suspicious glare, the kind one of Mr. Palmer's agents might give to a party in a checked suit steppin' off the train from Montreal with something bulgin' on the hip.

So it was kind of unfortunate that when Vee suddenly remembers the Airedale pup and asks where he is that I should say just what I did. "Buddy?" says I. "Oh, he's all right. I shut him up myself."

It was a fact. I had. And I'd meant well by it. For that's one of the things we have to look out for when Auntie's visitin' us, to keep Buddy away from her. Not that there's anything vicious about Buddy. Not at all. But being only a year old and full of pep and affection, and not at all discriminatin', he's apt to be a bit boisterous in welcomin' visitors; and while some folks don't mind havin' fifty pounds of dog bounce at 'em sudden, or bein' clawed, or havin' their faces licked by a moist pink tongue, Auntie ain't one of that kind. She gets petrified and squeals for help and insists that the brute is trying to eat her up.

So as soon as I'd come home and had my usual rough-house session with Buddy, I leads him upstairs and carefully parks him in the south bedroom over the kitchen wing. Being thoughtful and considerate, I call that. Not to Buddy maybe, who's used to spendin' the dinner hour with his nose just inside the dinin' room door; but to Auntie, anyway.

Which is why I'm so surprised, along about 9 o'clock when Auntie has made an early start for a good night's rest, to hear these loud hostile woofs comin' from him and then these blood curdlin' screams.

"For the love of Mike!" I gasps. "Where did you put Auntie?"

"Why, in the south bedroom this time," says Vee.

"Hal-lup!" says I. "That's where I put Buddy."

It was a race then up the stairs, with me tryin' to protest on the jump that I didn't know Vee had decided to shift Auntie from the reg'lar guest room to this one.

"Surely you didn't," admits Vee. "But I thought the south room would be so much sunnier and more cheerful. I—I'll explain to Auntie."

"It can't be done," says I. "Stop it, Buddy! All right, boy. It's perfectly all right."

Buddy don't believe it, though, until I've opened the door and switched on the light. Young as he is he's right up on the watch-dog act and when strangers come prowlin' around in the dark that's his cue for goin' into action. He has cornered Auntie scientific and while turnin' in a general alarm he has improved the time by tearin' mouth-fuls out of her dress. At that, too, it's lucky he hadn't begun to take mouthfuls out of Auntie.

As for the old girl, she's so scared she can't talk and so mad she can hardly see. She stands there limp in a tattered skirt with some of her gray store hair that has slipped its moorin's restin' jaunty over one ear and her eyes blazin' hostile.

"Oh, Auntie!" begins Vee. "It was all my—"

"Not a word, Verona," snaps Auntie. "I know perfectly well who is responsible for this—this outrage." With that she glares at me.

Course, we both tells her just how the mistake was made, over and over, but it don't register.

"Humph!" says she at last. "If I didn't remember a warning I had at dinner perhaps I might think as you do, Verona. But I trust that nothing else has been—er— arranged for my benefit."

"That's generous, anyway," says I, indulgin' in a sarcastic smile.

It's an hour before Auntie's nerves are soothed down enough for her to make another stab at enjoyin' a peaceful night. Even then she demands to know what that throbbin' noise is that she hears.

"Oh, that?" says I. "Only the cistern pump fillin' up the rain water tank in the attic. That'll quit soon. Automatic shut-off, you know."

"Verona," she goes on, ignorin' me, "you are certain it is quite all right, are you?"

"Oh, yes," says Vee. "It's one we had put in only last week. Runs by electricity, or some thing. Anyway, the plumber explained to Torchy just how it works. He knows all about it, don't you, Torchy?"

"Uh-huh," says I, careless.

I did, too. The plumber had sketched out the workin's of the thing elaborate to me, but I didn't see the need of spendin' the rest of the night passin' an examination in the subject. Besides, a few of the details I was a little vague about.

"Very well, then," says Auntie. And she consents to make one more stab at retirin'.

I couldn't help sighin' relieved when we heard her door shut. "Now if the roosters don't start crowin'," says I, "or a tornado don't hit us, or an earthquake break loose, all will be well. But if any of them things do happen, I'll be blamed."

"Nonsense," says Vee. "Auntie is going to have a nice, quiet, restful night and in the morning she will be herself again."

"Here's hoping," says I.

And if it's good evidence I'd like to submit the fact that within' five minutes after I'd rolled into my humble little white iron cot out on the sleepin' porch I was dead to the world. Could I have done that if I'd had on my mind a fiendish plot against the peace and safety of the only real aunt we have in the fam'ly? I ask you.

Seemed like I'd been asleep for hours and hours, and I believe I was dreamin' that I was being serenaded by a drum corps and that the bass drummer was mistakin' me for the drum and thumpin' me on the ribs, when I woke up and found Vee proddin' me from the next cot.

"Torchy!" she's sayin'. "Is that rain?"

"Eh?" says I. "No, that's the drum corps."

"What?" says she. "Don't be silly. It sounds like rain."

"Rain nothing," says I, rubbin' my eyes open. "Why, the moon's shining and—but, it does sound like water drippin'."

"Drippin'!" says Vee. "It's just pouring down somewhere. But where, Torchy?"

"Give it up," says I. "That is, unless it could be that blessed tank—"

"That's it!" says Vee. "The tank! But—but just where is it?"

"Why," says I, "it's in the attic over—over—Oh, good-night!" I groans.

"Well?" demands Vee. "Over what?"

"Over the south bedroom," says I. "Quick! Rescue expedition No. 2. Auntie again!"

It was Auntie. Although she was clear at the other end of the house from us we heard her moanin' and takin' on even before we got the hall door open. And, of course, we made another mad dash. Once more I pushes the switch button and reveals Auntie in a new plight. Some situation, I'll say, too. Uh-huh!

You see, there's an unfinished space over the kitchen well and the plumber had located this hundred-gallon tank in the middle of it. As it so happens the tank is right over the bed. Well, naturally when the fool automatic shut-off fails to work and the overflow pipe is taxed beyond its capacity, the surplus water has to go somewhere. It leaks through the floorin', trickles down between the laths and through the plaster, and some of it finds its way along the beams and under the eaves until it splashes down on the roof of the pantry extension. That's what we'd heard. But the rest had poured straight down on Auntie.

Being in a strange room and so confused to wake up and find herself treated to a shower bath that she hadn't ordered, Auntie couldn't locate the light button. All she could remember was that in unpackin' she'd stood an umbrella near the head of the bed. So with great presence of mind she's reached out and grabbed that, unfurled it, and is sittin' there damp and wailin' in a nice little pool of water that's risin' every minute. She's just as cosy as a settin' hen caught in a flood and is wearin' about the same contented expression, I judge.

"Why, Auntie, how absurd!" says Vee.

It wasn't just the right thing to say. Natural enough, I'll admit, but hardly the remark to spill at that precise moment. I could see the explosion coming, so after one more look I smothers a chuckle on my own account and beats it towards the cellar where that blamed pump is still chuggin' away merry and industrious. By turnin' off all the switches and handles in sight I manages to induce the fool thing to quit. Then I sneaks back upstairs, puts on a bathrobe and knocks timid on the door of the reg'lar guest room from which I hears sounds of earnest voices.

"Can I help any?" says I.

"No, no!" calls out Vee. "You—you'd best go away, Torchy."

She's generally right, Vee is. I went. I took a casual look at the flooded kitchen with an inch or more of water on the linoleum, and concluded to leave that problem to the help when they showed up in the mornin'. And I don't know how long Vee spent in tryin' to convince Auntie that I hadn't personally climbed into the attic, bugged the pump, and bored holes through the ceilin'. As I couldn't go on the stand in my own defense I did the next best thing. I finished out my sleep.

In the mornin' I got the verdict. "Auntie's going back to town," says Vee. "She thinks, after all, that it will be more restful there."

"It will be for me, anyway," says I.

I don't know how Vee and Master Richard still stand with Auntie. They may be in the will yet, or they may not. As for Buddy and me, I'll bet we're out. Absolutely. But we can grin, even at that.

CHAPTER XVIII

HARTLEY PULLS A NEW ONE

Looked like kind of a simple guy, this Hartley Tyler. I expect it was the wide-set, sort of starey eyes, or maybe the stiff way he had of holdin' his neck. If you'd asked me I'd said he might have qualified as a rubber-stamp secretary in some insurance office, or as a tea-taster, or as a subway ticket-chopper.

Anyway, he wasn't one you'd look for any direct action from. Too mild spoken and slow moving. And yet when he did cut loose with an original motion he shoots the whole works on one roll of the bones. He'd come out of the bond room one Saturday about closin' time and tip-toed hesitatin' up to where Piddie and I was havin' a little confab on some important business matter—such as whether the Corrugated ought to stand for the new demands of the window cleaners, or cut the contract to twice a month instead of once a week. Mr. Piddie would like to take things like that straight to Old Hickory himself, but he don't quite dare, so he holds me up and asks what I think Mr. Ellins would rule in such a case. I was just giving him some josh or other when he notices Hartley standin' there patient.

"Well?" says Piddie, in his snappiest office-manager style.

"Pardon me, sir," says Hartley, "but several weeks ago I put in a request for an increase in salary, to take effect this month."

"Oh, did you?" says Piddie, springin' that sarcastic smile of his. "Do I understand that it was an ultimatum?"

"Why—er—I hadn't thought of putting it in that form, sir," says Hartley, blinkin' something like an owl that's been poked off his nest.

"Then I may as well tell you, young man," says Piddie, "that it seems inadvisable for us to grant your request at this time."

Hartley indulges in a couple more blinks and then adds: "I trust that I made it clear, Mr. Piddie, how important such an increase was to me?"

"No doubt you did," says Piddie, "but you don't get it."

"That is—er—final, is it?" asks Hartley.

"Quite," says Piddie. "For the present you will continue at the same salary."

"I'll see you eternally cursed if I do," observes Hartley, without changin' his tone a note.

"Eh?" gasps Piddie.

"Oh, go to thunder, you pin-head!" says Hartley, startin' back for the bond room to collect his eye-shade, cuff protectors and other tools of his trade.

"You—you're discharged, young man!" Piddie gurgles out throaty.

"Very well," Hartley throws over his shoulder. "Have it that way if you like."

Which is where I gets Piddie's goat still further on the rampage by lettin' out a chuckle.

"The young whipper-snapper!" growls Piddie.

"Oh, all of that!" says I. "What you going to do besides fire him? Couldn't have him indicted under the Lever act, could you?"

Piddie just glares and stalks off. Having been called a pin-head by a bond room cub he's in no mood to be kidded. So I follows in for a few words with Hartley. You see, I could appreciate the situation even better than Piddie, for I knew more of the facts in the case than he did. For instance, I had happened to be in Old Hickory's private office when old man Tyler, who's one of our directors, you know, had wished his only son onto our bond room staff.

He's kind of a rough old boy, Z. K. Tyler, one of the bottom-rungers who likes to tell how he made his start as fry cook on an owl lunch wagon. Course, now he has his Broad Street offices and is one of the big noises on the Curb market. Operatin' in motor stocks is his specialty, and when you hear of two or three concerns being merged and the minority holders howlin' about being gypped, or any little deal like that, you can make a safe bet that somewhere in the background is old Z. K. jugglin' the wires and rakin' in the loose shekels. How he gets away with that stuff without makin' the rock pile is by me, but he seems to do it reg'lar.

And wouldn't you guess he'd be just the one to have finicky ideas as to how his son and heir should conduct himself. Sure thing! I heard him sketchin' some of 'em out to Old Hickory.

"The trouble with most young fellows," says he, "is that they're brought up too soft. Kick 'em out and let 'em rustle for themselves. That's what I had to do. Made a man of me. Now take Hartley. He's twenty-five and has had it easy all his life—city and country home, college, cars to drive, servants to wait on him, and all that. What's it done for him? Why, he has no more idea of how to make a dollar for himself than a chicken has of stirring up an omelette.

"Of course, I could take him in with me and show him the ropes, but he couldn't learn anything worth while that way. He'd simply be a copy-cat. He'd develop no originality. Besides, I'd rather see him in some other line. You understand, Ellins? Something a little more substantial. Got to find it for himself, though. He's got to make good on his own hook before I'll help him any more. So out he goes.

"Ought to have a year or so to pick up the elements of business, though. So let's find a place for him here in the Corrugated. No snap job. I want him to earn every dollar he gets, and to live off what he earns. Do him good. Maybe it'll knock some of the fool notions out of his head. Oh, he's got 'em. Say, you couldn't guess what fool idea he came back from college with. Thought he wanted to be a painter. Uh-huh! An artist! Asked me to set him up in a studio. All because him and a room mate had been daubin' some brushes with oil paints at a summer school they went to during a couple of vacations. Seems a long-haired instructor had been telling Hartley what great talent he had. Huh! I soon cured him of that. 'Go right to it, son,' says I. 'Paint something you can sell for five hundred and I'll cover it with a thousand. Until then, not a red cent.'

And inside of twenty-four hours he concluded he wasn't any budding Whistler or Sargent, and came asking what I thought he should tackle first. Eh? Think you could place him somewhere?"

So Old Hickory merely shrugs his shoulders and presses the button for Piddie. I expect he hears a similar tale about once a month and as a rule he comes across with a job for sonny boy. 'Specially when it's a director that does the askin'. Now and then, too, one of 'em turns out to be quite a help, and if they're utterly useless he can always depend on Piddie to find it out and give 'em the quick chuck.

As a rule this swift release don't mean much to the Harolds and Perceys except a welcome vacation while the old man pries open another side entrance in the house of Opportunity, Ltd., which fact Piddie is wise to. But in this ease it's a different proposition.

"Did you mean it, Tyler, handin' yourself the fresh air that way!" I asks him.

"Absolutely," says he, snappin' some rubber bands around, a neat little bundle.

"Who'd have thought you was a self starter!" says I. "What you going to do now?"

He hunches his shoulders. "Don't know," says he. "I must find something mighty quick, though."

"Oh, it can't be as desperate a case as that, can if?" I asks. "You know you'll get two weeks' pay and with that any single-footed young hick like you ought to—"

"But it happens I'm not single-footed," breaks in Hartley.

"Eh?" says I. "You don't mean you've gone and—"

"Nearly a month ago," says Hartley. "Nicest little girl in the world, too. You must have noticed her. She was on the candy counter in the arcade for a month or so."

"What!" says I. "The one with the honey-colored hair and the bashful behavin' eyes?"

Hartley nods and blushes.

"Say, you are a fast worker when you get going, ain't you?" says I. "Picked a Cutie-Sweet right away from all that opposition. But I judge she's no heiress."

"Edith is just as poor as I am," admits Hartley.

"How about your old man?" I goes on. "What did Z. K. have to say when he heard!"

"Suppose'we don't go into that," says Hartley. "As a matter of fact, I hung up the 'phone just as he was getting his second wind."

"Then he didn't pull the 'bless you, my children,' stuff, eh?" I suggests.

"No," says Hartley, grinnin'. "Quite the contrary. Anyway, I knew what to expect from him. But say, Torchy, I did have a pretty vague notion of what it costs to run a family these days."

"Don't you read the newspapers?" says I.

"Oh, I suppose I had glanced at the headlines," says Hartley. "And of course I knew that restaurant prices had gone up, and laundry charges, and cigarettes and so. But I hadn't shopped for ladies' silk hose, or for shoes, or—er—robes de nuit, or that sort of thing. And I hadn't tried to hire a three-room furnished apartment. Honest, it's something awful."

"Yes, I've heard something like that for quite a spell now," says I. "Found that your little hundred and fifty a month wouldn't go very far, did you?"

"Far!" says Hartley. "Why, it was like taking a one-gallon freezer of ice cream to a Sunday school picnic. Really, it seemed as if there were a thousand hands reaching out for my pay envelope the moment I got it. I don't understand how young married couples get along at all."

"If you did," says I, "you'd have a steady job explainin' the miracle to about 'steen different Congressional committees. How about Edith? Is she a help—or otherwise?"

"She's a good sport, Edith is," says Hartley. "She keeps me bucked up a lot. It was her decision that I just passed on to Mr. Piddie. We talked it all out last night; how impossible it was to live on my present salary, and what I should say if it wasn't raised. That is, all but the crude way I put it, and the pin-head part. We agreed, though, that I had to make a break, and that it might as well be now as later on."

"Well, you've made it," says I. "What now?"

"We've got to think that out," says Hartley.

"The best of luck to you," says I, as he starts toward the elevator.

And with that Hartley drops out. You know how it is here

in New York. If you don't come in on the same train with people you know, or they work in different buildin's, or patronize some other lunch room, the chances of your seein' 'em more 'n once in six months are about as good as though they'd moved to St. Louis or Santa Fe.

I expect I was curious about what was goin' to happen to Hartley and his candy counter bride, maybe for two or three days. But it must have been as many weeks before I even heard his name mentioned. That was when old Z. K. blew into the private office one day and, after a half hour of business chat, remarks to Old Hickory; "By the way, Ellins, how is that son of mine getting on?"

"Eh?" says Old Hickory, starin' at him blank. "Son of yours with us? I'd forgotten. Let's see. Torchy, in what department is young Tyler now?"

"Hartley?" says I. "Oh, he quit weeks ago."

"Quit?" says Z. K. "Do you mean he was fired?"

"A little of both," says I. "Him and Mr. Piddie split about fifty-fifty on that. They had a debate about him gettin' a raise. No, he didn't leave any forwardin' address and he hasn't been back since."

"Huh!" says Z. K., scratchin' his left ear. "He'd had the impudence to go and get himself married, too. Think of that Ellins! A youngster who never did a stroke of real work in his life loads himself up with a family in these times. Well, I suppose he's finding out what a fool he is, and when they both get good and hungry he'll come crawling back. Oh yes, I'll give him a job this time, a real one. You know I've been rebuilding my country home down near Great Neck. Been having a deuce of a time doing it, too—materials held up, workmen going out on strikes every few days. I'll set Hartley to running a concrete mixer, or wheeling bricks when he shows up."

But somehow Hartley don't do the homeward crawl quite on schedule. At any rate, old Z. K. was in the office three or four times after that without mentionin' it, and you bet he would have cackled some if Hartley had come back. All he reports is that the house rebuildin' is draggin' along to a finish and he hopes to be able to move in shortly.

"Want you to drive over and see what you think of it," he remarks to Mr. Robert, once when Old Hickory happens to be out. "Only a few plasterers and plumbers and painters still hanging on. How about next Saturday? I've got to be there about 2 o'clock. What say?"

"I shall be very glad to," says Mr. Robert, who's always plannin' out ways of revisin' his own place.

If it hadn't been for some Western correspondence that needed code replies by wire I expect I should have missed out on this tour of inspection to the double-breasted new Tyler mansion. As it was Mr. Robert tells me to take the code book and my hat and come along with him in the limousine. So by the time we struck Jamaica I was ready to file the messages and enjoy the rest of the drive.

We finds old Z. K. already on the ground, unloadin' a morning grouch on a landscape architect.

"Be with you in a minute, Robert," says he. "Just wander in and look around."

That wasn't so easy as it sounded, for all through the big rooms was scaffolds and ladders and a dozen or more original members of the Overalls Club splashin' mortar and paint around. I was glancin' at these horny-handed sons of toil sort of casual when all of a sudden I spots one guy in a well-daubed suit of near-white ducks who looks strangely familiar. Walkin' up to the step-ladder for a closer view I has to stop and let out a chuckle. It's Hartley.

"Well, well!" says I. "So you did have to crawl back, eh?"

"Eh?" says he, almost droppin' a pail of white paint. "Why, hello, Torchy!"

"I see you're workin' for a real boss now," says I.

"Who do you mean?" says he.

"The old man," says I, grinnin'.

"Not much!" says Hartley. "He's only the owner, and precious little bossing he can do on this job. I'm working for McNibbs, the contractor."

"You—you mean you're a reg'lar painter?" says I, gawpin'.

"Got to be, or I couldn't handle a brush here," says Hartley. "This is a union job."

"But—but how long has this been goin' on, Hartley?" I asks.

"I've held my card for nearly three months now," says he. "No, I haven't been painting here all that time. In fact, I came here only this morning. The president of our local shifted me down here for—for reasons. I'm a real painter, though."

"You look it, I must say," says I. "Like it better than being in the bond room?"

"Oh, I'm not crazy about it," says he. "Rather smelly work. But it pays well. Dollar an hour, you know, and time and a half for overtime. I manage to knock out sixty or so a week. Then I get something for being secretary of the Union."

"Huh!" says I. "Secretary, are you? How'd you work up to that so quick?"

"Oh, they found I could write fairly good English and was quick at figures," says he. "Besides, I'm always foreman of the gang. Do all the color mixing, you know. That's where my art school experience comes in handy."

"That ought to tickle the old man," says I. "Seen him yet?"

"No," says Hartley, "but I want to. Is he here?"

"Sure," says I. "He's just outside. He'll be in soon."

"Fine!" says Hartley. "Say, Torchy, stick around if you want to be entertained. I have a message for him."

"I'll be on hand," says I. "Here he comes now."

As old Z. K. stalks in, still red in the ears from his debate outside, Hartley climbs down off the step ladder. For a minute or so the old man don't seem to see him any more'n he does any of the other workmen that he's had to dodge around. Not until Hartley steps right up to him and remarks: "Mr. Tyler, I believe?" does Z. K. stop and let out a gasp.

"Hah!" he snorts. "Hartley, eh? Well, what does this mean—a masquerade?"

"Not at all," says Hartley. "This is my regular work."

"Oh, it is, eh?" says he. "Well, keep at it then. Why do you knock off to talk to me?"

"Because I have something to say to you, sir," says Hartley. "You sent a couple of non-union plumbers down here the other day, didn't you?"

"What if I did?" demands Z. K. "Got to get the work finished somehow, haven't I?"

"You'll never get it finished with scab labor, Mr. Tyler," says Hartley. "You have tried that before, haven't you? Well, this is final. Send those plumbers off at once or I will call out every other man on the job."

"Wh-a-a-at!" gasps Z. K. "You will! What in thunder have you got to do with it?"

"I've been authorized by the president of our local to strike the job, that's all," says Hartley. "I am the secretary. Here are my credentials and my union card."

"Bah!" snorts Z. K. "You impudent young shrimp. I don't believe a word of it. And let me tell you, young man, that I'll send whoever I please to do the work here, unions or no unions."

"Very well," says Hartley. With that he turns and calls out: "Lay off, men. Pass the word on."

And say, inside of two minutes there isn't a lick of work being done anywhere about the place. Plasterers drop their trowels and smoothing boards, painters come down off the ladders, and all hands begin sheddin' their work clothes. And while Z. K. is still sputterin' and fumin' the men begin to file out with their tools under their arms. Meanwhile Hartley has stepped over into a corner and is leisurely peelin' off his paint-spattered ducks.

"See here, you young hound!" shouts Z. K. "You know I want to get into this house early next month. I—I've simply got to."

"The prospects aren't good," says Hartley.

Well, they had it back and forth like that for maybe five minutes before Z. K. starts to calm down a bit. He's a foxy old pirate, and he hates to quit, but he's wise enough to know when he's beaten.

"Rather smooth of you, son, getting back at me this way," he observes smilin' sort of grim. "Learned a few things, haven't you, since you've been knocking around?"

"Oh, I was bound to," says Hartley.

"Got to be quite a man, too—among painters, eh?" adds Z. K.

Hartley shrugs his shoulders.

"Could you call all those fellows back as easily as you sent them off?" demands Tyler.

"Quite," says Hartley. "I wouldn't, though, until you had fired those scab plumbers."

"I see," says Z. K. "And if I did fire 'em, do you think you have influence enough to get a full crew of union men to finish this job by next Saturday?"

"Oh, yes," says Hartley. "I could put fifty men at work

here Monday morning—if I wanted to."

"H-m-m-m!" says Z. K., caressin' his left ear. "It's rather a big house for just your mother and me to live in. Plenty of room for another family. And I suppose a good studio could be fixed up on the third floor. Well, son, want to call it a trade?"

"I'll have to talk to Edith first," says Hartley. "I think she'll like it, and I'll bet you'll like her, too."

Uh-huh! From late reports I hear that Hartley was right both ways. A few days later Mr. Robert tells me that the Tylers are all preparin' to move out together. He had seen the whole four of 'em havin' a reunion dinner at the Plutoria, and says they all seemed very chummy.

"Just like they was members of One Big Union, eh?" says I. "But say, Hartley's right up to date in his methods of handlin' a wrathy parent, ain't he? Call a strike on 'em. That's the modern style. I wonder if he's got it patented?"

CHAPTER XIX

TORCHY GETS A HUNCH

Course, I only got my suspicions, and I ain't in position to
call for the real facts in the case, but I'll bet if it came to a
show down I could name the master mind that wished this
backache and the palm blisters on me. Uh-huh! Auntie. I
wouldn't put it past her, for when it comes to evenin' up a
score she's generally right there with the goods. Deep
stuff, as a rule, too.

I ain't denyin' either, but what Auntie had grounds for
complaint. Maybe you remember how she came out to
spend a quiet week-end with us after a nerve shatterin'
night in town and near got chewed up by Buddy, the
super-watch dog, and then was almost flooded out of bed
because the attic storage tank ran over? Not that I didn't
have a perfect alibi on both counts. I did. But neither
registered with Auntie.

Still, this before-breakfast sod-turnin' idea comes straight
from Vee. Ever try that for an appetizer? Go on, give it a
whirl. Ought to be willin' to try anything once, you know.
Some wise old guy said that, I understand. I'd like to find
the spot where he's laid away. I think I'd go plant a
cabbage on his grave. Anyway, he's got some little tribute
like that comin' from me.

Sewell Ford

Just turnin' up sod with a spade in the dewy morn. Listens kind of romantic, don't it! And you might like it first rate. Might agree with you. As for me, I've discovered that my system don't demand anything like that. Posi-tive-ly. I gave it a good try-out and the reactions wasn't satisfactory.

You see, it was this way: there's a narrow strip down by the road where our four-acre estate sort of pinches out, and Vee had planned to do some fancy landscape gardenin' on it—a bed of cannas down the middle, I believe, and then rows of salvia, and geraniums and other things. She had it all mapped out on paper. Also the bulbs and potted plants had arrived and were ready to be put in.

But it happens that Dominick, our official gardener, had all he could jump to just then, plantin' beans and peas and corn, and the helper he depended on to break up this roadside strip had gone back on him.

"How provoking!" says Vee. "I am so anxious to get those things in. If the ground was ready I would do the planting myself. I just wish"—and then she stops.

"Well, let's have it," says I. "What's your wish?"

"Oh, nothing much Torchy," says she. "But if I were strong enough to dig up that sod I wouldn't have to wait for any pokey Italian."

"Why couldn't I do it?" I suggests reckless.

"You!" says Vee, and then snickers.

Say, if she'd come poutin' around, or said right out that she didn't see why I couldn't make myself useful now and then, I'd have announced flat that gardenin' was way out of my line. But when she snickers—well, you know how it is.

"Yessum! Me," says I. "It ain't any art, is it, just stirrin' up the ground with a spade? And how do you know, Vee, but what I'm the grandest little digger ever was? Maybe it's a talent I've been concealin' from you all along."

"But it's rather hard work, turning old sod, and getting out all the grass roots and rocks," says she. "It takes a lot of strength."

"Huh!" says I. "Feel of that right arm."

"Yes," says she, "I believe you are strong, Torchy. But when could you find the time?"

"I'd make it," says I. "All I got to do is to roll out of the cot an hour or so earlier in the morning. Wouldn't six hours do the job? Well, two hours a day for three days, and there you are. Efficiency stuff. That's me. Lead me to it."

Vee gazes at me admirin'. "Aren't you splendid, Torchy!" says she. "And I'm sure the exercise will do you a lot of good."

"Sure!" says I. "Most likely I'll get the habit and by the end of the summer I'll be a reg'lar Sandow. Now where's that kitchen alarm clock? Let's see. M-m-m-m! About 5:30 will do for a starter, eh?"

Oh, I'm a determined cuss when I get going. Next mornin' the sun and me punched in at exactly the same time, and I don't know which was most surprised. But there I was, associatin' with the twitterin' little birds and the early worms, and to show I was just as happy as they were I hums a merry song as I swings out through the dewy grass with the spade over my shoulder.

Say, there's no fake about the grass being dewy at that hour, either. I hadn't gone more 'n a dozen steps through it before my feet were as soggy as if I'd been wadin' in a brook. I don't do any stallin' around, same as these low brow labor gangs. I pitches right in earnest and impetuous, makin' the dirt fly. Why, I had the busy little bee lookin' like he was loafin' on a government contract.

I was just about gettin' my second wind and was puttin' in some heavy licks when I hears somebody tootin' a motor horn out in the road. I looks up to find that it's that sporty neighbor of mine, Nick Barrett, who now and then indulges a fad for an early spin in his stripped roadster. He has collected his particular chum, Norris Bagby, and I expect they're out to burn up the macadam before the traffic cops go on duty.

"What's the big idea, Torchy?" sings out Nick. "Going to bury a cat, or something?"

"Nothing tragic like that," says I. "Just subbin' in for the gardener. Pulling a little honest toil, such as maybe you've read about but haven't met."

"Doing it on a bet, I suppose?" suggests Norris.

"Ah, run along and don't get comic," says I.

And with that I tears into the sod again, puttin' both shoulders and my back into the swing. I don't let up, either, until I think it must be after 7 o'clock, and then I stops long enough to look at my watch. It's just 6:20. Well, I expect I slowed up some from then on. No use tryin' to dig all over that ground in one morning. And at

6:35 I discovers that I'd raised a water blister on both palms. Ten minutes later I noticed this ache in my back and arms.

"Oh, well!" says I, "gotta take time to change and wash up."

At that I didn't feel so bad. After a shower and a fresh outfit from the socks up I was ready to tackle three fried eggs and two cups of coffee. On the way to the station I glanced proud at what I'd accomplished. But somehow it didn't look so much. Just a little place in one corner.

Course, goin' in on the 8:03 I had to stand for a lot of kiddin'. They're a great bunch of humorists, them commuters. Nick and Norrie has spread the news around industrious about my sunrise spadin' stunt, and everybody has to pull his little wheeze.

"How's the old back feel about now; eh, Torchy?" asks one.

"Great stuff!" says another. "Everybody does it—once."

"The boy's clever with the spade, I'll say," adds Nick. "Let's all turn out tomorrow morning and watch him. He does it regular, they tell me."

I grinned back at 'em as convincin' as I could. For somehow I wasn't just in the mood for grinnin'. My head was achin' more or less, and my back hurt, and my palms were sore. By noon I was a wreck. Absolutely. And when I thought of puttin' in two or three more sessions like that I had to groan. Could I do it? On the other hand, could I renig on the job after all that brash line of talk I'd given Vee?

Say, it was all I could do to limp out to luncheon. I didn't want much, but I thought maybe some tea and toast would make me feel better. And it was in a restaurant that I ran across this grouchy Scotchman, MacGregor Shinn, who sold me the place here a while back.

"Maybe you don't know it, Mac," says I, "but you're a wise guy."

"Am I, though?" says he. "I hadn't noticed it myself. Just how, now?"

"Unloadin' that country property on me," says I. "I used to wonder why you let go of it. I don't any more. I've got the right hunch at last. You got up bright and early one morning and tried digging around with a spade. Eh?"

Mac stares at me sort of puzzled. "Not me," says he. "Whatever put that in your mind, me lad?"

"Ah, come!" says I. "With all that land lyin' around you was bound to get reckless with a spade some time or other. Might not have been flower beds you was excavatin' for, same as me. Maybe you was specializin' on spuds, or cabbages. But I'll bet you had your foolish spell."

Mr. Shinn shakes his head. "All the digging I ever did out there," says he, "was with a niblick in the bunkers of the Roaring Rock golf course. No, I'm wrong."

"Ha, ha!" says I. "I thought so."

"Yes," he goes on, rubbin' his chin reminiscent, "I mind me of one little job of digging I did. I had a cook once who had a fondness for gin that was scandalous. Locking it up was no good, except in my bureau drawers, so one time when I had an extra case of Gordon come in I sneaked out at night and buried it. That was just before I sold the place to you and—By George, me lad!"

Here he has stopped and is gazin' at me with his mouth open.

"Well?" says I.

"I canna mind digging it up again," says he.

"That doesn't sound much like a Scotchman," says I, "being so careless with good liquor. But you were in such a rush to get back to town maybe you did forget. Where did you plant it?"

Mac scratches his head. "I canna seem to think," says he.

And about then I begins to get a glimmer of this brilliant thought of mine. "Would it have been in that three-cornered strip that runs along by the road?" I asks.

"It might," says he.

I didn't press him for any more details. I'd heard enough. I finished my invalid's lunch and slid out. But say, when I caught the 5:13 out to Harbor Hills that afternoon I had something all doped out to slip to that bunch of comic commuters. I laid for 'em in the smokin' car, and when Nick Barrett discovers me inspectin' my palm blisters he starts in with his kidding again.

"Oh, you'll be able to get out and dig again in a week or so," says he.

"I hope so," says I.

"Still strong for it, eh?" says he.

"Maybe if you knew what I was diggin' for," says I, "you'd—well, there's no tellin'."

"Eh?" says he. "Whaddye mean?"

I shakes my head and looks mysterious.

"Isn't it green corn, or string beans that you're aimin' at, Torchy?" he asks.

"Not exactly," says I. "Vegetable raisin' ain't in my line. I leave that to Dominick. But this—oh, well!"

"You don't mean," insists Nick, eyein' me close, "buried treasure!"

"I expect some would call it that—in these days," says I.

Uh-huh! I had him sittin' up by then, with his ear stretched. And I must say that from then on Nick does some scientific pumpin'. Not that I let out anything in so many words, but I'm afraid he got the idea that what I was after was something money couldn't buy. That is, not unless somebody violated a sacred amendment to the grand old constitution. In fact, I may have mentioned casually that a whole case of Gordon was worth riskin' a blister here and there.

As for Nick, he simply listens and gasps. You know how desperate some of them sporty ginks are, who started out so gay only a year or so ago with a private stock in the cellar that they figured would last 'em until the country rose in wrath and undid Mr. Volstead's famous act? Most of 'em are discoverin' what poor guessers they were. About 90 per cent are bluffin' along on home brew hooch that has all the delicate bouquet of embalmin' fluid and produced about the same effect as a slug of liquid T. N. T., or else they're samplin' various kinds of patent medicines and perfumes. Why, I know of one thirsty soul who tries to work up a dinner appetite by rattlin' a handful of shingle nails in the old shaker. And if Nick Barrett has more 'n half a bottle of Martini mixture left in the house he sleeps with it under his pillow. So you can judge how far his tongue hangs out when he gets me to hint that maybe a whole case of Gordon is buried somewhere on my premises.

"Torchy," says he, shakin' me solemn by the hand, "I wish you the best of luck. If you'll take my advice, though, you won't mention this to anyone else."

Oh, no, I didn't. That is, only to Norrie Bagby and one or two others that I managed to get a word with on the ride home.

Vee was mighty sympathetic about the blisters and the way my back felt. I was dosed and plastered and put to bed at 8:30 to make up for all the sleep I'd lost at the other end of the day.

"And we'll not bother any more about the silly old flowers," says she. "If Dominick can't find time to do the spading we'll just let it go."

"No," says I, firm and heroic. "I'm no quitter, Vee. I said I'd get it done within three days and I stick to it."

"Torchy," says she, "don't you dare try getting up again at daylight and working with your poor blistered hands. I—I shall feel dreadfully about it, if you do."

"Well, maybe I will skip tomorrow mornin'," says I, "but

somehow or other that diggin' has got to be done."

"I only wish Auntie could hear you say that," says Vee, pattin' me gently on the cheek.

"Why Auntie?" I asks.

"Oh, just because," says Vee.

With that she fixes me up all comfy on the sleepin' porch and tells me to call her if I want anything.

"I won't," says I. "I'm all set for slumber. It's goin' to be a fine large night, ain't it!"

"Perfect," says Vee.

"Moon shinin' and everything?" says I.

"Yes," says she.

"Then here's hoping," says I.

"There, there!" says Vee. "I'm afraid you're a little feverish."

Maybe I was, but I didn't hear another thing until more 'n ten hours later when I woke up to find the sun winkin' in at me through the shutters.

"Did you have a good night's rest?" asks Vee.

"As good as they come," says I. "How about you!"

"Oh, I slept fairly well," says she. "I was awake once or twice. I suppose I was worrying a little about you. And then I thought I hear strange noises."

"What sort of noises?" I asks.

"Oh, like a lot of men walking by," says she. "That must have been nearly midnight. They were talking low as they passed, and it almost sounded as if they were carrying tools of some sort. Then along towards morning I thought I heard them pass again. I'm sure some of them were swearing."

"Huh!" says I. "I wonder what they could have been peeved about on such a fine night?"

"Or I might have been simply dreaming," she adds.

"Yes, and then again," says I, smotherin' a chuckle.

I could hardly wait to dress and shave before rushin' out to inspect the spot where I'd almost ruined myself only the mornin' before. And it was something worth inspectin'. I'll say. Must be nearly half an acre in that strip and I expect that sod has been growin' for years untouched by the hand of man. At 6 P. M. last night it was just a mass of thick grass and dandelions, but now—say, a tractor plough and a gang of prairie tamers couldn't have done a more thorough job. If there was a square foot that hadn't been torn up I couldn't see it with the naked eye.

Course, it aint all smooth and even. There was holes here and there, some of 'em three feet deep, but about all the land needed now was a little rakin' and fillin' in, such as Dominick could do in his spare time. The cheerin' fact remains that the hard part of the work has been done, silent and miraculous, and without price.

I shouts for Vee to come out and see. It ain't often, either, that I can spring anything on her that leaves her stunned and bug-eyed.

"Why, Torchy!" says she, gaspy. "How in the world did you ever manage it? I—I don't understand."

"Oh, very simple!" says I. "It's all in havin' the right kind of neighbors."

"But you don't mean," says she, "that you persuaded some of our—oh, I'm sure you never could. Besides, you're grinning. Torchy, I want you to tell me all about it. Come, now! Exactly what happened last night?"

"Well," says I, "not being present myself I could hardly tell that. But I've got a good hunch."

"What is it!" she insists.

"From your report of what you heard," says I, "and from the looks of the ground 'n everything, I should judge that the Harbor Hills Exploring and Excavating Co. had been making a night raid on our property."

"Pooh!" says Vee. "I never heard of such a company. But if there is one, why should they come here?"

"Oh, just prospectin', I expect," says I.

"For what?" demands Vee.

"For stuff that the 18th amendment says they can't have," says I. "Gettin' down to brass tacks, for a case of dry gin."

Even that don't satisfy Vee. She demands why they should dig for any such thing on our land.

"They might have heard some rumor," says I, "that MacGregor Shinn went off and left it buried there. As though a Scotchman could ever get as careless as that. I don't believe he did. Anyway, some of them smart Alec commuters who were kiddin' me so free yesterday must have worked up blisters of their own. My guess is that they lost some sleep, too."

You don't have to furnish Vee with a diagram of a joke, you know, before she sees it. At that she squints her eyes and lets out a snicker.

"I wonder, Torchy," says she, "who could have started such a rumor?"

"Yes, that's the main mystery, ain't it?" says I. "But your flower bed is about ready, ain't it?"

CHAPTER XX

GIVING 'CHITA A LOOK

I got to admit that there's some drawbacks to being a 100 per cent perfect private see. Not that I mind making myself useful around the general offices. I'm always willin' to roll up my sleeves any time and save the grand old Corrugated Trust from going on the rocks. I'll take a stab at anything, from meetin' a strike committee of the Amalgamated Window Washers' Union to subbin' in as president for Old Hickory at the annual meetin'. And between times I don't object to makin' myself as handy as a socket wrench. That is, so long as it's something that has to do with finance, high or low.

But say, when they get to usin' me in strictly fam'ly affairs, I almost work up a grouch. Notice the almost. Course, with this fair-and-warmer disposition of mine I can't quite register. Not with Mr. Robert, anyway. He has such a matey, I-say-old-chap way with him. Like here the other day when he comes strollin' out from the private office rubbin' his chin puzzled, stares around for a minute, and then makes straight for my desk.

"Well," says he, "I presume you noted the arrival of the prodigal son; eh, Torchy?"

"Meaning Ambrose the Ambler?" says I.

"The same," says he.

"They will come back even from South America," says I. "And you was figurin', I expect, how that would be a long, wet walk. But then, nothing was ever too wet for Amby, and the only fear he had of water was that he might get careless some time and swallow a little."

"Quite so," says Mr. Robert, grinnin'.

You see, this Ambrose Wood party is only an in-law once removed. Maybe you remember Ferdy, who had the nerve to marry Marjorie Ellins, the heavyweight sister of Mr. Robert's, here a few years back? Well, that was when the Ellinses acquired a brunette member of the flock. Ambrose is a full brother of Ferdy's. In every sense. That is, he was in the good old days when Mr. Volstead was only a name towards the end of roll call.

I ought to know more or less about Amby for we had him here in the general offices for quite some time, tryin' to discover if there wasn't some sphere of usefulness that would excuse us handin' him a pay envelope once a week. There wasn't. Course, we didn't try him as a paper weight or a door stop. But he had a whirl at almost everything else. And the result was a total loss.

For one thing, time clocks meant no more to Amby than an excursion ad. would to a Sing Sing lifer. Amby wasn't interested in 'em. He'd drift in among the file room or bond clerks, or whatever bunch he happened to be inflicted on that particular month, at any old hour, from 10 A. M. up to 2:30 P. M. Always chirky and chipper about it, too. And his little tales about the parties he'd been to on the night before was usually interestin'. Which was bad for the general morale, as you can guess. Also his light and frivolous way of chuckin' zippy lady stenogs under the chin and callin' 'em "Dearie" didn't help his standin' any. Yeauh! He was some boy, Amby, while he lasted. Three different times Brother Ferdie was called from his happy home at night to rush down with enough cash bail to rescue Ambrose from a cold-hearted desk sergeant, and once he figured quite prominent on the front page of the morning papers when he insisted on confidin' to the judge that him and the young lady in the taxi was really the king and queen of Staten Island come over to visit upper Broadway. I don't doubt that Amby thought he was something of the kind at the time, too, but you know how the reporters are apt to play up an item of that kind. And of course they had to lug in the fact that Ambrose was a near-son-in-law of the president of the Corrugated Trust.

That was where Old Hickory pushed the button for me. "Young man," says he, chewin' his cigar savage, "what should you say was the longest steamer trip that one could buy a ticket for direct from New York?"

"Why," says I, "my guess would be Buenos Ayres."

"Very well," says he, "engage a one way passage on the next boat and see that Mr. Ambrose Wood stays aboard until the steamer sails."

Which I did. Ambrose didn't show any hard feelin's over it. In fact, as I remember, he was quite cheerful. "Tell the old hard boiled egg not to worry about me," says he. "He may be able to lose me this way for a while, but I'm not clear off the map yet. I'll be back some day."

Must have been more 'n three years ago, and as I hadn't heard Amby's name mentioned in all that time I joined in the general surprise when I saw him trailin' in dressed so neat and lookin' so fit.

"On his way to hand Ferdy the glad jolt, eh?" I asks.

"No," says Mr. Robert. "Ambrose seems quite willing to postpone meeting his brother for a day or so. He has just landed, you see, and doesn't care to dash madly out into the suburbs. What he wishes most, as I understand, is to take a long, long look at New York."

"Well, after three years' exile," says I, "you can hardly blame him for that."

Mr. Robert hunches his shoulders. "I suppose one can't," says he. "Only it leaves him on my hands, as it were. Someone must do the family honors—dinner, theatre, all that sort of thing. And if I were not tied up by an important committee meeting out at the country club I should be very glad to—er—"

"Ye-e-es?" says I, glancin' at him suspicious.

"You've guessed it, Torchy," says he. "I must leave them to you."

"Whaddye mean, them?" says I. "I thought we was talking about Ambrose."

"Oh, certainly," says Mr. Robert. "But Mrs. Wood is with him, he says. In fact they came up together. Same boat. They would, you know. Charming young woman. At least, so I inferred from what Ambrose said. One of those dark Spanish beauties such as—"

"Check!" says I. "That lets me out. All the Spanish I know is 'Multum in parvo' and I forget just what that means now. I couldn't talk to the lady a-tall."

But Mr. Robert insists I don't have to be conversational with her, or with Ambrose, either. All he wants me to do is steer 'em to some nice, refined place regardless of expense, give 'em a welcome-home feed that will make 'em forget that the Ellins family is only represented by proxy, tow 'em to some high-class entertainment, like "The Boudoir Girls," and sort of see that Ambrose lands back at his hotel without having got mixed up with any of his old set.

"Oh!" says I. "Kind of a he-chaperone act, eh?"

That seems to be the general idea, and as he promises to stop in at the house and fix things up for me at home, and pushes a roll of twenties at me to spray around with as I see fit, of course, I has to take the job. I trails in with Mr. Robert while he apologizes elaborate to Ambrose and explains how he's had to ask me to fill in.

"Perfectly all right, old man," says Ambrose. "In fact— well, you get the idea, eh? The little wife hasn't quite got her bearings yet. Might feel better about meeting her new relatives after she's been around a bit. And Torchy will do fine."

He tips me the wink as Mr. Robert hurries off.

"Same old cut-up, eh, Amby?" says I.

"Who me?" says he. "No, no! Nothing like that. Old married man, steady as a church. Uh-huh! Two years and a half in the harness. You ought to see the happy hacienda we call home down there. Say, it's forty-eight long miles out of Buenos Ayres. Can you picture that! El Placida's the name of the cute little burg. It looks it. They don't make 'em any more placid anywhere."

"I wonder you picked it then," says I.

"I didn't exactly," says Ambrose. "El Placida rather picked me. Funny how things work out sometimes. Got chummy with an old boy going down on the boat, Senor Alvarado. Showed him how to play Canfield and Russian bank and gave him the prescription for mixing a Hartford stinger. Before we crossed the line he thought I was an ace. Wanted to know what I was going to do down in his great country. 'Oh, anything that will keep me in cigarettes,' says I. 'You come with me and learn the wool business,' says he. 'It's a bet,' says I. So instead of being stranded in a strange land and nibbling the shrubbery for lunch, as my dear brother and the Ellinses had doped out, I lands easy on my feet with a salary that starts when I walks down the gank plank. Only I have to be in El Placida to draw my pay."

"But you made good, did you?" I asks.

"I did as long as Senor Alvarado was around to back me up," says Amby, "but when he slides down to the city for a week's business trip and turns me over to that Scotch superintendent of his the going got kind of rough. Mr. McNutt sends me out with a flivver to buy wool around the country. Looked easy. Buying things used to be my long suit. I bought a lot of wool. But I expect some of them low-browed rancheros must have gypped me good and plenty. Anyway, McNutt threw a fit when he looked over my bargains. He didn't do a thing but fire me, right off the reel. Honest, I'd never been fired so impetuous or so enthusiastic. He invites me to get off the place, which means hiking back to Buenos Ayres.

"Well, what can you do with a Scotchman who's mad

clear to the marrow? Especially a rough actor like McNutt. I'd already done a mile from the village when along comes 'Chita in her roadster. You know, old man Alvarado's only daughter. Some senorita, 'Chita is. You should have seen those black eyes of her's flash when she heard how abrupt I'd been turned loose. 'We shall go straight to papa,' says she. 'He will tell Senor McNutt where he gets off.' She meant well, 'Chita. But I had my doubts. I knew that Alvarado was pretty strong for McNutt. I'd heard him say there wasn't another man in the Argentine who knew more about wool than McNutt, and if it came to a showdown as to which of us stayed on I wouldn't have played myself for a look in.

"So while 'Chita is stepping on the gas button and handing out a swell line of sympathy I begins to hint that there's one particular reason why I hated to leave El Placida. Oh, we'd played around some before that. Strictly off stage stuff, though; a little mandolin practice in the moonlight, a few fox trot lessons, and so on. But before the old man I'd let on to be skirt shy. It went big with him, I noticed. But there in the car I decides that the only way to keep in touch with the family check book is to make a quick bid for 'Chita. So I cut loose with the best Romeo lines I had in stock. Twice 'Chita nearly ditched us, but finally she pulls up alongside the road and gives her whole attention to what I had to say. Oh, they know how to take it, those sonoritas. She'd had a whole string of young rancheros and caballeros dangling around her for the past two years. But somehow I must have had a lucky break, for the next thing I knew we'd gone to a fond clinch and it was all over except the visit to the church."

"And you married the job, eh?" says I. "Fast work, I'll say. But how did papa take it?"

"Well, for the first ten minutes," says Ambrose, "I thought

I'd been caught out in a thunderstorm while an earthquake and a sham battle were being staged. But pretty soon he got himself soothed down, patted me on the shoulder and remarked that maybe I'd do as well as some others that he hadn't much use for. And while he didn't make McNutt eat his words or anything like that, he gave him to understand that a perfectly good son-in-law wasn't expected to be such a shark at shopping for wool. Anyway, we've been getting along fairly well ever since. You have to, in a place like El Placida."

"And this is a little postponed honeymoon tour, eh?" I suggests.

"Hardly," says Ambrose. "I hope it's a clean break away from the continent of South America in general and El Placida in particular."

"Oh!" says I. "Will Senor Alvarado stake you to that?"

"He isn't staking anybody now," says Ambrose. "Uh-huh! Checked out last winter. Good old scout. Left everything to 'Chita, the whole works. And I've been ever since then trying to convince her that the one spot worth living in anywhere on the map is this little old burg with Broadway running through the middle."

"That ought to be easy," says I.

"Not with a girl who's been brought up to think that Buenos Ayres is the last word in cities," says Ambrose. "Why, she's already begun to feel sorry for the bellhops and taxi drivers and salesladies because she's discovered that not one of 'em knows a word of Spanish. Asks me how all these people manage to amuse themselves evenings with no opera to go to, no band playing on the plaza, and so on. See what I'm up against, Torchy?"

Sewell Ford

"I get a glimmer," says I.

"That's why I'm glad you are going to tow us around," he goes on, "instead of Bob Ellins. He's a back number, Bob. Me, too, from having been out of it all so long. Why, I've only been scouting about a little, but I can't find any of the old joints."

"Yes, a lot of 'em have been put out of business," says I.

"Must be new ones just as good though," he insists. "The live wires have to rally around somewhere."

"I don't know about that," says I. "This prohibition has put a crimp in—"

"Oh, you can't tell me!" breaks in Ambrose. "Maybe it's dimmed the lights some in Worcester and Toledo and Waukegan, but not in good old Manhattan. Not much! I know the town too well. Our folks just wouldn't stand for any of that Sahara bunk. Not for a minute. Might have covered up a bit—high sign necessary, side entrances only, and all that. But you can't run New York without joy water. It's here. And so are the gay lads and lassies who uncork it. We want to mingle with 'em, 'Chita and yours truly. I want her to see the lights where they're brightest, the girls where they're gayest. Want to show her how the wheels go 'round. You get me; eh, Torchy?"

"Sure!" says I.

What was the use wastin' any more breath? Besides, I'd been hearin' a lot of these young hicks talk big about spots where the lid could be pried off. Maybe it was so. Ambrose and 'Chita should have a look, anyway. And I spent the rest of the afternoon interviewin' sporty acquaintances over the 'phone, gettin' dope on where to hunt for active capers and poppin' corks. I must say, too, that most of the steers were a little vague. But, then, you can't tell who's who these days, with so many ministers givin' slummin' parties and Federal agents so thick.

When I sails around to the Plutoria to collect Amby and wife about 6:30 I finds 'Chita all gussied up like she was expectin' big doings. Quite a stunner she is, with them high voltage black eyes, and the gold ear hoops, and in that vivid colored evening gown. And by the sparkle in her eyes I can guess she's all primed for a reg'lar party.

"How about the old Bonaparte for the eats?" I says to Ambrose.

"Swell!" says he. "I remember giving a little dinner for four there once when we opened—"

"Yes, I know," says I. "Here's the taxi."

Did look like kind of a jolly bunch, too, down there in the old dining-room—orchestra jabbin' away, couple of real Jap girls floatin' around with cigars and cigarettes, and all kinds of glasses on the tables. But you should have seen Amby's jaw drop when he grabs the wine list and starts to give an order.

"What the blazes is a grenadine cocktail or—or a pineapple punch?" he demands.

"By me," says I. "Why not sample some of it?"

Which he does eager. "Bah!" says he. "Call that a cocktail, do they? Nothing but sweetened water colored up. Here, waiter! Call the chief."

All Ambrose could get out of the head waiter, though,

was shoulder shrugs and regrets. Nothing doing in the real red liquor line. "The champagne cider iss ver' fine, sir," he adds.

"Huh!" says Ambrose. "Ought to be at four fifty a quart. Well, we'll take a chance."

Served it in a silver bucket, too. It had the familiar pop, and the bubbles showed plain in the hollow stemmed glasses, but you could drink a gallon of it without feelin' inspired to do anything wilder than call for a life preserver.

The roof garden girl-show that we went to afterwards was a zippy performance, after it's kind. Also there was a bar in the lobby. Amby shoved up to that prompt—and came back with two pink lemonades, at 75 cents a throw.

"Well," says I, "ain't there mint on top and a cherry in the bottom?"

"And weak lemonade in between," grumbles Ambrose. "What do they take me for, a gold fish?"

"We'll try a cabaret next," says I.

We did. They had the place fixed up fancy, too, blue and green toy balloons floatin' around the ceilin', a peacock in a big gold cage, tables ranged around the dancin' space, and the trombone artist puttin' his whole soul into a pumpin' out "The Alcoholic Blues." And you could order most anything off the menu, from a poulet casserole to a cheese sandwich. Amby and 'Chita splurged on a cafe parfait and a grape juice rickey. Other dissipated couples at nearby tables were indulgin' in canapes of caviar and frosted sarsaparillas. But shortly after midnight the giddy revellers begun to thin out and the girl waiters got yawny.

"How about a round of strawb'ry ice cream sodas; eh, Amby?" I suggests.

"No," says he, "I'm no high school girl. I've put away so much of that sweet slush now that I'll be bilious for a week. But say, Torchy, honest to goodness, is Broadway like this all the time now?"

"No," says I. "They're goin' to have a Y.W.C.A. convention here next week and I expect that'll stir things up quite a bit."

"Sorry," says Amby, "but I shan't be here."

"No?" says I.

"Pos-i-tively," says Ambrose. "'Chita and I will be on our way back by that time; back to good old Buenos Ayres, where there's more doing in a minute than happens the whole length of Broadway in a month. And listen, old son; when we open a bottle something besides the pop will come out of it." "Better hurry," says I. "Maybe Pussyfoot Johnson's down there now monkeying with the constitution."

Choose from Thousands of 1stWorldLibrary Classics By

A. M. Barnard
Ada Leverson
Adolphus William Ward
Aesop
Agatha Christie
Alexander Aaronsohn
Alexander Kielland
Alexandre Dumas
Alfred Gatty
Alfred Ollivant
Alice Duer Miller
Alice Turner Curtis
Alice Dunbar
Allen Chapman
Alleyne Ireland
Ambrose Bierce
Amelia E. Barr
Amory H. Bradford
Andrew Lang
Andrew McFarland Davis
Andy Adams
Angela Brazil
Anna Alice Chapin
Anna Sewell
Annie Besant
Annie Hamilton Donnell
Annie Payson Call
Annie Roe Carr
Annonaymous
Anton Chekhov
Archibald Lee Fletcher
Arnold Bennett
Arthur C. Benson
Arthur Conan Doyle
Arthur M. Winfield
Arthur Ransome
Arthur Schnitzler
Arthur Train
Atticus
B.H. Baden-Powell
B. M. Bower
B. C. Chatterjee
Baroness Emmuska Orczy
Baroness Orczy
Basil King
Bayard Taylor
Ben Macomber
Bertha Muzzy Bower
Bjornstjerne Bjornson

Booth Tarkington
Boyd Cable
Bram Stoker
C. Collodi
C. E. Orr
C. M. Ingleby
Carolyn Wells
Catherine Parr Traill
Charles A. Eastman
Charles Amory Beach
Charles Dickens
Charles Dudley Warner
Charles Farrar Browne
Charles Ives
Charles Kingsley
Charles Klein
Charles Hanson Towne
Charles Lathrop Pack
Charles Romyn Dake
Charles Whibley
Charles Willing Beale
Charlotte M. Braeme
Charlotte M. Yonge
Charlotte Perkins Stetson
Clair W. Hayes
Clarence Day Jr.
Clarence E. Mulford
Clemence Housman
Confucius
Coningsby Dawson
Cornelis DeWitt Wilcox
Cyril Burleigh
D. H. Lawrence
Daniel Defoe
David Garnett
Dinah Craik
Don Carlos Janes
Donald Keyhoe
Dorothy Kilner
Dougan Clark
Douglas Fairbanks
E. Nesbit
E. P. Roe
E. Phillips Oppenheim
E. S. Brooks
Earl Barnes
Edgar Rice Burroughs
Edith Van Dyne
Edith Wharton

Edward Everett Hale
Edward J. O'Biren
Edward S. Ellis
Edwin L. Arnold
Eleanor Atkins
Eleanor Hallowell Abbott
Eliot Gregory
Elizabeth Gaskell
Elizabeth McCracken
Elizabeth Von Arnim
Ellem Key
Emerson Hough
Emilie F. Carlen
Emily Bronte
Emily Dickinson
Enid Bagnold
Enilor Macartney Lane
Erasmus W. Jones
Ernie Howard Pie
Ethel May Dell
Ethel Turner
Ethel Watts Mumford
Eugene Sue
Eugenie Foa
Eugene Wood
Eustace Hale Ball
Evelyn Everett-green
Everard Cotes
F. H. Cheley
F. J. Cross
F. Marion Crawford
Fannie E. Newberry
Federick Austin Ogg
Ferdinand Ossendowski
Fergus Hume
Florence A. Kilpatrick
Fremont B. Deering
Francis Bacon
Francis Darwin
Frances Hodgson Burnett
Frances Parkinson Keyes
Frank Gee Patchin
Frank Harris
Frank Jewett Mather
Frank L. Packard
Frank V. Webster
Frederic Stewart Isham
Frederick Trevor Hill
Frederick Winslow Taylor

Friedrich Kerst
Friedrich Nietzsche
Fyodor Dostoyevsky
G.A. Henty
G.K. Chesterton
Gabrielle E. Jackson
Garrett P. Serviss
Gaston Leroux
George A. Warren
George Ade
Geroge Bernard Shaw
George Cary Eggleston
George Durston
George Ebers
George Eliot
George Gissing
George MacDonald
George Meredith
George Orwell
George Sylvester Viereck
George Tucker
George W. Cable
George Wharton James
Gertrude Atherton
Gordon Casserly
Grace E. King
Grace Gallatin
Grace Greenwood
Grant Allen
Guillermo A. Sherwell
Gulielma Zollinger
Gustav Flaubert
H. A. Cody
H. B. Irving
H.C. Bailey
H. G. Wells
H. H. Munro
H. Irving Hancock
H. R. Naylor
H. Rider Haggard
H. W. C. Davis
Haldeman Julius
Hall Caine
Hamilton Wright Mabie
Hans Christian Andersen
Harold Avery
Harold McGrath
Harriet Beecher Stowe
Harry Castlemon
Harry Coghill
Harry Houidini

Hayden Carruth
Helent Hunt Jackson
Helen Nicolay
Hendrik Conscience
Hendy David Thoreau
Henri Barbusse
Henrik Ibsen
Henry Adams
Henry Ford
Henry Frost
Henry James
Henry Jones Ford
Henry Seton Merriman
Henry W Longfellow
Herbert A. Giles
Herbert Carter
Herbert N. Casson
Herman Hesse
Hildegard G. Frey
Homer
Honore De Balzac
Horace B. Day
Horace Walpole
Horatio Alger Jr.
Howard Pyle
Howard R. Garis
Hugh Lofting
Hugh Walpole
Humphry Ward
Ian Maclaren
Inez Haynes Gillmore
Irving Bacheller
Isabel Cecilia Williams
Isabel Hornibrook
Israel Abrahams
Ivan Turgenev
J.G.Austin
J. Henri Fabre
J. M. Barrie
J. M. Walsh
J. Macdonald Oxley
J. R. Miller
J. S. Fletcher
J. S. Knowles
J. Storer Clouston
J. W. Duffield
Jack London
Jacob Abbott
James Allen
James Andrews
James Baldwin

James Branch Cabell
James DeMille
James Joyce
James Lane Allen
James Lane Allen
James Oliver Curwood
James Oppenheim
James Otis
James R. Driscoll
Jane Abbott
Jane Austen
Jane L. Stewart
Janet Aldridge
Jens Peter Jacobsen
Jerome K. Jerome
Jessie Graham Flower
John Buchan
John Burroughs
John Cournos
John F. Kennedy
John Gay
John Glasworthy
John Habberton
John Joy Bell
John Kendrick Bangs
John Milton
John Philip Sousa
John Taintor Foote
Jonas Lauritz Idemil Lie
Jonathan Swift
Joseph A. Altsheler
Joseph Carey
Joseph Conrad
Joseph E. Badger Jr
Joseph Hergesheimer
Joseph Jacobs
Jules Vernes
Julian Hawthrone
Julie A Lippmann
Justin Huntly McCarthy
Kakuzo Okakura
Karle Wilson Baker
Kate Chopin
Kenneth Grahame
Kenneth McGaffey
Kate Langley Bosher
Kate Langley Bosher
Katherine Cecil Thurston
Katherine Stokes
L. A. Abbot
L. T. Meade

L. Frank Baum
Latta Griswold
Laura Dent Crane
Laura Lee Hope
Laurence Housman
Lawrence Beasley
Leo Tolstoy
Leonid Andreyev
Lewis Carroll
Lewis Sperry Chafer
Lilian Bell
Lloyd Osbourne
Louis Hughes
Louis Joseph Vance
Louis Tracy
Louisa May Alcott
Lucy Fitch Perkins
Lucy Maud Montgomery
Luther Benson
Lydia Miller Middleton
Lyndon Orr
M. Corvus
M. H. Adams
Margaret E. Sangster
Margret Howth
Margaret Vandercook
Margaret W. Hungerford
Margret Penrose
Maria Edgeworth
Maria Thompson Daviess
Mariano Azuela
Marion Polk Angellotti
Mark Overton
Mark Twain
Mary Austin
Mary Catherine Crowley
Mary Cole
Mary Hastings Bradley
Mary Roberts Rinehart
Mary Rowlandson
M. Wollstonecraft Shelley
Maud Lindsay
Max Beerbohm
Myra Kelly
Nathaniel Hawthrone
Nicolo Machiavelli
O. F. Walton
Oscar Wilde

Owen Johnson
P.G. Wodehouse
Paul and Mabel Thorne
Paul G. Tomlinson
Paul Severing
Percy Brebner
Percy Keese Fitzhugh
Peter B. Kyne
Plato
Quincy Allen
R. Derby Holmes
R. L. Stevenson
R. S. Ball
Rabindranath Tagore
Rahul Alvares
Ralph Bonehill
Ralph Henry Barbour
Ralph Victor
Ralph Waldo Emmerson
Rene Descartes
Ray Cummings
Rex Beach
Rex E. Beach
Richard Harding Davis
Richard Jefferies
Richard Le Gallienne
Robert Barr
Robert Frost
Robert Gordon Anderson
Robert L. Drake
Robert Lansing
Robert Lynd
Robert Michael Ballantyne
Robert W. Chambers
Rosa Nouchette Carey
Rudyard Kipling
Saint Augustine
Samuel B. Allison
Samuel Hopkins Adams
Sarah Bernhardt
Sarah C. Hallowell
Selma Lagerlof
Sherwood Anderson
Sigmund Freud
Standish O'Grady
Stanley Weyman
Stella Benson
Stella M. Francis

Stephen Crane
Stewart Edward White
Stijn Streuvels
Swami Abhedananda
Swami Parmananda
T. S. Ackland
T. S. Arthur
The Princess Der Ling
Thomas A. Janvier
Thomas A Kempis
Thomas Anderton
Thomas Bailey Aldrich
Thomas Bulfinch
Thomas De Quincey
Thomas Dixon
Thomas H. Huxley
Thomas Hardy
Thomas More
Thornton W. Burgess
U. S. Grant
Upton Sinclair
Valentine Williams
Various Authors
Vaughan Kester
Victor Appleton
Victor G. Durham
Victoria Cross
Virginia Woolf
Wadsworth Camp
Walter Camp
Walter Scott
Washington Irving
Wilbur Lawton
Wilkie Collins
Willa Cather
Willard F. Baker
William Dean Howells
William le Queux
W. Makepeace Thackeray
William W. Walter
William Shakespeare
Winston Churchill
Yei Theodora Ozaki
Yogi Ramacharaka
Young E. Allison
Zane Grey